Crossroads

Baby Blue Publishing—Edison, NJ
Paperback ISBN: 979-8-9871604-3-5
Hardcover ISBN: 979-8-9871604-4-2
Library of Congress Control Number: 2022919399
Title: *Crossroads*
Author: Adam Klein
Digital distribution | 2022
Paperback | 2022
Hardcover | 2022

Crossroads

Adam Klein

Dedication

To my Dad, who always provided me with the support and encouragement I needed. Miss you Dad!

Chapter 1

The setting was perfect. It was just the way he liked it; a dark house with everyone asleep. No matter how many times he experienced this setting, he always got a rush knowing that nobody knew he was there or what he was about to do. In fact, sometimes he became so excited, he forgot why he was there.

As he made his way through the living room and kitchen, it became clear that there was nobody downstairs. Just to be sure, he checked the bathroom, garage, and guest bedrooms. Nothing. Not one person or animal in the area, which kind of disappointed him. He always liked a little appetizer before the main event.

He began to make his way upstairs, taking one step at a time. The steps were made of dark mahogany and did not have any carpet on them. He was sure his shoes would make enough noise that it would wake someone up. To his delight, he made it up all fourteen stairs without a hitch. First up would be the room immediately to his right.

As he walked into the room, he could see stars on the ceiling and hear music coming from the headphones that were on the floor. He began to smile realizing that he can use the music to drown out his attack. He then started thinking to himself that they are making this way too easy for him. *At least give me a challenge* is what he thought as he approached a little girl in the bed sound asleep. Without hesitation, he placed his hands on the back of the head of the little girl, pushed down, and smothered her face into the pillow she was laying on. Once her head was firmly pressed down, he grabbed her by the hair, tilted her head back and slit her throat from ear to ear. One down, who knows how many to go.

He exited the girl's room and went down the hall to the first room on the left, where he saw a teenage boy lying on his back, holding a gaming controller. He could tell the boy was asleep because when he looked at the TV, the game was paused and there was a message in the upper right corner of the screen that read *wireless controller disconnected because of inactivity.*

He knew he would have to be much more careful with the boy because he looked like he lifted weights and could cause a problem if he was woken up. The room was a mess with plates, cups, forks, and spoons all over the floor. There were also several papers scattered all over, which would surely wake up the boy if stepped on. Making his way through the maze on the floor proved easier than he thought it would be, which brought a smile to his face. As he made his way to the boy's bed, he thought of waking him for a moment to see the fear in eyes, but he thought better of it, not wanting to take any chances. He put his hand over the boy's mouth and pressed his head down into the pillow with all of his strength, and slit his throat ear to ear, just as he had done to the little girl.

There were two more rooms on the upper level of the home, one of them being the master bedroom, and the other seemed like it was a den. He carefully approached the next door on the right, being careful not to be in the direct beam of the lamp that was on. He peeked inside and saw a teenage girl on a computer typing at a very rapid pace. He thought for a moment to save her for last because there would be nobody around to stop him from doing what he wanted to her, but then thought if she heard him in the master bedroom, she could sneak away and call the police without him knowing it.

He entered the room in a crouch, as if he were in stealth mode during a top-secret mission. The girl was typing so fast, he wondered what she could possibly be working on at this early morning hour that allowed her to have so much energy. When he got closer to her, he saw she was on a Zoom meeting with what was probably her boyfriend. He stayed perfectly still about ten feet from the girl trying to think of his next move. The live feed with her boyfriend put a damper on his plan and forced him to look around the room for anything that would help him get rid of the boyfriend. After a minute or two of some thought, he saw the plug for the computer was plugged into a surge protector that was plugged in right next to him. *This is perfect* he thought to himself, although he knew he had to act quickly, in order to not get caught. Once he worked up enough courage, he unplugged the surge protector and in one motion jumped up behind the girl, covered her mouth, tilted her head, and just like the other two, sliced her throat ear to ear.

After the girl fell on the floor, he needed to take a breather before heading into the final room. He had exerted way more energy than he ever had before, and he was not prepared for it. After five minutes of rest, he rose to his feet and approached the master bedroom to finish what he had started.

Entering the room, he immediately could see that both the father and mother of the children were sound asleep. He would need to deal with the father first because he posed more of a threat. He also knew that he would have to finish both of them quickly before it became a two on one situation. The father was sleeping on the left side of the bed, which was furthest from the door. He tiptoed his way around the bed, avoiding the clothes on the floor. When he made his way to the side of the bed where the father was, without thinking, he plunged the knife into the father's chest. The father let out a low groan and then went limp. Just to be sure, he took the knife out of the father's chest, and slit his throat.

He began to smile an even bigger smile than he had before at this point because he knew all that was left was the tiny one hundred ten-pound mother, who did not wake up when her husband was butchered to death. He didn't want to waste any time, so he rolled her over onto her back and slashed her throat from ear to ear; just like everyone else.

He felt so proud of himself at that point that he decided to revisit each room to admire his handiwork. He had done mass murders before, but not with the grace and precision as he did on this night. Not one victim had woken up and given him a problem. Not one single issue the entire night. Either he was getting really good at this, or he got lucky. He concluded his escapade by cleaning out the jewelry drawers, the wallets of both the father and mother, and the piggy bank of the young girl. He made one last sweep around the house to make sure he was not leaving any evidence behind. When he felt satisfied, he went out the back door to slip away into the deep, dark night only to find out he was not alone anymore.

"Freeze! NYPD. Don't move, put the weapon and bag down, get on your knees, and put your hands behind your head," An NYPD police officer screamed.

"I want Sal Amici! You hear me? *I WANT SAL AMICI*," he screamed back as he was being put in the back of a police car. His world as he knew it was over.

Chapter 2

Walking into the office with a clear mind is one of the greatest feelings in the world. It sets up the entire day to be positive and allows me to think without any distractions. I have not had many positive experiences over the past year, so it was refreshing to enjoy that feeling on what was one of the coldest January days New York City has had in over fifty years. The temperature was minus two degrees, with a wind chill of minus twenty-three. On days like these, I will drive into work instead of taking public transportation to take advantage of the heat in the car.

Being a partner at a law firm has many perks; however, one of the best perks is the reserved parking spot. I had taken the parking spot of Thomas Greenwood, who passed away last year from a massive stroke. Thomas had been my mentor and father figure in the office. He was beloved by everyone in the office, but nobody revered him more than me. Even though fourteen months had passed since his death, I was still in shock and disbelief that he was no longer with us.

I pulled into my parking spot and hurried to get to the elevator, in order to avoid the bitter cold. Once I was in the elevator, I received a text message. I took off my scarf so my face scan could open my phone and smiled when I saw who the text message was from.

Miss you already! Call me when you can. Xoxo. Nicole.

I did not intend to get into another relationship so soon after divorcing my ex-wife, but sometimes fate cannot be controlled.

My ex-wife Danielle had been found guilty of the first-degree murders of her parents and the family of Sean Lancaster; the scumbag I successfully defended last year. As a result, she was sentenced to life in prison without the possibility of parole. Danielle had been the mastermind behind the plot to have Sean's family killed and caused the auto accident that killed her parents by cutting the break line on their car. Never in a million years would I have suspected Danielle was capable of something like that, but as time passed and I got to know more details of just how evil she was, it became easier to let her go and move on.

I text Nicole back that I missed her too right before arriving on the fifth floor of our office building. Upon walking out of the elevator, I always glanced at the portrait we have of Thomas Greenwood in the lobby and smiled. Beneath the portrait, is an engraved plaque that reads *Play to Win*. It was Thomas's favorite saying and something he said at the end of every trial brief.

On my way to my office, I passed by my assistant Jill, who had recently received her degree in paralegal studies. She was having an animated conversation on the phone, when I gave her a look that said you better tell me later what that is about and went into my office. When I opened the door, I had an unexpected visitor waiting for me.

"Hey Sal. How are you? Alan Lowery asked me.

"I am great, Alan. How are you?"

"I am great as well. You want to know why I am great?

"Why Alan?" I asked curiously.

"The police finally caught the Night Slasher."

The night slasher had been terrorizing all five boroughs of New York City for the better part of seven months. He would only strike at night, usually targeting families of five or more. He managed to elude police by not leaving any evidence behind. He was very meticulous with his actions and always seemed to back track and collect anything that might lead to his capture.

"I saw that on the news. That's great. We can sleep without fear now," I said.

"And guess who he asked for?" Alan said with a grin ear to ear.

"No! No way Alan. I do not need another high-profile case after what I just went through. *NO!*"

"Wasn't it you that said you want to continue practicing trial law?" Alan questioned.

"Yes, but not this. Can't we give this to Schmidt or Phillips?" I pleaded.

"Sal, I need the best lawyer we have on this and that is you."

I knew Alan was right, yet still did not want to take the case. Sean Lancaster's case had taken everything out of me, and I vowed to myself to never get involved in something like that again. I was a partner now and would be able to turn down a case if I didn't want it.

However, I knew Alan wanted me in this case badly and I didn't want to disappoint him.

"I will think about it Alan. That is the best I can give you now."

"Fair enough Sal. How are you doing with the Danielle situation?"

"I am ok. Having a tough time with the kids because they keep asking questions about her that I am not ready to answer yet," I said, feeling ashamed.

"Sal, it's been over a year since she was arrested. Don't you think it's time to tell them what happened? They are going to find out sooner or later."

"I know, but they are still too young. I am not ready yet."

"Ok, Sal. I get it. Have you heard any updates on- you know who?"

"Not in a few weeks. I can't believe nobody has been able to catch him yet. I am constantly looking over my shoulder and taking extra precautions every day and I need it to stop," I said, anxiously.

"I am sure he will be caught eventually. Everyone slips up at some point," Alan said, as he exited my office.

Sean Lancaster had disappeared after he showed up at my house and told me about how Danielle was involved in his family's murder. He left my house that day with David Flores, another client I successfully defended that ended up committing murder, and never gave any clue that he was about to pull a Houdini act. He called me a while later and dropped a hint that he was in Italy, which he later confirmed in a text message. I alerted the authorities, which promptly got the Polizia di Stato, and Interpol involved; however, Sean has been able to evade both law enforcement agencies. I had not heard from Sean since he confirmed his location, something that terrified me every day.

Chapter 3

I got home around six pm and found my twelve-year-old son playing his new Nintendo Switch game and my seven-year-old daughter playing in her playroom that I had built for her last year. I loved my kids and would do anything for them, but I also had to protect them. I knew they deserved to hear the truth about their mother, but I did not know how to describe it to them. Do I come right out and say what she did, or do I ease into it and give them general details? Whichever path I decided to take, I felt the time to tell them was now.

"Gio. Angela. Can you guys come into the kitchen please? I want to talk to you both," I said as my nerves began to kick in.

Both of my kids came running into the kitchen, seemingly excited to hear what I had to say. I rarely called them together at the same time and when I did, it was usually to announce that we were going on a trip.

"Where are we going this time daddy?" Angela asked.

"Yeah, dad. Where are we off to this time?" Gio echoed.

"Sorry kids. We aren't going anywhere. I need to talk to you both about your mother."

The smiles on the faces of both Angela and Gio wiped away and were replaced with looks of concern.

"Did something happen to her?" Gio asked.

"Is she coming home daddy?" Angela asked me while holding her hands together like she was praying.

I knew I was going to have one shot at this, and I still had no idea how I was going to tell them. I will usually prepare myself for situations like this but in this case, I had not. I decided it was best to just go with whatever came to mind and not think too much about it.

"No angel. She isn't coming home, and nothing happened to her," I said as sweat began to pour down my face. "I need to talk to you about where she is and why she is there."

"You mean she isn't at Aunt Kate's?" Gio asked.

"No Gio," I said and took one of the deepest breaths I have ever taken. "She is in prison."

The stunned look on the faces of Angela and Gio told me that they had not known that is where Danielle was and that I had made a mistake. I wasn't sure if I should continue talking or let what I had told them sink in. Either way, it was not going to alleviate the pain they felt in that moment.

"What do you mean in prison? What did she do?" Gio asked.

"How can she be in prison? Isn't that where bad people go?" Angela asked innocently.

"Yes, angel it is. Your mother did something very bad and now she is being punished for it."

"What did she do dad?" Gio asked, fighting back tears.

"You know how sometimes people do things that aren't like them? Or sometimes people don't act themselves and they don't know why?"

"Yeah," Gio said confused.

"Well, your mother got involved in something and acted in a way that was not like her and she got caught," I said hoping that would be the end of the discussion.

"Daddy, I don't understand. Is mommy a bad person?" Angela asked.

For some reason, that question had caught me off guard and my emotions went into overdrive. I did not want to tell Angela that Danielle was an evil person that conned everyone and is a mass murderer, yet I did not want to lie to her either. Both of my kids deserved to know the truth because they would be going through this with me whether they knew or not. I also felt that this would set the tone for the rest of our lives together and I wanted them to know they could trust me.

"Yes, angel she is. She was not who any of us thought she was. She is a bad person and did some very bad things that she needs to pay the price for," I said calmly. "She won't be coming home anytime soon. I am sorry."

"Dad, *what did she do*?" Gio asked, losing his patience.

I took another deep breath before I answered. "She helped set up the murder of someone's family Gio. That is what she did."

"YOU'RE A LIAR. SHE DID NOT!" Gio screamed and ran upstairs.

"What does murder mean daddy and why did it upset Gio so bad?" Angela asked.

"Is it ok if we talk about this later angel? I promise I will explain everything to you, but right now, daddy needs some time alone."

"Ok, daddy. But you promise you tell me what murder means?"

"Yes, angel. I promise," I said with remorse. "Why don't you go back to playing in your playroom."

"Ok daddy," Angela said as she walked away dragging her feet and lowering her head.

I knew that Gio would react the way he did, but I did not expect that Angela would not know what murder meant. I guess it is a good thing that a seven-year-old does not know what murder means, even if it was going to make my job as a father that much harder. I was going to go upstairs to speak to Gio, but I decided to give him space and let him come to me when he was ready.

After my kids went their separate ways, I continued to sit at the kitchen table in deep thought. The clear mind I had earlier in the day was nothing but a distant memory. It had now been supplanted by grief, sorrow, and anger. I was still furious with Danielle for what she had done and did not know if I would ever be able to move past it. She not only destroyed the lives of those involved in her scheme, but she also obliterated my family. My children were hurting because of her selfish actions and most likely would hurt for the rest of their lives. I knew I could not do anything to ease their pain, but I could do something to release the built-up anger I had raging inside me. I needed to visit Danielle in prison for the first time.

Chapter 4

No matter how many times I visit a prison, I never get used to the loud buzzing when doors are opened or the clanging of steel on steel when they close. The musty smell is also something to be forgotten; however, it serves as a quick reminder of how lucky I am to not have spent my days and nights in this hellhole.

Walking through the corridors of the Bedford Hills Correctional Facility, I got a quick flashback to my visits with both David Flores and Sean Lancaster. Both men partnered with Danielle to murder Sean's family so they all can get rich. Sean got away before he could be apprehended, David was murdered in his home, and Danielle was in this place.

Once I was through all the security checks, I was escorted to a private visitation area. I was not sure why my meeting with Danielle had been set up this way, but I knew I didn't have a say in the matter because I was not there as her attorney. As I waited for Danielle, a million thoughts went through my head, including how I would react to seeing her for the first time in over a year and if I would be able to control myself from strangling her.

Just as I was to get up and ask what was taking so long, I heard a loud buzzer. The steel door squeaked open and in walked Danielle. She was in the typical orange jumpsuit with shackles around her ankles and her hands were in handcuffs. She had lost weight and her hair was a lot shorter and grayer than it had been. She also looked like she hadn't slept in days and smelled like she hadn't showered in an equal amount of time.

The guards that had escorted her to this meeting sat her in a chair behind a table that was bolted to the floor. On the table, there was a steel bar with slots for the inmates' hands. Danielle complied with all the directions from the guard, without incident, and when she was secured to the table, the guards left us alone.

"You look like shit," I said.

"Hello to you too," Danielle replied.

"I must admit, this look suits you. Matches the black hole inside you."

"Sal, if all you are going to do is insult me, I am leaving," Danielle said angrily.

"You are not in a position to hurt me anymore sweetheart. I am over you and have moved on. Got me a nice little relationship budding, I see my kids every day, and I am a partner at my firm. Life is pretty damn good."

"Yeah? Where's Sean? Bet that is still weighing on your mind."

"Don't pay much attention to it anymore," I said, trying to hide a bit of fear. "Anyway, the reason I came here was to talk to you about what you did to our family. I finally told Gio and Angela what you did and where you are. I was tired of lying to them and letting them think you were this sweet innocent person who was spending time at her sister's house."

The look on Danielle's face was something I wish I had taken a picture of. We had made an agreement through our divorce attorneys that the kids would not know what Danielle had done until we both felt the time was right. I had obeyed our arrangement but could not do so any longer. Danielle was in no position to make demands and eventually, I stopped caring what she might think.

"How dare you tell *our* kids the truth without asking me first?" Danielle said, trying to be intimidating.

"Uh, I don't think you are in a position to negotiate Danielle. You lost the right to be a parent when you decided to shack up with Sean and plot the murder of his family."

"You will be hearing from an attorney on this Sal, you can beat your ass on that."

"Danielle, I don't care what you want or do anymore. You can't hurt me anymore. You can't threaten me anymore. Gio and Angela will grow up in my house, quite possibly with a new mother as well."

"You son of a bitch. You better be looking in every direction from now mister. I still can hurt you from inside here," Danielle said. "GUARD!"

The two guards that escorted Danielle to the private visitation area opened the door and prepared her to go back to her cell. Before they took her away, I had one more comment for her.

"Guys, can you wait a sec please? I have one more thing to say," I asked as I leaned toward Danielle's ear and whispered. "I should have let that foul ball hit you in the head. Rot in hell you bitch."

Chapter 5

One of the most exciting parts of being a defense attorney is representing a client when they are being questioned by the police. There is unspoken distrust among lawyers and law enforcement that sometimes interferes with the interrogation process, with no explanation as to why. My job as an attorney is to make sure my client does not say anything that will incriminate him/herself and that the questions being asked are fair and related to the case; a fact sometimes lost by the police when they want to nail someone to the wall.

I stepped into the seventy-eighth precinct police station on sixth avenue in Brooklyn not knowing what to expect. I do not normally take cases outside of Manhattan; however, this was a special case, and as a partner, I wanted this case for the firm. I was exhausted from a lack of sleep and from my emotional reunion with Danielle, but I knew I had to be here on this day at this time.

The station sounded and smelled like any other, which immediately put me in my comfort zone. I had been in dozens of police stations before and always felt right at home. As I looked around and realized I did not know anyone or where to go, I began to feel a little less secure. I must have looked like a deer in headlights because the desk sergeant immediately asked if I needed help.

"Uh, yes. Thank you, sir. I am Sal Amici. I am hoping you can point me in the right direction. I am here to represent Joseph Millstone."

"Ah, yes. The night slasher. Good luck with that one," the desk sergeant remarked.

"Gee, yes, thank you for clearing that up. Where is he?"

"Smart ass. You think cuz you are this hot shot lawyer now people are going to bow down to you?"

"Um, no. I just want to know where my client is. Can you please tell me where I can find him? Thank you," I said sarcastically.

"Down the hall, third interrogation room on the left, asshole."

"Thank you," I said and bowed to the desk sergeant.

As I made my way toward my client, I had an immediate flashback of when I first met Sean Lancaster at Rikers Island. Sean had been a sarcastic, conceited jerk that loved to play games. I had not expected that from someone who was about to be charged with murder, so it threw me off my game. However this time, I was prepared for anything Joseph Millstone would throw at me, despite facing a quintuple murder charge.

When I reached the correct interrogation room, I opened the door to find my client all by himself and it looked like he didn't have a care in the world. I was surprised at how small he was, given the nature of why he was arrested. He had thinning brownish hair, with a little gray above the ear. He looked to be in his early thirties and definitely did not go to the gym. His eyes had a weird oval shape to them, which didn't match the rest of his physique. If this was the guy the police claim murdered all those people, he must have a secret because it looked like *I* could kick his ass.

"Hello Joseph. I am Sal Amici, and I am here to represent you. I am sure you knew that already since that is the only thing you told the police when they arrested you."

"Call me Joe. Yes, that is correct. I asked for you. Who wouldn't want the great Sal Amici as his attorney? What you did with Flores and Lancaster makes you a legend. It is an honor to meet you," Joe praised.

"Ok, then. Thank you, but let's tone down the high praise for a bit, ok?"

"Sure thing."

"So Joe, tell me what happened?"

"What happened with what?" Joe asked.

"What do you mean with what? With…"

Suddenly the interrogation room burst open and two arrogant NYPD detectives with a smug look on both their faces came charging in.

"Gentlemen, let's get this over with, shall we? I am Detective Jones, and this is Detective Slater. We are with the homicide division here in Brooklyn."

"Pleased to meet you gentlemen," I said and extended my hand. "You may proceed with your questioning."

After shaking my hand, Detective Jones came out firing right away. "Mr. Millstone, what were you doing at the home of the King's last night and why did you kill everyone in the house?"

"Excuse me detective, my client has not been charged with anything and I would appreciate you not accusing him of such crimes," I interjected.

"Your client, *counselor*, was caught with a chef knife on his person, covered in blood. Our lab is processing that knife as we speak. I wonder what we will find?" Detective Jones answered.

"Well, then until the examination is complete, do not accuse my client of any wrongdoing again. Carry on."

"Mr. Millstone"

"Joe. Please call me Joe, I hate being addressed so formally."

"Ok. Joe. Why were you at the King's house last night?"

I put my finger up toward Detective Jones and leaned into Joe's ear to whisper instructions on how to answer that question. I knew they had Joe trespassing because he had been caught leaving the house, but that didn't mean he needed to answer the question directly.

"I don't recall being there last night," Joe answered.

"You don't recall being there? Joe, you were arrested right outside of their home. They were all dead inside. How do you not remember?" Detective Slater asked angrily.

"What does the family being dead have to do with my client's answer? He was asked a question and answered it. Move on," I demanded.

"Is this how this is going to go? If so, I am not wasting my time here. We will hold your client for the full forty hours if we have to, in order to get some answers," Detective Jones said.

"Fine by me. My client has nothing more to say. By the way, you only have twenty-one hours left to hold him, which means my client will be home by dinner time tomorrow."

"Detectives, we have something you need to see," a voice said over the intercom.

"Be right there," Detective Jones answered. "Would you mind waiting here, counselor? I have a feeling this is about our mutual friend."

"Sure."

When the detectives left the room, I gave Joe further instructions not to talk because the room is most likely wired for sound and anything we say will be picked up. Joe nodded and sat back in his chair with his arms folded. We did not say a word to each other for the next twenty minutes, which was when the detectives returned with huge smiles on their faces.

"So, the fingerprints on the knife are a match to you Joe," Detective Jones said smiling. "Joseph Millstone, please stand up. You are under arrest for the murders of Harold, Donna, Tim, Karen, and Megan King. You have the right to remain silent…"

"Joe, do not say a word to anyone until we meet again. I am going to look over all of the details of their investigation and schedule a time to meet with you tomorrow. Remember, not a word."

Joseph nodded his head and complied with what the detectives told him to do. After he was taken away, I exited the room and waited to find out where they were taking him. I was informed that he was being taken to the Central Court Building to be formally charged and processed and then transported to Rikers Island. I was also informed that I would be able to meet with him in two days.

As I left the police station, I started to wonder if I was setting myself up for failure. This case seemed to be as air tight as I have ever seen, and I had no idea how I would be able to defend Joe. I also knew that I had not looked at any evidence or arrest reports so there was bound to be information I did not have yet. Still, I could not help but think here we go again- another high-profile murder case that will test my limits.

Chapter 6

Joseph Millstone was born and raised in Sarasota, Florida. His father left when he was just two years old and never returned. His mother died of ovarian cancer when he was eleven, which put him into foster care. He bounced around from foster home to foster home, never seeming to find that one family that wanted to keep him. He was always a quiet kid but was the complete opposite on the inside.

He moved to New York City to attend college at NYU and when he graduated with a degree in economics, decided to stay in New York because he loved the energy the city gave him. He got a job as a bartender and quickly made a name for himself as one of the elite bartenders in NYC. He began to see an almost endless flow of cash due to the high tips he received, which he then invested in hedge funds and made a fortune.

Sitting in his cell in Rikers Island, Joseph Millstone wondered what he did that went wrong that night. He ensured when he cut the glass to the back door he was as quiet as he could be. He made sure he slit the throats of all five members of the family and was extremely quiet while traversing the house. He made sure he did not make noise while rummaging through the dresser drawers. What did he miss?

Joseph knew that it was a possibility that he would be caught one day, but he never put a plan together if he was. When was apprehended, the first and only thing he could think of was asking for Sal Amici. He was not sure why he had done that, but he was glad he did. He knew of Sal's work from the news coverage of Sean Lancaster's trial and the follow up interviews that took place over the next year, in which Sal was portrayed as a messiah in the media.

He also knew that surviving in Rikers Island was a matter of not only being tough, but also being smart. He asked around the moment he arrived at Rikers who to look out for and who to align with. He got some advice but mostly was told to fuck off.

As Joseph thought of how he was going to survive in this place, his cell door began to open. He turned around to see two guards and an inmate staring right at him. Right away, he got a chill that ran down his spine and put a sense of fear in him that he had never felt before.

"Get up, inmate," one of the guards commanded.

"Who is this?" Joseph asked.

Without giving it any thought, the guard took out his baton and whacked Joseph square in the knee, knocking him down to the ground like a collapsing building. "When I say move, you move. Got it inmate?"

"Yes boss. I got it," Joseph said, as he struggled to get back to his feet.

"Good. Now, this is Whitaker. He is a bad person so behave yourself. Have fun you two," the guard laughed, as he slammed the cell door shut.

"I'm Millstone," Joseph said as he extended his hand.

"This ain't no business negotiation. Put your hand away son."

"Whatever," Joseph said and returned to his cot.

Whether it was being in Rikers Island or his new cellmate, Joseph began to feel a great deal of fear and it made him queasy. He began to take deep breaths, but not so loud so Whitaker could hear him. If he was going to stay alive and unharmed, he was going to have to work on his ability to show no fear; something he had never had to do before.

Chapter 7

There is nothing worse than being woken up out of a deep sleep. It had been a long time since I was able to sleep as well as I have been lately, which is why I was angry when I was awakened by my children screaming at each other at six-thirty in the morning.

"SHE DID NOT. STOP SAYING THAT."

"WHY WOULD HE LIE YOU WEIRDO."

"*HEY!* Knock it off. What's going on?" I yelled.

"Angela won't admit that mom is a bad person," Gio answered.

"He keeps saying she is a bad person, and he never wants to see her again. That is just mean. And he keeps calling me names too," Angela whined.

"Alright, both of you, stop it! Come here and sit down. I will make breakfast and we will then talk about this again, ok?" I said hoping to restore peace.

"Fine."

"Ok, Daddy. Thank you."

I spent the next ten minutes making pancakes, bacon, sausage, and home fries. I wanted my kids to stuff their faces so they would have less energy to talk. When I finished cooking, I set a plate for Gio and Angela in front of them at the table and sat down to join them. I knew this was going to be a tough conversation, but I also wanted to be transparent with them.

"Ok, so what's going on?" I started.

"Like I said, Angela doesn't believe you about mom. I told her she needs to move on and accept it but she won't listen to me," Gio said, as he stuffed two pieces of bacon in his mouth.

"Angela, is that true?" I asked.

"Why would mommy do bad things? I love her and don't think she is a mean person."

"Angela, I know it is tough and sometimes hard to believe. I also am having a hard time believing it."

"You are?" Angela asked, surprised.

"Of course. We all love your mother and did not anticipate any of this, but we also have to realize that sometimes people hide who they really are. Mommy is not the person we all thought she was, and she hurt a lot of people. That doesn't mean we can't still love her. It just means she deserves to be punished for what she did."

"How long will she be punished for?" Angela asked.

"I don't know angel," I said, not wanting to tell Angela that Danielle was never coming home.

"When will you know?"

"Soon angel. Soon. I promise."

"She is probably never coming home after what she did," Gio said, underneath his breath.

"That is enough Gio. You got it. *Enough.*".

After they finished their breakfast, Gio and Angela went to watch TV in the living room. Saturday mornings are filled with programs that they both enjoy, even though those programs do not match the Saturday morning cartoons I grew up with. Before I cleaned the table, I took a moment to look at both of them and took the moment in. They grow up so fast, I wanted to make sure I savored every minute of their youth. They looked so innocent and carefree, something I hoped would stay with them for the rest of their lives. I was so wrapped up in the moment, I didn't hear my phone going off for a good five seconds.

"This is Sal," I answered.

"Sal, sorry to be calling this early, but I wanted to let you know that you have received clearance to visit Joe today. I want you to go as soon as you can," Alan Lowery said.

"Why the urgency Alan?"

"I want to find out what his story is before it is all over the news."

"Why would it be all over the news?"

"Because that son of a bitch is threatening to tell his story to anyone who will listen."

"Ok, I will head over there in an hour or so. How can he expect to get a good defense of multiple homicides if he talks before the trial?"

"I don't know. That is why you need to get there and straighten him out."

"Will do Alan. I will let you know what happens after I visit him."

When I hung up the phone and began to clear the table, I was startled by Gio just staring at me. He looked like he had heard something that piqued his interest. His eyes were wide open, and he had a grin on his face that reminded me of something evil.

"What is it Gio?" I asked.

"I want to know more about the multiple homicide case you have. It seems interesting."

Chapter 8

I decided to go to the office before I went to see Joseph in Rikers Island because I wanted to speak to both Alan and Steven to get their opinions on how I should proceed with questioning Joseph. Even though I was a partner, I still felt the need to run ideas and plans by Alan and Steven. It was more a sign of respect than anything else.

On the way to the office, I like to listen to sports radio. WFAN is the number one sports station in NYC and they always have both lively hosts and guest callers. Today's topic centered around the putrid play of the New York Football Giants. The Giants have been a bad football team for almost a decade now and there seems to be no end in sight. I usually do not call into radio stations, but that morning, I felt like venting my frustrations and letting the Giants ownership know how their fanbase feels. I brought up my phone on the car's infotainment system and dialed the number for the station. To my surprise, I was able to get through on the first try. I told the producer why I was calling and my name and was then placed on hold. Suddenly, I became nervous about being on the radio, which was an odd feeling for me. As I was on hold, a call came through without a caller ID. With so many robocalls recently, I always let these calls go to voicemail; however, I was in such a nervous state of mind, I switched over and picked up the call.

"Hello, this is Sal," I answered.

"Well. Well. Well. If it isn't my favorite defense attorney turned divorcee."

If I wasn't nervous enough waiting to speak on the radio, I surely was now. In fact, I became so overwhelmed with nerves and anxiety, I almost smashed into the car in front of me. I didn't respond for a few seconds because I could not speak. In order to avoid a sure accident, I pulled over in front of a Starbucks.

"What the hell are you doing calling me?" I asked.

"I didn't want you to think I forgot about you," Sean Lancaster said.

"Now why would I think that?"

"Ha-ha. So how are you buddy? Miss me yet?"

"First of all, I am not your buddy. Second, I have no interest in schmoozing with you Sean. What do you want?"

"Ok, I get it. You are pissed at me and have a right to be. You're right. There is something I want to talk to you about," Sean said.

"So talk already. My god Sean, you are worse than a child," I said, getting angry.

"First I want to know how Danielle is. I understand you went to see her at Bedford."

"Uh-uh. We are not doing this. I have my own shit to worry about. I am going to ask you for the last time. What do you want?"

"Fine. But don't come to me when you need a friend to talk to," Sean said sarcastically. "I want to help you with your case by providing some background information for you on Joseph Millstone."

Once again, I froze while talking to Sean Lancaster. He has a way of doing this to me virtually every conversation we have. I had no idea how he gets the information he does and if there is a limit to the amount of resources he has, but he sure knows how to use them.

"What did you say?" I questioned.

"Joseph Millstone. He is your client, isn't he? He was arrested for the murders of the King family, correct?"

"That's right, how do you know about that? Are you back in the United States?"

"Oh we haven't gotten that intimate yet. I am going to be sending you the information that you need soon. You won't know when or how it will come, but when it does, you will know," Sean said and then hung up.

When I went to click back over to the radio station I was on hold with, they had hung up on me as well. Wondering what had just happened, I continued to sit in my car in disbelief. Not only was I about to defend another murderer, but I also now had Sean Lancaster back in my life. I had worked incredibly hard over the past year to move on from him and the damage he did, and now it was all for naught. If I was going to be able to juggle everything that was going on in my life, I would have to find someone to talk to. Someone who

I knew would have the answers for me. Someone who I had gotten close to over the past few months; Dr. Nicole Adams.

25

Chapter 9

Before I made the call to Nicole, I needed to talk to Alan and Steven about my case. I was also torn as to whether or not I should mention my phone call with Sean. Full transparency, which is what I am practicing with my children, should also be applied in my professional life.

I got into the elevator to ascend to the fifth floor with a laser focus. I was not going to let Sean derail what I had prepared for Alan and Steven, nor was I going to let him ruin the mood I was in. However, once the elevator doors opened and I stepped out onto the fifth-floor lobby, the anxiety that I had suppressed came roaring back like a tidal wave. I began to sweat profusely and got very lightheaded. Everything around me started to cave in and get out of focus. My legs became weak and wobbly. My head began to pound like never before and felt a tingling throughout my body. I knew I was having a major panic attack and needed to get to the bathroom before I passed out on the lobby floor.

When I reached the bathroom, I immediately went to the sink and splashed cold water on my face. I do not know what the science is, or even *if* there is a science behind cold water being the remedy for anxiety, but it worked like a charm. The cold water seemed to wake me up a little, as well as slow my heart rate down. I went into one of the stalls and began taking heavy, deep breaths. After five minutes or so, I was starting to get my bearings back and my surroundings were coming back into focus. I needed to see Nicole sooner than I thought.

After I was able to stabilize and clean myself up, I made my way to Alan's office. I knew he was not expecting me, but I also knew he would not turn me away. I continued to take deep breaths as I got closer to his office, in order to prevent another panic attack. It seemed to work because when I approached Alan's door, I was as calm as I had been all morning.

"Alan, do you have a minute?" I asked.

"Hey Sal. Sure, come on in. To what do I owe the pleasure?"

"Do you mind if we call in Steven as well? I just want to throw a few ideas at the both of you."

"Sure. Peggy, can you ask Mr. Hill to come to my office?" Alan asked his secretary via intercom.

"How are things at home Sal?" Alan asked, making small talk.

"They are ok. Could be better. Angela is as sweet as ever and is oblivious to everything that is going on. Gio on the other hand- "

"Hey Sal. You wanted to see me?" Steven asked as he sat in the chair next to me.

"Yeah, Steven, thank you for coming by. Guys, I want to run a few ideas and strategies by you before I go see Joe later today."

"Sal, you know you don't have to do this anymore. You are a partner now. An equal. We trust you," Alan said with confidence.

"I know you do, and I thank you for that, but I have always liked getting your input," I replied.

"Ok then. Shoot," Alan directed.

"I have been reviewing the notes from the arrest and a few things stood out to me. The first item is that Joe was caught exiting the backdoor, which seems odd to me because why would the police only be at the backdoor and not cover both exits? The second item is when he was caught, he only mentioned my name. Why? I have not had any interactions with this guy, nor have I ever crossed paths with him. The last item, and this is the big one, is the police claim that Joe's fingerprints were on the knife that was recovered at the scene. How can that be if it is also in the arrest report that, and I quote, "suspect was apprehended successfully without incident. Suspect was wearing a black Adidas hoodie, black Nike sweatpants, black Air Jordan sneakers, and black driving gloves". If he was wearing gloves, how could his fingerprints be on the murder weapon? So my question to both of you is, how do I approach Joe about all of this, and should I be passive or aggressive?"

Both Alan and Steven looked at each other with a tiny smirk on both of their faces. It seemed they either knew something I did not know or were about to bestow their wisdom on me.

"Sal, you already know the answer. You do exceptional work and your craft in the courtroom is the best in the firm. There is nothing we can tell you that you haven't already thought of. However, I will tell you this. Never forget that he is *your* client. You work for him. You don't want to piss him off so much that he fires you, yet you need to press him harder than you would any other client because of the nature of the crime," Steven told me.

"Thank you for the confidence, Steven, I really appreciate it. I am going to go hard at him. He seems like a passive type of guy; despite the crimes he is being charged with. I will also be mindful not to push too hard though." I thought for a second or two about telling Alan and Steven about my call with Sean but decided against it. I would tell them at a more appropriate time.

I left Alan's office to head over to Rikers Island to see Joseph Millstone. I had a plan in mind of what I would ask, the order in which I would ask it, and how I would ask it. I was not going to leave that jail without getting all of the answers I was looking for. I was not going to let Joseph manipulate me like Sean did. My guard would be up from the moment I entered Rikers Island to the moment the trial ended.

I got into my car to drive over to Rikers Island with a much clearer head than I had just thirty minutes ago. I put on *Seek and Destroy* by Metallica to get me in the mood. Even though it was twenty-one degrees outside, I put the window down; enjoying the crisp winter air. There wasn't much traffic on the Manhattan streets, which was odd for that time of day, so I figured I would get to Rikers in record time.

I didn't see or hear it. It seemed to come out of nowhere, yet it sent me flying in the air. When the tumbling was done, I ended up smashed against a parked taxicab and all I could hear was people running over to me and asking me questions. I didn't understand any of them and I didn't know where I was. I could not move at all, and I had glass all over my face. I seemed to be lying upside down and when I tried to speak, nothing came out. I began to hear sirens; however, the closer they got, the softer they became. Within the next few seconds, everything went dark and quiet. I do not remember anything else after that.

Chapter 10

Chow time in jail is usually not something inmates look forward to. The food is awful, there is usually a fight or two, and the guards use this time to flex their muscles on those they do not like. For Joseph Millstone, chow time would be an opportunity to assess who he could trust and who he would be watching.

After getting his repulsive food, Joseph went to sit at the end of the table closest to the exit. He wanted to be separated from everyone so he could get a good look around the room and begin his evaluation process. Once he was settled in with his food, he began to survey the room. Most of the inmates were either eating the food or talking; however, there was one inmate who sat by himself staring at the floor. This would be Joseph's first contact inside Rikers Island.

"Mind if I join you?" Joseph asked the inmate.

The inmate just stared at Joseph. He didn't say a word or make a sound. Joseph was not sure he heard him, so he repeated his question a little louder. Again, the inmate did not respond. Annoyed, Joseph whispered in the inmate's ear if he wanted company. The inmate nodded and moved over a few inches so Joseph could sit down next to him.

"So what's the story? Do you not talk? Are you a monk? What?" Joseph asked.

"I don't like talking with people here. They all think I am a freak and make fun of me," the inmate replied.

"I see. Well, I am not them. I am looking for someone who I can trust and is willing to be my pal. Are you ok with being my pal?"

"I guess. What's your name?" the inmate asked timidly.

"Joseph Millstone. What is your name?"

"Franklin Thompson, but please, call me Frankie."

"Alright, Frankie. Nice to meet you. What are you in for?"

"Armed robbery. You?"

That surprised Joseph because Frankie looked so timid and frail, it was hard to picture him robbing somewhere or someone.

"Murder, like everyone else in here probably," Joseph answered.

Frankie began to shift uncomfortably in his spot on the bench. He clearly was afraid of what Joseph had said and was not shy about hiding it. Not exactly the ideal behavior in Rikers Island.

"Calm down Frankie, innocent till proven guilty, right?"

"Well, did you do it.?" Frankie asked with a shaking voice.

"Ah, that I can't talk about, but what we can talk about is- "

"Yo, fish. Why are you hanging around freaky deaky over here?" a large man asked.

"Excuse me? Who are you?" Joseph asked, annoyed.

"Damn homie, chill out. Just trying to make conversation."

"Ok, sorry. I'm obviously new here and still need to learn how things work. I thought I would speak to Frankie over here because he seemed lonely and I felt bad, that's all."

"Aw, isn't that cute? We have a softy here fellas," the man said to his fellow inmates.

"Hey look, I am not looking for trouble, alright? I'll just go about my business, and you can go about yours, ok?" Joseph said.

"Yeah, that's not going to work for me because well, you embarrassed me in front of my crew."

"Huh? How did I embarrass you?" Joseph asked, as he began to get angry.

"I don't have to explain myself to you. Just apologize," the man demanded.

"You want me to apologize? Ok. Let's shake hands first. To show everyone we have come to a deal," Joseph said.

"Sounds good."

Joseph approached the man and extended his hand. When he had the man's hand in his grasp, he quickly grabbed the man's middle and pointer fingers and with one swift movement, snapped both of them backwards. There was a loud crunching sound that accompanied the screaming that was heard coming from the man's mouth.

"You broke my fingers man. AAHH. What the hell?"

Joseph walked behind the man, grabbed his other hand, and held it in his hand with a tight grip.

"Don't you know who I am? I am the night slasher. You ever talk to me or Frankie like that again, and you will have bigger problems than two broken fingers. You got that?"

"Yeah, I got it," the man said through pain.

"I can't hear you. Do you got it?

"*YEAH, I GOT IT,*" The man yelled.

"Good. Make fucking sure you do."

Chapter 11

The sound of constant beeping, along with a tube inside your nose, is not the greatest way to wake up. I tried to look around to see where I was, but my neck was in a brace, and I had very limited movement. My eyes kept closing involuntarily as I tried to focus on the person looking down at me. It appeared to be a nurse, but I was not entirely sure. Then it hit me. I was in a car accident, and I must be in the hospital. I was alive, so it must not have been too bad. But I was also in a hospital bed with tubes and wires all over the place. I tried to speak, but nothing came out. I would have to wait until I was more awake to find out what was wrong with me.

As the next few hours passed by, I went in and out of consciousness. One moment I was ready to try and lift my head and the next, I was comatose. I began to get frustrated because I was not able to communicate with the nurses and nobody would tell me what was going on when I was awake. Finally, after about seven hours of torture, I had one of the longest stretches of awareness and I was able to get the attention of the nurse changing my IV medication by grabbing the line and pulling on it. She tried to pull it back from me, but I kept tugging until she realized I wanted to talk to her; only I couldn't speak. I assumed it was because my throat was still sore from being intubated, but I wasn't sure. I began to move my hand back and forth, signaling I wanted to write down my questions. The nurse grabbed a notepad, and I began to write as legibly as I could what I wanted to know.

I handed the nurse my note that read:

What happened to me?

She began to write her answer, but I moved my pointer finger back and forth and pointed to my mouth and then to her. She understood what I was saying and then proceeded to tell me what I wanted to know.

"Mr. Amici, I am Nurse Bellinger. I am here to help you in any way I can," Nurse Bellinger said, trying to ease me into what was sure to be difficult news to hear. "You suffered a ruptured spleen, which we had to remove because of the extensive damage. You can live without a spleen; however, you will be more susceptible to conditions such as pneumonia, influenza, and other bacterial infections. We will discuss this more when you are fully aware. You also suffered numerous broken ribs and a broken nose. Fortunately, the airbag saved you from having further damage done, but it could not prevent the ruptured spleen. Finally, and this may be worse than the spleen, both of your legs were severely bruised and you have a sprained knee. Although you suffered terrible injuries, the good news is that they are not life threatening."

As stoically as I could, I grabbed the notepad and wrote:

How long will I be here?

"That is yet to be determined. Based on your injuries and the extensive treatment you need, I estimate it will be a few weeks before we can release you."

How long have I been here for?

"Nine days. You were put into a medically induced coma while we operated on your injuries. This was done to both keep you stable and prevent you from having to deal with too much pain."

Where are my kids?

"Your parents took them when you got into the accident. They have been here a few times, not with the kids though. Very lovely people," Nurse Bellinger said with a smile.

Thank you. I appreciate your patience. I know this isn't an easy way of communicating.

"Not a problem Mr. Amici. I am glad to help."

Just one more question. Do you know if my colleagues at the law firm know what is going on?

"Yes, they do. Alan, Steven, and Jill have all been here. Alan asked to receive a call once you were awake. Shall I call him for you?"

Yes, please. But let him know I can't talk and need to write on this ridiculous pad.

"Will do. Here is your remote and call button. Please don't hesitate to call me if you need anything. I will be back to check on you soon," Nurse Bellinger said as she left my room.

I was really impressed at both her patience and bedside manner. It is very uncommon to see that level of care in a hospital, but I guess it is somewhat of a requirement to work in the ICU. After flipping through the channels a few times, I grew frustrated at not recognizing any programs and tossed the remote over the side of the bed. I tried to stay awake as long as I could to see if I would get my bearings, but it proved harder than I thought it would be and I slipped into a deep sleep once again.

Chapter 12

When I awoke, I was pleasantly surprised to see both Gio and Angela sitting across from me. I still couldn't talk, but that didn't stop me from smiling ear to ear when I saw them. I grabbed the pad that I had used with Nurse Bellinger and began to write a message that would have to be basic so Gio could read it to Angela.

You have no idea how happy I am to see you guys. How did you get here?

"Grandma took us here. She is in the bathroom," Gio answered as he gave a hug.

"Daddy I am so glad you are awake. I have been waiting so long to talk to you," Angela said and gave me a hug as well.

I bet you have. Did anyone tell you about what happened?

"Not much. Just that you were in a car accident, and you got hurt pretty bad. Does it hurt?" Gio asked.

Not really. I am on a lot of pain medication, the good stuff.

Gio and Angela both laughed at my poor attempt at humor. When they finished laughing, my mother came out of the bathroom with a concerned look on her face. I knew what that look meant, and I wanted to do what I could to put her at ease.

Mom, I am ok. Nothing that won't heal in time. No need to worry.

After reading my note, my mom began to tear up and then gave me the best motherly hug one can give. While holding me, she whispered in my ear, "You have been through so much, I know you will prevail from this. I just wish like hell it was me instead of you. I love you son."

Thank you, mom. I love you too.

The next few minutes were spent in silence as I began to drift in and out again. The combination of the morphine, antibiotics, and other medications, was making me very groggy. I wanted to stay awake and talk with my family forever, but I knew that I would be asleep soon and wanted to let them know they didn't need to hang around.

I am very tired and will be asleep soon, so why don't you all go back home, and I will have someone call you when I am more awake. Hopefully, I will be able to call myself.

With that, my mom, Gio, and Angela each gave me a hug and kiss goodbye and told me that they would see me soon. I did my best to reciprocate but I was too sleepy to do anything other than raise my eyebrows to acknowledge their gesture.

Once my family left, I turned the TV off and turned on my side to go to sleep. I was relieved I was able to move more freely now that the neck collar was removed. Once I was comfortable, I closed my eyes, only to be interrupted by the nurse coming in to give me more medication.

"Sorry to wake you Mr. Amici, but it is time for your early evening medication. I also have something for you," Nurse Bellinger said.

Nurse Bellinger handed me two pills and a cup of water to take them with. Once she collected the medicine cup from me, she handed me a sealed envelope with nothing written on the front. I was extremely tired, so I decided to open the envelope when I woke up in the morning; however, curiosity got the better of me. When the nurse left the room, I turned on the light and opened the envelope with both anxiety and excitement.

Inside the envelope was a flash drive that had my name on it. It was obviously sent to me by someone who wanted to either show me something or send a message. I had grown accustomed to this sort of cryptic nonsense since the Sean Lancaster case. In fact, I kind of liked it. I enjoyed trying to solve puzzles and connect the dots. But I also grew tired of these antics very quickly because they usually led to a situation that would not bode well for me. I was not sure if my laptop was retrieved from my car and brought to my room or if it was still in working condition.

I paged Nurse Bellinger to see if it was in the room, but she could not find it. I then wrote her a note asking if she had a laptop I could borrow and showed her the flash drive. She offered to see what was on the flash drive for me, but I told her I was not sure it was meant for anyone else's eyes but mine. She seemed to understand because she immediately went to get her workstation laptop. When she entered the room again, she handed me her laptop and put her finger to her mouth to tell me not to tell anyone. I winked at her in acknowledgment and inserted the flash drive.

After a few seconds, a clickable icon appeared to play a video. My anxiety was kicking up several notches waiting for the video to load. Once the video loaded, I pressed play and was immediately confused by what I saw. The camera angle was high above an intersection in NYC and there were cars passing each other, nothing out of the ordinary. What was this? Why would someone send me a video of normal flowing traffic in New York City? Twenty-three seconds into the video, a car came speeding into view from the left side of the video, ran a red light, and crashed directly into a car crossing the intersection. The car that was hit went flying in the air and then tumbled until it smashed into a parked taxicab. Immediately, my heart sank, and I began to panic. This was a video of my car accident. Someone had filmed it, almost as if they knew what was coming. Once the video of the accident faded, a message appeared on the screen.

Sometimes, things are not an accident at all.

Chapter 13

Alan Lowery and Steven Hill sat in the main conference room pondering what to do with Sal's case. After his accident, there was no way Sal could defend Joseph Millstone, yet they did not have anyone that they trusted with a case of this magnitude. Both of them had not been in a courtroom setting in a decade and a half so they were not suitable replacements for Sal. After several hours of deliberation, they were still at an impasse.

"Steven, we cannot let this case go. It means too much to the firm and our reputation. We are still riding the wave of popularity that Sean Lancaster gave us and if we gave this up, it would derail us for years to come," Alan stated.

"I get that Alan, but who else do we have that can take on this case? Sal is the only one qualified to do it and let's face it, he is the only one with enough credibility to do it also," Steven rebutted.

"We can attend the arraignment. That is not a big deal. We can also begin the discovery phase as well. Do you really think we forgot how to review evidence? The hope is that at that point, Sal will be well enough to take over the trial."

Steven looked at Alan with a confused look on his face. In all the years he had known Alan, he had never once heard him offer to split up the responsibilities on a case. The idea that the case meant so much to the firm was clear; however, Steven also knew that just as much damage could be done if the firm seemed unorganized or lacked faith in its other attorneys.

"Alan. You really want to split up the responsibilities on this case? Won't that make us look unorganized and desperate?"

"How, exactly? It will show quite the opposite. It will demonstrate that we have a pulse on what's going on and can make adjustments as needed to ensure our clients are represented in the best, most professional way."

Steven knew that Alan was the unofficial boss of the firm even though Alan's name is a part of the firm's name. Since the passing of Thomas Greenwood a little over a year ago, Alan has assumed the responsibility of making critical decisions for the firm. Alan will sometimes consult Steven and Sal, but for the most part, he makes judgment calls on most issues by himself.

"Ok Alan. If that is what you want to do. Just know that I am on record as saying I am opposed to this and think we need to assign this case to another attorney. I love Sal and I know he is the right person for this case, but the truth is, we do not know when or if he will be back at full capacity," Steven stated.

"Duly noted Steven," Alan replied.

As both Alan and Steven were packing up and readying themselves to head back to their offices, Jill Lawson came waltzing in, looking like she had something important to tell them.

"Sorry to bother you two, but I just got a call from Sal's mother with an update on Sal's condition," Jill said. "She said he is doing ok but that he cannot speak. The doctors think there was damage to his vocal cords and that he may not be able to speak for a while."

"Thank you, Jill. We appreciate you giving us an update," Alan said.

After Jill left the conference room, Alan and Steven looked at each other with a look of great concern. They realized that everything they had just discussed was for naught and they needed to change their strategy immediately.

"Well that sucks, doesn't it?" Alan said.

"Sure does. What do we do now?" Steven asked.

"The only thing we can do. Go see Sal and assess the situation ourselves."

Chapter 14

Preparing food for the inmates is one of the safest jobs one can have in prison. Rarely will there be a fight in the kitchen because everyone wants to eat and is not willing to do anything to disrupt that process. It is also not easy to get a job like that. It normally takes a number of bribes, intimidation, and power to be offered a position in the kitchen; however, for Danielle Amici, it did not require any of those methods. She had been offered the job of head chef from day one because of her celebrity.

Revered for her sophisticated and elaborate plan to help murder the family of Sean Lancaster, Danielle was a hero from the moment she arrived at Bedford Hills. Nobody messed with her or even thought to double cross her on anything. She embraced the stature she had and used it to her advantage on most occasions, including running the kitchen.

"I made meatloaf for them last week. These bitches will just have to learn that they eat what I give them," Danielle said hastily.

"True, but you also do not want the wrong people getting angry at you. You may be hot shit around here, but you aren't untouchable," Kim Martinez said.

Kimberly Martinez was Danielle's cell mate at Bedford Hills. The two were as different as you can get; however, they prove the theory that opposites do indeed attract. Danielle was about elegance and grace, whereas Kim was about toughness and grit. She was in an abusive marriage for years when she finally snapped. She took a metal baseball bat and beat her ex-husband over the head thirteen times and then broke both his kneecaps. Miraculously, her ex-husband survived the attack; however, he suffered severe brain damage and will never walk again. As a result of the attack, Kim was in Bedford Hills on two aggravated assault charges, with each charge carrying a sentence of twenty years.

"I know Kim, but I am not letting anyone walk all over me. You know this," Danielle answered.

"Ok. But don't say I didn't warn you."

Danielle proceeded to continue to prepare dinner for all of the inmates when she received a message from one of the guards that she had a phone call. She was awarded certain privileges because of her status in the prison, but also because of her incredibly deep pockets. She can pay off anyone and often supplied the guards with hefty bonuses for allowing her to bend the rules.

"Who is this?" Danielle asked.

"Is that anyway to answer the phone?"

"OMG. I am so sorry. How are you? Where are you?" Danielle said with excitement.

"You know I can't tell you where I am, but I am doing ok," Sean Lancaster said. "How are you? How is life at the top treating you?"

"You were right. Money is king around here. I can't believe the shit I am able to get away with. I just wish you could come visit me so we can have conjugal visits over and over."

"In time, we might be able to, but not in the near future. I have to keep a low profile while I am being hunted. Speaking of which, have you heard anything?"

"Not recently. My contact at the NYPD said they have no new leads and are recycling the ones they do have. You really have them spinning their tails," Danielle said with a grin.

"Good. They will never catch me. I am too smart for them, and I have unlimited resources as well," Sean said with cockiness. "One last question. That pain in the ass ex-husband of yours. Any word on how he is doing?"

"Last I heard he was not able to speak and is still in critical condition."

"And the video?"

"I arranged to have it sent to him. I am assuming he has watched it by now, so I should hear something soon."

"Good, because this has to go as planned. If he starts asking questions and finds out you set the accident up, he will come at you with everything he has," Sean said cautiously.

"Don't worry. Sal will not make it out of the hospital alive."

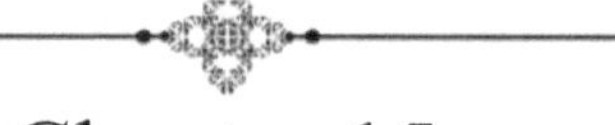

Chapter 15

After a few days, I was beginning to feel a little better. I was able to move around in the bed a little, which was good because bed sores were beginning to kick in. I got my voice back, although it was very raspy and low, making it difficult for others to hear me. I was also beginning to realize that I would be taken off the Millstone case and that I would be in this shithole for a while.

"Mr. Amici, sorry to bother you, but you have some visitors. Would you like me to send them in?" the nurse asked me.

Anytime I got a visitor, it was a welcomed distraction to my situation. It didn't matter who the visitor was because I was glad to be able to talk to someone and not have to listen to the TV all day and all night. My mother and children were my normal visitors, but I also received visits from a few friends and colleagues. What surprised me the most about those that came and did not come to see me, was that Alan and Steven had not stopped by. I knew they were busy trying to see what needed to get done for the Millstone case, but I was a partner in the firm and felt they should have stopped by at least once.

"Sure, send them in," I said as I tried to sit up the best I could.

To my amazement, Alan and Steven came waltzing into my room with a bouquet of beautiful flowers.

"Hey partner. How are you feeling?" Alan asked me.

"Been better. It's so nice to see you both," I said in a deep raspy voice.

"You sound like shit, but at the least you sound like something," Steven said laughing.

I began to chuckle but had to limit myself because of the pain I had in my ribs. I tried not to show how much pain I was in, but I did not do a very good job because Steven grimaced and told me he would not make any more jokes.

"It's ok Steven. That's who you are. Don't change on my behalf," I reassured Steven.

"So what have the doctors told you about your recovery?" Alan asked.

"Doctors. These guys are almost as useless as prosecutors. They have no idea. One says I will be here for a few weeks then go to an inpatient rehab center, while another tells me I will be out in a few days and will require outpatient therapy three times a week."

"Well that doesn't help. Why the different opinions?" Alan asked.

"Probably a pissing contest. Who knows. All I do know is that I need a straight answer and I am not getting one," I said with frustration.

"I bet. Want me to ruffle some feathers?" Steven said. "Oops, sorry. I forgot. No jokes."

"I don't think you can do that Steven, but I'll tell you what you can do for me. You can grab that pitcher of water and pour me a glass."

As Steven was pouring my water, Alan gave me a look that I recognized right away. It was the look I had seen too many times recently. One that I was all too familiar with. Now I understood why Alan and Steven had not come to see me yet.

"Listen, Sal. I hate to bring this up, I really do, but we have to talk about how Joseph Millstone's case will be handled. Obviously in the immediate future you are not able to represent him, so Steven and I will attend the arraignment and begin the discovery phase. We plan on using a few of the newer colleagues to assist us. After that…well after that we have no idea."

"Alan, do you think it is best to take me off the case completely so you can assign it to someone that can devote his/her full attention to the case from day one?" I asked.

"I was thinking that, but Steven doesn't trust anyone else in the firm to handle a case of this magnitude," Alan answered.

"Well it's true, isn't it?" Steven said.

"To a degree, yes, but what about this? What if we assign the case to someone and then when Sal gets better, he can join as co-counsel?"

"Who can we give the case to?" I asked confused.

"Kelly Esteves," Alan answered.

"Kelly is young, ambitious, and definitely a different direction, but she also just passed her bar exam and does not have any courtroom experience," I responded.

"That is true, but that is what you will teach her," Steven said.

"How? From my hospital bed?"

"Exactly," Alan said with an ear-to-ear smile.

"How is that going to work? I won't be in the courtroom to observe her."

"You don't need to be. Sal, all you need to teach her is courtroom etiquette and procedure. She will provide the facts of the case, what happened that day, and where she feels she needs improvement. It is perfect," Alan said, still smiling.

"I don't know guys, but I am willing to try it. Have her stop by here sooner than later so we can get started. And make sure to tell her right away that she is co-counsel. Once I am better, I will join her, but it will still be her show."

"Will do Sal. Get some rest. We will see you in a few days with more details," Alan said and gave me a fist pump.

"Take care Sal. Get well soon," Steven said and gave me a hug.

"Thanks guys. Don't forget to run this by Joseph as well. After all, we work for him."

Chapter 16

Joseph Millstone sat in the courtroom waiting for the inevitable to happen. He knew that the judge would not grant him bail so why go through the hassle of getting dressed up to appear in court. He also was aware of Sal's accident but had not been told what the plan was moving forward.

The arraignment went as planned, only lasting a few minutes. As expected, the judge denied bail and remanded Joseph back to Rikers Island for the duration of his trial. After the judge's decision, Joseph was brought to the courthouse jail awaiting transfer back to Rikers Island. While sitting in his cell, he began to think of his next move and how he would survive in Riker's. Before he had a chance to complete his thoughts, his defense team came to pay him a visit.

"Joseph, I would like to formally introduce you to Kelly Esteves. Kelly will be lead counsel until Sal is well enough to return to work. At that time, he will join Kelly as co-counsel; however, Kelly will remain lead counsel for the duration of the trial," Alan explained.

"I didn't agree to this. Did you think to run this by me first before you made these decisions?" Joseph answered with great anger.

"What do you think we are doing now dipshit?" Steven replied.

"Mr. Millstone. I understand and respect that you want Sal Amici as your defense attorney. He is a fantastic lawyer with a proven track record of success. But the fact of the matter is, he is laid up in a hospital bed and not getting out anytime soon. Now, unless you want to spend the next few weeks interviewing attorneys and losing time that could be spent building your defense, I suggest you roll with what we are offering and keep your mouth shut," Kelly said.

Her response shocked both Alan and Steven. They had never seen her like this before, but they loved it. She was both frank and tough. No bullshit, just hard truth with an ultimatum. They both looked at each other in amazement and excitement. It was then that they realized they had chosen the right person to step in and it didn't even take the first witness to whip her into shape.

"Wow. That was impressive counselor. You do that in the courtroom, and we are golden. Now, what do you need from me?" Joseph asked.

"What I need from you, is to listen to what I say and do what I say without question. It is very important that we are on the same page because if the DA or jury think for one instance that we are not, it is game over," Kelly instructed.

"Got it ma'am."

"No need to call me ma'am. Kelly will be fine. I am going to come see you tomorrow at Riker's to get your story about what happened that night."

"Which night?" Joseph asked.

Alan, Steven, and Kelly were confused by Joseph's question because Joseph was being charged with crimes that occurred on only one night. What did he mean by which night?

"What do you mean which night?" Kelly asked.

"Is there another way to say it? There have been so many nights I can talk about; I honestly lose track easily."

"Explain," Alan said.

"I will, but first, we have attorney-client privilege right?" Joseph asked.

"Yes, we do," Kelly answered.

"Ok then, here we go. Well, you know they call me the night slasher, right?"

"We have heard that in the news, but we didn't think it applied to you. It seemed too convenient for the police to pin all those murders on you," Steven said.

"Oh it applies to me alright. See, they only reported on six cases, but in fact, there are so many more that they don't know about," Joseph said with an evil stare.

"How many more cases?" Kelly asked nervously.

"Oh who keeps count of these things? Just know that six is just the beginning."

Alan, Steven, and Kelly looked at each other with both fear and nervousness. Was their client actually admitting to them that he is the serial killer the police have been after for all these months? And if he is, would they want to continue to defend him?

"Are you telling us that you are the night slasher and that the police haven't found all of your victims?" Alan asked.

"Now counselor, I am not saying anything to that effect, but I will tell you this. If the police think they can find a pattern or MO, they are mistaken. There isn't one. If they think there are only six cases, they are mistaken. If they think this will end because I am here, it won't. In other words, the people of New York City should be scared," Joseph said as he leaned into Kelly's eyes, stared for a few seconds, and finally whispered, "very scared."

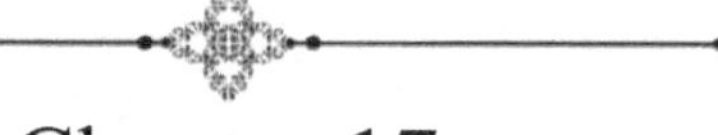

Chapter 17

Over the next few days, I continued to improve both physically and mentally. I was able to get out of bed now and walk to the other side of the room with a walker. I was also able to go to the bathroom by myself, which is a very underrated ability. I was also beginning to warm up to the idea that I had a long road of recovery ahead of me and I would need to give everything I had to that and not be so worried about when I was going to get back to work.

Most of my days consisted of eating breakfast, lunch, and dinner, physical therapy, and watching TV. I occasionally got visitors, which threw a welcome wrinkle in my day; however, they did not come as often as I would like. All of my visitors were the same people, so I knew what to expect. That is why when Kelly Esteves came to see me, I was taken back a bit, unsure of what to expect.

"Hi Sal. How are you?" Kelly asked.

"Hi Kelly. I am ok. Getting better every day. Hopefully I will be getting out of here soon."

"That's good because I need your help with this one."

"Joseph Millstone?" I asked.

"Yeah. Sal, I got a real bad feeling about this guy," Kelly answered.

"Why? I mean I know he is being charged with murdering five people, but we have seen something like this before."

"Not like him. Sal, he basically admitted to being the night slasher and said that the police have not nearly uncovered all of his murders."

"He said that? In those exact words?" I asked nervously.

"Well not those exact words, but he insinuated that. Then he stared at me in the evilest way and said that this was not over and that the people of New York City should be very scared."

I could see the terror in Kelly's eyes growing and right away I knew something was terribly wrong. Joseph had put such a scare into her that it would have taken a miracle for her to be in the same room as him, let alone be able to defend him by herself.

"Are you going to be ok defending him alone? If not, I need to know now."

"No, I will be fine. I was just caught off guard by the way he acted and what he said. Sal, how are we supposed to, in good conscience, defend someone who admitted to being a serial killer?" Kelly asked, scared.

"Listen, Kelly. I know how upsetting this must be and how scared you are. I would be too. But there is something you can do about it. I know you did not know Thomas Greenwood, but I am sure you have heard of his legend. He was like a father to me, and he gave me a piece of advice when I was starting out, just like you, that I have carried with me to this day. He told me, 'Son, you are about to enter a world of deceit and lies. As long as you are always cognizant of where you are going and how to get there, you will be ok.' Take that for what it is worth but if you let your clients intimidate you, it will destroy your career faster than you can say career change."

"But how do I do that? I know the next time I see him I'm going to be scared and I do not hide my emotions well."

"You have to remember that he needs you and it is not the other way around. You always hold the upper hand. You can walk away anytime you like. You can threaten him."

"That is all well and good but what if I am not cut out for that?" Kelly asked.

"Why did you want to become a lawyer, more specifically, a defense attorney? And don't give the political bullshit answer of `I want to see justice done.'"

"I like to argue and be a voice for those who need it most," Kelly responded.

"Noble, but naïve don't you think?"

"What is your point?"

"My point is that at some point when you decided to pursue law as a career, you knew you would eventually have a career defining case. A case that would test your resolve and courage. This is *that* case for you. You have the opportunity right now to seize the moment, Carpe Diem. What you do with it will define who you will be as an attorney. Just know that you have the resources and support of the entire firm behind you. You are not alone," I said hoping to reassure Kelly.

I could see a change in her demeanor and posture after my pep talk. She no longer looked timid and frail. She sat up in her seat as if she had found new hope and had a gleam in her eye. I could tell that she resonated with what I said and would be able to use that motivation to move forward with the case.

"You're right Sal. Thank you. I needed that," Kelly graciously said.

"You're welcome. Now tell me how your meeting went with Joe."

Chapter 18

Once Kelly left, I got a visit from my primary doctor. She told me that I was progressing really well and that I was projected to be released by the end of the week. She also mentioned that I would need extensive outpatient physical therapy, which I was not looking forward to. Regardless of the prospect of facing months of physical therapy, I was happy to know that I would be home with my kids soon.

When my doctor left, I called Alan and let him know the good news and that I intended to get back to work, even if that meant working from home. He was elated that I was doing so well and would be able to get back to work sooner than we expected. He also told me that Kelly had reached out to him after our visit with a new sense of confidence and direction. He thanked me for speaking with her and told me to let him know if there were any further details.

For the first time since the accident, I was feeling optimistic and hopeful. I could now see the light at the end of the tunnel and began to think about what life would be like when I got out. I knew that I was going to have to take it slow, which would be a challenge for me because I only knew one speed and that was to go. I also knew that I would have support that I could rely on, which I definitely intended to use.

After a few hours of rest, I was woken up by someone standing next to my bed. I was so groggy and confused waking from such a deep sleep, that I did not recognize the person hovering over me. Even after regaining my bearings and vision, I still was not sure of who this person was. I soon realized there was only one way to find out.

"Who are you?" I asked.

"Name is Detective Randolph, NYPD. Sorry to wake you Mr. Amici but I have a few questions I would like to ask you," the detective stated.

"I already talked to the police and gave them my full statement. I do not know how much more I can add."

"I understand sir, but I am looking to ask some questions that maybe nobody else thought of. I am only asking for five minutes of your time."

"Ok, but just five minutes. I need to go back to sleep."

"Understood Mr. Amici," the detective began. "I am sure you have been asked this but do you know anyone who would want to harm you?"

"Harm me? This was an accident. Why would I think anybody did this on purpose?" I asked, confused.

"I'm not saying that sir. I am merely asking if you think it is possible someone wanted to harm you."

"Detective, I am a criminal defense attorney in New York City. I will always have enemies"

"I see. Well it was just a thought. You know from the fallout from last year."

"Meaning what?" I asked. starting to get agitated.

"Meaning you don't think it possible Sean Lancaster or Danielle want you dead?" the detective asked as he moved closer to me.

His line of questioning was odd to say the least, which got me suspicious of who he was. I had had the same suspicions last year when two detectives showed up at my front door to tell me David Flores had murdered his family, but those two gentlemen were actual detectives. I wanted to give this man the benefit of the doubt, but something inside me told me to be on my guard.

"Who sent you?"

"The police commissioner," the detective replied with a smirk. "Who do you think sent me?"

Just as he finished his sentence, he lunged toward me and covered my mouth and nose with a pillow. He was pressing down on my face so hard, I could not move. Even if I was at full strength, I would be no competition for him. He seemed to be applying more and more force as the seconds ticked away on what I thought was sure to be the end for me.

As he continued to smother my face, my arms began the flail in every direction. My vision was blurry so I did not have a good view of where he was. I managed to hit him a few times, which lightened his force a little each time, allowing me to catch my breath a bit. I knew that I was going to die if I didn't do something quick. I searched for the call button but could not find it. I reached for my phone but it had been knocked to the ground in the struggle. There was only one thing left I could do to save my life, but it would cause excruciating pain like I never felt before.

With all my strength and my will to live, I swung my right leg and hit him in the head. The pain started right away and shot right up my body, all the way to my head. At that point, adrenaline took over and I continued to kick again and again until the man finally fell to the floor.

I didn't have much time before he would recover, so I grabbed the first thing I could find, my metal bedpan, and whacked him over the head a few times. It didn't seem to do much damage because he got right back up and started charging toward me again.

Even though I had failed to knock him out, I was hopeful I caused enough ruckus that a nurse or doctor would come in to see what was going on. Nobody showed up immediately, but when I screamed as loud as I could before the pillow was back on my face, two nurses and a janitor came barging into my room.

"What the hell is this?" the janitor asked.

Without hesitation, the man turned his attention to subdue my rescuers. He quickly charged the janitor and knocked him down and began to pummel his face with punch after punch. He became so wrapped up in the janitor, that he forgot about the two nurses who accompanied him. One of the nurses was a bodybuilder in his spare time and quickly was able to grab the man and pin him to the floor until the police came. My horrifying ordeal had come to an end.

It took five minutes or so for the police to arrive, which was no problem for the nurse. When the police arrived, they quickly put the man in handcuffs and began to haul him away. As he was leaving my hospital room, he uttered, "Danielle says hi."

Chapter 19

"What do you mean he got arrested? He is supposed to be the best. I paid that man one hundred thousand dollars and he gets arrested? What the hell am I paying you for if you can't get me someone competent," Danielle said softly into the phone.

"Well why don't you just send someone else than. I know a guy—" a voice on the other end said.

"I can't send someone else to kill him now. Don't you think it would be too much of a coincidence if there was another attempt on Sal's life so soon after your mess up?"

"Good point. Alright well I will be in touch then." the voice replied and hung up.

Danielle hung up the phone seething with as much anger as she had had in a long time. She knew her plan had a chance of failure but she didn't think it would go this bad. She also knew that she would surely be implicated in the murder attempt on her ex-husband, thus adding to the laundry list of charges she had been convicted of. She asked the guard to allow her to make one more phone call and slipped her a fifty-dollar bill.

"We have a problem," Danielle said.

"I know, I heard."

"How did you hear that already?" Danielle questioned.

"Danielle, really? You need to ask that?" Sean joked.

"I know, you are resourceful. Blah, blah, blah."

"What's with the attitude?" Sean asked, getting annoyed. "If there is anyone who *doesn't* deserve an attitude, it is me."

"You're right. I am sorry. I am just really pissed and scared because this went south."

Danielle was hoping for comfort from Sean because she was not going to get it from anywhere else. She had wanted to take out Sal, but did not know how to do it. The attempt on Sal's life in the hospital had been his idea and she was pressured into it. The trouble for Danielle now was that nobody knew it was his idea. She had to find a way to get him to implicate himself; something that was near impossible to do.

"When am I going to see you again? I miss you," Danielle said softly,

"Soon enough. I am closer than you think."

"Are you in New York City?"

"Darling you know I can't tell you that. Just know that this fucking cold is killing me. I'll be in touch soon. Love you," Sean said and then hung up.

Based on his cryptic answer, Danielle assumed Sean was back in the United States and somewhere that is cold. It was a good guess to think he was back in New York City to finish what he had started with Sal. If he was in New York City, she knew he would find a way to go see her.

Realizing there was nothing more she could do, Danielle made her way back to her cell to try and get some rest. When she arrived at her cell, there was a woman sitting on her cot with a guard standing behind her wielding a baton.

"Who the hell are you?" Danielle asked angrily.

"Doesn't matter. What does matter is that your boyfriend is in danger," the woman said.

"What are you talking about?"

"Don't play coy with me Danielle. I know you were just speaking to Sean Lancaster."

"So. Why do you care and what do you want with Sean?"

"No need to be hostile. I just came to tell you that he is in danger and better watch his back. He is gonna pay for what he did to my fiancée."

"Why? Who is your fiancé?" Danielle asked.

"Titus Baxter."

Chapter 20

After the attempt on my life in the hospital, I thought it was best to go home and get any necessary medical treatment there. I was able to convince the doctors to allow me to go home, but had to have a nurse twenty-four hours a day, seven days a week as part of the deal. Not a bad gig when I thought about it because I would have someone on hand to assist me with anything I needed, whenever I needed it.

When I arrived home, there was a greeting party for me that was unexpected. My kids both ran up to me in my wheelchair and almost knocked me over. My parents were also there to offer their support and help with the kids. To my surprise, Nicole was there as well. I hadn't really spoken too much to her since the accident, but was glad she was there.

The living room had been turned into my bedroom, which was yet another great surprise. My fifty-inch 4K UHD television was brought downstairs and mounted on the wall. My gaming systems were connected, as well as the DirecTV receiver. There was also a mini fridge, stocked with Diet Ginger Ale and beer. My family and friends had done a terrific job making sure I was as comfortable as possible.

When I got settled into my bed, my nurse asked if there was anything I needed before she went to the pharmacy to pick up my prescriptions. At first, I thought the idea of a live-in nurse was nice and would be beneficial; however, for some reason, I was feeling the opposite. I felt claustrophobic and agitated when she asked me if I needed anything. Rather than start an argument, I decided to wait and see if I would feel better later in the afternoon and told her I was fine.

"Daddy, I am so glad you are home. I missed you so much," Angela said.

"I missed you too Angela. How has it been staying with Grandma and Pop Pop?" I asked.

"It is ok. Grandma doesn't let me play as much as I want to."

"Well I am sure she has her reasons," I said and turned my attention to Gio. "How's it going Gio?"

"Good, dad. I have been following your case on the news. Did you know that Joseph Millstone grew up in Sarasota, Florida and went to NYU?"

"I was not aware of that son. I have not had a chance to look into the case details. Why the sudden interest in Joseph Millstone?" I asked, concerned.

"No reason. I just find this sort of thing interesting," Gio responded.

"Well, maybe you can help me sort through the evidence when Kelly brings over the case files."

"Really? That would be awesome!"

"Just a few items. You are not ready to see all of the details yet," I told Gio.

"Something is better than nothing. Thanks dad!" Gio said and ran off to his room pumping his fists in the air.

I had not seen Gio in such a good mood in a long time. It was a pleasure to see and it really helped to set my mind at ease about how he was handling the whole ordeal with Danielle and me.

Once the kids left the room, it was just me and Nicole left. I had missed her but not to the point that I was dying to talk to her. I had so much going on, I really did not have the time to think about anything else other than myself. She had been so patient with me to this point, which made me feel guilty about not missing her too much.

"Well, I finally have you all to myself," Nicole said and gave me a kiss. "I've missed you Sal."

"I missed you too Nicole," I said hoping she wouldn't notice I was less than truthful.

"I know we haven't exactly gotten off to the smoothest of starts and I know you have this thing with Danielle, but I want you to know I am here for you and am not going to rush you into anything."

"Thank you, Nicole. That means a lot to me. I promise I will give you what I can, but right now, I need you as my therapist. Is that ok?" I asked, sensing I had just disappointed her.

"Of course, Sal. Whatever you need," Nicole said as she broke her hand away from mine.

"I'm sorry. I know that is not what you want to hear right now, but it is what I need."

"I get it, Sal. I understand and it's fine. Tell me what I can do to help."

"Well, let me know when we can have a session. I really need someone to unload all this shit I have built up inside."

"I'll check my schedule and have my secretary get back to you."

"Nicole, don't be like that. I just need time. Please understand that," I asked, almost begging.

"I do understand Sal. I also think it is best if you address me as Dr. Adams for now."

"Ok, Dr. Adams. I look forward to hearing from your secretary."

"Take care Sal," Nicole responded and left.

I felt bad because I knew I had upset Nicole and that is the last thing I wanted to do; however, I needed to be selfish and think of myself to get to where I want to be. If that meant getting a new therapist as well, then so be it.

Chapter 21

The apartment was a much smaller living quarter than he was used to, but for Sean Lancaster, it served its purpose, which was to provide him with a safe place to stay while he devised his plan. He had spent the last year on the move in Europe, never staying in one location for more than two weeks. It became both grueling and tiresome to travel so much, which is why he decided that on the one-year anniversary of his disappearance, he would return to New York City to finish what he started.

Sean knew that he could not overdo it when it came to reaching out to Sal, but he wanted to play his game in the worst way every day. He wanted to torment and antagonize Sal so much that he would be leaking anxiety out of every pore in his body. He wanted Sal to know that he could be nearby or one thousand miles away. He also wanted Sal to know that he hadn't forgotten what he did to Danielle and that one day he would pay for it.

Even though he was still getting situated, Sean decided it was time to take action. His first act was to contact Sal and get a sense of where he is mentally and physically after being released from the hospital. Unlike the year before, Sean did not have anybody watching Sal's house or following his every move; however, he did have someone getting him real time details of Sal's whereabouts and condition.

"Did you find out where he is?" Sean asked.

"Yes. He is at his house. I can't believe he would be that dumb," a voice said to Sean

"Sal may be a brilliant lawyer, but he sure is not street smart. How mobile is he?"

"Not very. He gets around in a wheelchair and is confined to the living room."

"Excellent. Did you get his contact information for me?"

"Yes sir. I'll text it to you."

"Great job! Continue to monitor him and report back if anything changes."

"Will do, sir. Till next time," Samuel Porter said and hung up.

Sean knew he could rely on Samuel and that is his information was rock solid. Samuel Porter had been the one to actually commit the murder of Sean's family last year. After a handsome payout, he disappeared for a while and had become an afterthought, until Sean needed someone he trusted. Samuel Porter is that guy.

Sean also liked the irony that Samuel was Sal's first case at Lowery, Hill, and Greenwood. He liked to manipulate people and play on their emotions. He had heard Sal speak on numerous occasions about Samuel's case and how it was a sense of pride for him. What better way to tug at Sal's strings than to use his first proud moment as a lawyer to get his game going.

Sean pondered whether he should contact Sal now or let him settle in first so he is relaxed when he made contact. Sean tried his hardest to calm down the adrenaline he had flowing through every part of his body, but it was to no avail. He couldn't resist the urge to kick off his game and see how much Sal Amici was willing to play.

Chapter 22

Kelly Esteves sat across from Joseph Millstone scared out her mind listening to the details of the gruesome murder of the King family. She had gotten most of the details from the police reports and the subsequent forensic investigation, but she was not prepared to hear it from someone as evil as Joseph Millstone.

"So next thing I knew, I was in the house and everyone was asleep, just the way I like it," Joseph Millstone continued. "In fact, all of my murders were committed with everyone asleep. Did you know that counselor?"

"No. Keep going," Kelly answered wanting this to end as soon as possible.

"Why Kelly, why the attitude?" Joseph asked.

"Because Joseph, your trial begins in one week and I don't have any details that I feel I can use in court. You haven't given me anything and if you continue this charade, I will not be able to represent you to the best of my ability."

"To the best of my ability? What am I searching for a new ad campaign? That was pretty weak," Joseph tormented.

"Enough with the bullshit Joseph. Do you want me to represent you or not?" Kelly asked as her voice got louder, echoing off the prison walls.

"NO! I want Sal Amici to represent me. Not some rookie who doesn't know her head from her ass."

Kelly was taken back a little by Joseph's response. She knew he was going to be a tough client, but she did not know he would be as stubborn as he was. She did not want to give in to him but she also knew that she could not take any more of this. She was at a breaking point and knew that this would be an early crossroad in her career.

"Well Sal isn't ready to come back yet, so you got me. You also have Alan Lowery and Steven Hill, who have over sixty years of combined experience practicing law. If that isn't good enough for you Mr. Millstone, then we will end this interview right now."

Joseph Millstone looked hard and long into Kelly's deep blue eyes. She was the typical blond hair and blue eyes woman he adored. One that he dreamed would be his next victim. He even thought about her meeting her demise right there in the jail interrogation room, but thought better of it in the end. Still, his hunger for murder only intensified by how strikingly beautiful she was.

"Continue Ms. Esteves," Joseph said and motioned his hand toward her seat.

"Thank you. As you were saying earlier, you entered the house and everyone was asleep. What happened next?" Kelly asked.

"You know what happened. You have the report right there. Or do you want to know exactly how I killed everyone in that house? How I ended their lives without them even knowing I was there? Or maybe how when I killed Mrs. King, I got an erection. Is that what you mean?"

"Never mind. I got what I came for, "Kelly said disgusted. "Mr. Millstone, you better start thinking of cooperating more. I am the last line of defense between you and a life in prison without parole. I need something I can use in court that puts doubt into the jury's minds. Something that shows someone else committed these crimes. Something that proves you were somewhere else when these crimes occurred. Do you get what I am saying?" Kelly desperately asked.

"I get what you mean, yes. You want answers to your questions, or better yet, you want the information you can use in court?"

"Yes, Mr. Millstone. That is what I have been trying to tell you. What do you have for me?"

"I don't have anything, but if you want answers, you need to find someone else first."

"Who?" Kelly asked intrigued.

"Sean Lancaster."

Chapter 23

I was enjoying my time at home with my kids while I was recovering from both the car accident and the attempt on my life. Angela was entertaining me every day with her doll shows and Gio was helping me sift through dozens of case files that Kelly had brought over for me to look at.

One thing I did not care for was the physical therapy. I had a therapist come to my house three times a week for a one-hour session. Each season was more grueling than the previous one, but it seemed to be working because I was gaining more strength with each passing day. On this day, my physical therapy session was interrupted by a surprise visit.

"Dad, Kelly is here. She said it's urgent she speaks to you," Gio shouted from the other room.

"Ok, send her in here," I answered.

I had not expected Kelly to come to my house or call me for that matter until the trial began, which was still a week away. Whenever she popped up, something is usually either wrong or she needs to be calmed down. In this case, it was both.

"Hi Kelly. Didn't expect to see you so soon. Everything ok?" I asked.

"Depends on what you mean by ok. I met with Joseph Millstone earlier. He told me something that I don't know what to make of."

"I am sure whatever it is, we can figure it out," I said, trying to reassure Kelly.

"He told me that if I want the information I can use to help set him free, I need to find Sean Lancaster."

I went completely still after hearing what Kelly had told me. I knew that Sean Lancaster was still out there and that he spun a very large web, but I did not think for one second that he would be involved in this case. I thought maybe Kelly had misheard Joseph, but the likelihood of that being the case was very slim.

"Are you sure he said Sean Lancaster?" I asked, knowing full well she had.

"Yes, Sal. I am positive. Why do you think I came straight here?"

"Uh, Pamela, I think we are going to have cut this session short. We can make it up tomorrow right?' I asked my therapist.

"Ok Sal, but you still have to do your exercises when you are done," Pamela answered.

"I will, I promise. Thank you," I said and waited for Pamela to leave. "Ok, tell me what you know."

"Well, like I said, he told me I need to find Sean Lancaster when I pressed him for information. I told him I needed something that I can use for his defense and this is what he gave me."

"It doesn't make any sense. At no time during Sean's trial or my interactions with him did Joseph Millstone come up. I find that hard to believe. You think he is just trying to buy some time?"

"I don't know Sal. That is why I am here to see what you think."

"Did you tell Alan and Steven?"

"No, I came here first. Isn't that what you told me to do?" Kelly answered, getting angry.

"Calm down, it was just a question. Alright, we need to keep digging through these files. The answer has to be here somewhere," I said pointing to dozens of boxes scattered in my living room.

"What boxes have you already been through? I will revisit them to begin."

After I pointed out the boxes Gio and I had already been through, I called Jill and asked her if she was able to come to my house to assist with this daunting task. If we were going to find the connection between Sean and Joseph, I needed all hands-on deck. Turns out, all the help I needed was with me all along.

"Dad, I think I found something. Here, take a look at this," Gio said as he handed me a photo.

"Thanks Gio, but this photo is of Samuel Porter and Sean Lancaster holding a fish, not Joseph Millstone," I said, informing my son.

"I know that, but who is this?" Gio said pointing to the far-right side of the photo.

I took the photo to examine it more closely but still could not see what Gio was talking about. I had looked over this photo at least two dozen times last year after I had won the Sean Lancaster case. At the time, I was trying to figure out who was toying with me over the phone. It turned out to be David Flores, who killed his family after I had set him free; however, the photograph helped me find out the whole truth about the murders of Sean's family.

"I don't see it son."

"RIGHT HERE!" Gio shouted and pointed to a name tag on the right side of someone's shirt.

I looked closely at the photo again, but this time, focusing on what Gio had pointed out. When I held a water bottle up to the photo to see what the name tag read, my heart began to beat rapidly. I couldn't believe my twelve-year old son had discovered what could be the evidence we needed to make the connection.

"Gio, this is fantastic. How did you see that?" I asked in astonishment.

"I am twelve years old. Not old like you," Gio joked.

"Sal, what did he find?" Kelly asked.

"This photo. The one I used last year to get the truth from Sean. There is a name tag on a person's shirt on the far-right corner of the photo."

"What name is on it?" Kelly asked anxiously.

"Joseph M."

Chapter 24

The night before his trial was set to begin, Joseph Millstone found himself pacing in his cell. He was not sure why he was so nervous, but he knew that his life was about to change one way or another. His roommate, only known to everyone as Whitaker, was growing tired of his pacing and decided to do something about it.

"Yo, man. Quit it. You're giving me a headache," Whitaker said.

"Man, I'm nervous about tomorrow. Sorry if I'm bothering you, I can't help it," Joseph answered.

"Yeah, well you ain't gonna make it to court tomorrow if you keep this up."

"Really? Am I supposed to be scared or something?"

Whitaker jumped down from the top bunk and got right up in Joseph's face. He had an intimidating snarl and eyes so dark, they blended in with the rest of his dark complexion.

"Don't make me hurt you dude. I don't wanna do that," Whitaker said.

"Listen, I know you are a big shot around here and I am supposed to be scared of you, but listen fella, I ain't scared of nobody. Ok?" Joseph answered without moving an inch.

The standoff between the two cellmates was coming to a boiling point, yet neither man was backing down. As the tension grew, Joseph let his natural instincts take over and before he knew it, he began pounding Whitaker's midsection like Rocky Balboa hitting raw meat. Blow after blow eventually caused Whitaker to go down rather quickly, which gave Joseph an even bigger advantage. Joseph continued his assault by kicking Whitaker in the face two times, then kicking his stomach another two times. Finally, Joseph finished off the beating with a stomp to Whitaker's nuts.

Joseph knew the guards were on their way, so he turned around, put his hands behind his back, and waited for them to take him away.

Before they were able to get there, Joseph had one more message for Whitaker.

"You think this was bad, just wait until we are alone again punk. You ain't seen nothing yet," Joseph said.

Joseph continued to stand with his hands behind his back for another two minutes until he realized that nobody was coming. The entire floor had seen what happened and were cheering Joseph on, so it would stand to reason that the guards would be on their way. Another minute passed by and nothing. Joseph began to get a little worried because he now faced the prospect of being in the cell with Whitaker after beating him so badly. Finally, a guard came to their cell, but not for the reason Joseph thought.

"You do this Millstone?" the guard asked.

"Do you see anyone else here?"

"Knock off the wiseass comments. Did you do this Millstone?"

"Yes boss," Joseph answered, resigning to his fate.

"I didn't see anything. Carry on," the guard said and walked away.

Joseph tried to resist but could not help letting a small smirk fall on his face. He clearly should have been sent to solitary confinement but instead, he was left in his cell with the man he almost beat to death.

After a few minutes, Whitaker began to get up and shake off the beating. Joseph wasn't sure how things would turn out from that point, but he *was* sure that would be ready to give another beating if he had to.

"Damn, you sure fight hard. Kudos to you man," Whitaker said.

"Uh, thank you," Joseph said, confused.

"I mean he told me to make it look convincing but I wasn't expecting to get my ass handed to me like that. I don't think I will be having kids anytime soon thanks to you."

"I'm sorry, who told you to make what look convincing?" Joseph asked, still confused.

"Your lawyer, Sal Amici. He asked me to pick a fight with you and let you win so your cred goes up. When your cred goes up, you get special privileges," Whitaker answered, shocking Joseph.

"Nice of him to tell me his plan."

"I think that was the point. To make it as authentic for you as possible. His plan worked dude. The guard just looked the other way."

"Now all I need to know is why Sal wants me to have special privileges."

"You really don't get it do you?" Whitaker said. "Special privileges allow you to meet with people during non-visitation hours. They allow you extra yard time. They also allow you extra phone time."

"And why do I need all that? I am doing just fine the way things are now," Joseph asked, more confused than ever.

"Because my narrow-minded cellie, the more phone time and visitation you have, the easier it is for you here."

Chapter 25

One Week Later

There is nothing like the anticipation of the first day of a trial. It was a new chapter in my career; however, I still liked the intensity of cross examinations and disproving a theory the prosecution has. All the hard work that goes into preparing a defense and identifying what obstacles I would be sure to encounter at some point during the trial is something I enjoyed as well. However, getting dressed and getting into the car has never been an obstacle I thought I would ever face. Welcome to my new life.

I was advised by both my doctor and live-in nurse that going to court would not be the best option for me at this stage of my recovery. They both seem to feel that my body is not ready to handle the activities involved in being in a courtroom. Although they were probably correct, there was not a chance I was going to miss making an opening statement and seeing how the trial went. I also thought that if I surprisingly showed up, that the jury would be distracted from the DA's opening statement.

When I got to the courthouse, my nurse wanted to bring me inside in a wheelchair; I was having none of that. I was determined to not let anyone, especially the jury, see me in a weakened state. Instead, I grabbed the steel cane that had been given to me by Alan and Steven and made my way to the courtroom on my own two feet. On my way to the courtroom, I was greeted with applause from the passing attorneys and clerks I have worked with over the years. It was a great feeling to know that so many people were aware of what happened to me and they were in my corner.

As I entered the courtroom, I had to maneuver my way around the multiple television cameras and the wires that protruded from them. I rejected any help offered to me in an effort to show strength and determination. This day was about Joseph Millstone, but it was also

69

my only opportunity to show everyone that I am stronger than people think.

When I approached the defense table, Kelly was already there. She was reviewing her notes and was a bit startled when I tapped her on the shoulder to announce my presence. She looked fantastic for the occasion. She had asked me what to wear to make an impression and I told her just look like you own a yacht and you will be fine. She took my words literally because she was wearing a Valentino midnight black pencil skirt with a silk blouse in nature white made by Valerie. Her shoes were also Valentino and matched her skirt. If someone saw her for the first time, they would never have known this was her first high profile case.

"How much did you spend on that outfit? My god," I asked Kelly.

"Don't ask. Let's just say we better win this case or I will be homeless," Kelly replied.

"Well you look magnificent," I said, hoping to give her confidence.

"Thank you."

We spent the next few minutes reviewing the case notes she had compiled and came to a decision that I would conduct the opening statement, but she would have the floor the rest of the day, with me observing. I could tell she was nervous and unsure of herself, but I reminded her that she was here for a reason and that Alan, Steven, and myself have nothing but the highest confidence in her. That confidence was about to be tested when I saw who the judge was.

"All rise," the bailiff ordered. "This court, with the Honorable Victoria Santino presiding, is now in session."

I was suddenly in a catatonic state for a few seconds. With all of the rehab I was doing and everything else that was going on in my life, I had forgotten to ask who the judge was. I had not put together the fact that we were in Brooklyn and Victoria Santino was a judge there.

"Did you know Santino was the judge? I asked Kelly.

"Yes. You didn't know?"

"Does this look like the face of someone who knew?" I snapped back, pointing to my face with one finger. .

"Oh, well sorry. I thought you did. Is it going to be a problem?" Kelly asked me.

"We will see."

When Judge Santino entered the courtroom, she sat down, ordered everyone else to sit, then asked the bailiff to bring Joseph Millstone into the courtroom. This was the first time I had seen him without his shackles and orange jumpsuit. He looked like a normal guy who works a nine to five job and has a family. That would hopefully work in our favor.

After the jury was sworn in, Judge Santino wasted no time in addressing the elephant in the room.

"Mr. Amici, it is good to see you here today. How do you feel?"

"I am ok judge, thank you for asking," I answered avoiding eye contact.

"It is quite impressive that you were able to make the recovery that you did," Judge Santino said.

"Once again, thank you judge," I answered wanting to take the attention off of me.

"Ok then. Calling the case of the People of the State of New York versus Joseph Millstone. Are both sides ready to begin?"

"Yes, Your Honor," Kelly said.

"Yes, Your Honor. I can't wait to battle you again Sal," Bryce Weatherford said.

Once again, I had forgotten to check on the details of the case. Bryce Weatherford was the DA on the Sean Lancaster case and is very good at what he does. I was not aware that he was transferred out of Manhattan and was now the District Attorney for the borough of Brooklyn. Some of his examinations were tough to overcome and quite frankly, I didn't know if I could, yet somehow, I had won that case.

"Same here Bryce," I said, while not looking at him.

For the next five minutes, Bryce gave a powerful and accurate opening statement. Nothing he claimed was untrue or misleading. He laid the entire case out for the jury with fact and unmistakable confidence. It seems he had learned from the last case because his opening statement in the Sean Lancaster case lasted for forty-five minutes and contained way too much information for the jury to process so early in the case. I could tell right away that I was up against a much more formidable opponent.

"Your opening statement, counselor," Judge Santino said when Bryce was finished.

"Thank you, Your Honor," I began and rose to my feet. "Ladies and Gentlemen of the jury. I would first like to apologize for not walking over your jury box, but as you can see, I have aged quite a bit since my last case. What we have here is something of a conundrum. One on hand, you have my client, Joseph Millstone, caught red handed after the brutal murders of the King family. On the other hand, you have the blatant mishandling of evidence by the NYPD and the complete disregard for chain of custody. Most of you, I assume, have watched at least one courtroom drama on television or in the movies. Mostly all of those screenings depict a case where there are facts uncovered and theories disproved, which brings a great deal of excitement. This will not be one of those cases. As Mr. Weatherford stated, Joseph Millstone was caught exiting the backdoor of the King's residence directly after their murders took place. He was covered in blood and asked for me right away. Those facts are undeniable, in fact, the defense has stipulated to those facts. What you will hear is testimony from several eyewitnesses that saw the NYPD contaminate the evidence at the crime scene and fail to secure the front of the residence when they arrested my client. You will also see how the evidence was passed along, which was in direct violation of chain of custody protocols. Once you have heard all the testimonies and seen all the evidence, I have no doubt in my mind that you will see the only option is to vote not guilty. Thank you."

When I finished my opening statement, I needed assistance from Kelly to sit back down. It was embarrassing and I tried to shrug her off, but I figured it would be better for me to take her help than to cause a panic by falling on the floor. Once I was seated, Judge Santino asked Bryce to call his first witness.

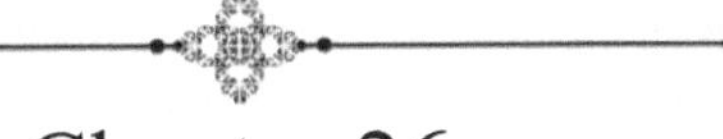

Chapter 26

Danielle sat nervously in the private interrogation room waiting for her attorney to show up. She had wanted to meet with her to go over the appeal process and what she should expect. Danielle knew that the chances of her conviction being overturned stood somewhere between zero and nil, but she still needed to try.

While she was deep in thought about her future, Danielle heard a noise. When she turned around, she saw that the steel door began to open. She turned expecting to get a wise remark from her attorney, but instead, saw a tall, thin, and handsome man enter the room. She peeked around him to see if her attorney was behind him, but the guard closed the door eliminating any hope of that coming true.

"Who are you? Where is Maris?" Danielle asked.

"Maris? Oh she is sick and asked me to come talk to you for her," the stranger said.

"Bullshit. She would have told me if that was the case. So I will ask you again. Who are you?"

"You didn't think I would come here and not dress up, did you?"

Danielle suddenly froze and got a massive head rush. She felt adrenaline flow through her body for the first time in ages and got a warm feeling in her heart. She did not know what was going on, but she had an inkling. The only way to confirm her suspicions was to address the stranger head on.

"Sean?" she asked timidly.

"Hey baby!" Sean replied quietly.

"How did…when did…how did?" Danielle said, not able to complete a sentence.

"It's a long story, but you can now add master of disguise to my list of accomplishments."

"I can't believe it is really you!" Danielle said, as she leaned in to kiss Sean.

"Whoa, whoa. No can do. I am your attorney. Remember?"

"I guess," Danielle answered sadly. "So how do we proceed?"

"Well, my name is now Terence Callahan. Call me Terry though. I was born in Shaker Heights, Ohio to a very wealthy family. My father is a retired vascular surgeon and my mother is still working as a high school principal. I went to Stanford Law School and have been practicing law for seven years," Sean explained.

"Wow. I don't know what to say. That is impressive, but what happened to Maris?"

"She received a message to come later because you were meeting with a family friend to discuss your case. I told the guards I was co-counsel and that she would be stopping by later."

Danielle could not help but have the biggest smile on her face. She loved seeing Sean in action, but this took it to new heights. Never before had he played the role of someone else and created an entirely new persona. She was surprised by how much it turned her on.

"Sean, I can't resist much longer. I don't know what it is, but I am so hot for you right now."

"Me too, but we have to play this safe. There will be plenty of time for us to be together when the time is right. For now, we need to discuss your ex-husband."

Any kind of lust or desire Danielle felt was now deflated like a flat tire. The mere mention of Sal was enough to cool her down and make her nauseous. She knew Sean did not mean for that to happen, but she was still a bit upset at his rejection of her advances.

"Before we do that, there is something I need to tell you. I got a visitor a while back that told me you are in danger. She said that her fiancé was Titus Baxter and you better be looking behind your back from now on."

"Did you get her name?" Sean asked.

"No. She left immediately after she told me this. Do you think she is right? Are you in danger?" Danielle asked worriedly.

"I have no idea, but I doubt it. Thank you for letting me know. I will have to hire a few bodyguards now. I am sure it won't be an issue. Now, Sal."

"What about him?"

"Do you think you can get him here?" Sean questioned.

"I am not sure. It would have to be for a very good reason. Why?"

"Because I want you to deliver a message to him. Something he needs to hear in person."

"What is the message?"

"Not now. When the time is right, I will let you know. For now, just work on getting him here," Sean ordered.

"Ok, but that's not fair. I deserve to know. I have done everything you have asked for and have not questioned anything," Danielle said, with a bit of anger.

"I said, *when the time is right.* Now drop it," Sean said, getting up to leave.

"Whatever Sean. But you might want to watch how you treat me because I might wake up one day and ask someone to do some research on Terence Callahan."

"Is that a threat?" Sean asked, squinting his eyes in anger.

"It is what you want it to be."

"Got it. I will watch how I act from now on. I will see you another time," Sean said, as he banged on the door for the guard to let him out.

"Oh and one more thing Danielle," Sean said as he turned back toward her. "When he comes, tell him to bring the kids. It would be a shame if something happened to them when he wasn't home."

Chapter 27

"T"he state would like to call Detective Landis," Bryce Weatherford said.

I had never met Detective Landis so I did not know what to expect from him. When he stood up to walk to the witness stand, I was surprised the courtroom ceiling was high enough for him to stand upright. He must have been seven feet tall. He was very well built, well groomed, and wore his police blues. He seemed to own the room with his gargantuan presence, which made him very intimidating, something he surely used to his advantage. After taking the witness oath, Bryce began his questioning.

"Would you please state your name and occupation for the court please?" Bryce said.

"Detective Timothy Landis, NYPD, seventy-eighth precinct."

"Thank you for your time today detective. How long have you been an officer in the NYPD?"

"Eighteen years. Nine as a detective."

"That is an amazing career. Congratulations."

"Thank you," Detective Landis replied with pride.

"Can you please explain how you became involved in this case?" Bryce asked.

"I was the first to respond to a 911 distress call made from the King's residence," Detective Landis answered.

"What was the nature of the call?"

"The person making the call could barely speak, so I did not know more than that."

"Did the caller identify themselves?"

"No. The caller hung up before an identification was given."

"Do you have any clues as to who made that call?"

We were only thirty seconds into the case, and I could already tell that Bryce had sharpened his interrogation skills. He was leaving very little, if any, room for objections or ambiguities. If we were going to win this case, I would need to assist Kelly much more than I previously anticipated.

"Yes. We now know that the caller was Tim King," Detective Landis said, causing the first gasp from the court audience.

"And how do you know this to be true?" Bryce asked.

"Because we found him in his room with the phone in his hand, barely breathing."

"Tim King is alive?" Bryce asked.

I squeezed Kelly's leg to make sure she was paying attention. I whispered out the side of my mouth to object, but she didn't move. Her eyes were wide open and her mouth was slightly open as well. I squeezed her leg a little harder this time and whispered again to object. This time, she got the hint.

'Objection, Your Honor. Defense was not provided with this information during discovery," Kelly shouted.

"Your Honor, this information was kept private to protect Mr. King. The NYPD was not sure if his life was in any further danger and decided the best course of action was to keep him hidden," Bryce retorted.

"While that is both admirable and smart Mr. Weatherford, it is also against protocol. Objection sustained," ruled Judge Santino.

Kelly seemed to get her senses back after the ruling on her objection. She now had a pep in her step and gave me a wink and a smile to let me know she was ok.

"Did Tim King state where he was in the house when he called?" Bryce asked.

"Objection. Your Honor?" Kelly said, as she motioned her hand toward Bryce.

"Sustained. Mr. Weatherford, no more questions on this topic. Understood?" Judge Santino asked.

"Yes, Your Honor," Bryce answered. "Detective Landis, can you describe what took place when you arrived on the scene?"

"Well, as I mentioned earlier, I was the first to arrive. Before entering, I waited for back up to arrive before entering the house. When they did, I made my way toward the back to make sure the perpetrator could not escape that way. As soon as I and two other officers got to the back door, the defendant came out of the house. Officer Pendleton instructed the defendant to freeze and then proceeded to make the arrest."

"Did the defendant resist?"

"No, he did not."

"Can you describe the scene inside the home when you went inside?"

Detective Landis had to take a moment to compose himself before continuing. There was no denying his emotions were real, given the gravity of the crime; however, that doesn't mean I wish he had not had to do it.

"It was the worst crime scene I have ever worked. All of the family members were either deceased or gravely injured. We knew the 911 call came from inside the house, so there was at least one person alive, we just didn't know which one."

"What were the injuries you observed during your investigation?"

"Objection! Witness is a Detective, not a medical doctor. His observations of the victims lying in a pool of their own blood would be amateur at best," Kelly shouted.

"Sustained," Judge Santino ruled.

I was pleasantly surprised at how Kelly was performing to this point. She was composed and to the point, but still needed some guidance on the words she chose to use.

"Nice job," I whispered to Kelly. "But next time don't use such a description of the crime scene that your client is responsible for."

"Oh shit, you are right. Sorry," Kelly said as she covered her mouth.

"No worries. Just move on" I whispered back.

"Detective, can you tell the court what methods were used to collect evidence from the crime scene?" Bryce asked.

"Well that is for the forensics team to describe, but what I can tell you is that we followed every protocol to the letter and took extra caution in preserving the crime scene for them."

"Thank you, detective. No more questions, Your Honor."

"Ms. Esteves, care to cross?"

"Yes, Your Honor," Kelly answered, clearly nervous.

"Go get 'em tiger!" I said, trying to pep Kelly up.

"Detective Landis, thank you again for being here today. I would like to revisit the moment when my client allegedly exited the house through the rear door. How many officers did you say were present at the rear door?" Kelly began.

"There were two when I arrived. Once I was on the scene, another four arrived."

"Arrived where?" Kelly asked.

"At the rear entrance."

"How many officers in total were on the scene when my client was arrested?"

"Seven, including myself."

"So if there were seven officers total on the scene and all seven were at the rear door, who secured the front entrance?"

Detective Landis lowered his head and paused for a few seconds before answering Kelly's question. "Nobody."

"*Nobody?* You mean to tell me that in your nine years of experience as a detective, it did not occur to you to secure all possible exits in case there was more than one perpetrator?" Kelly attacked.

"In the heat of the moment, no it did not occur to me since the defendant was in our custody within a matter of seconds of me arriving on the scene."

"Do you know for certain that there were no other perpetrators in the home that could have left through the unguarded front door?"

"The evidence does not show that a second person committed these crimes," Detective Landis stated.

"But the evidence also does not exclude the theory that someone may have exited through the front door, does it?"

"No it does not," Detective Landis answered.

"Thank you Detective. No more questions."

When Kelly returned to the defense table both Joseph and I had smiles on our faces. Kelly had taken her first at bat and hit it out of the park. She was tremendous and Joseph obviously was pleased with her work as well.

"I am sorry I ever doubted you Kelly," Joseph said.

"That is ok. I am here to not only prove you wrong, but to prove them wrong as well," Kelly said, as she pointed to Bryce's table.

"Calm down kid. This is just the first witness. There is still a way to go."

"I know, but can't a girl enjoy a victory for a moment?" Kelly asked.

"Not now. Here comes the next witness."

Chapter 28

"Gio what do you think you are doing?" asked Molly, the teenage babysitter hired by Sal to watch over his children while he was in court.

"Dad said I can go through his files and help. Now leave me alone," Gio answered.

"Not until I verify that with him. Leave those files alone and come back in here."

"Not a chance Molly. Sorry," Gio said and locked the door so Molly could not get in.

Molly began to bang on the door to the den, but it was to no avail. After three minutes of constant banging and yelling, she decided to give up and go back to her book. She knew Gio was a handful, but he had never been this defiant before. She chalked it up to him being a pre-teen and hormone changes.

As Gio went through the files over and over, he did not spot anything new, which frustrated him a great deal. He was supposed to be able to help his father find evidence that linked Sean Lancaster to Joseph Millstone, yet all he could find was the photo he already showed his dad and Kelly. He began to doubt his skills as a detective and wondered whether he was worthy enough of the task his father had given him. Dejected, Gio opened the door and went to his room to play some video games, in order to take his mind off of the case for a little while.

For the next three hours, Gio spent his time playing *Phoenix Wright: Ace Attorney*, a game that takes place in a courtroom with the player taking on the role of the lead attorney, in hopes of sharpening his detective skills. After winning the first three cases, Gio was no closer to having more confidence in himself than he was before he started playing. Suddenly, before the fourth case was about to begin, he had an idea.

Gio ran back to the den and opened the file that contained the photograph of Sean Lancaster, Samuel Porter, and Joseph Millstone. He looked closer at the photo to see if Joseph Millstone had the same facial appearance as he does now or if he looked different back then. Unfortunately, Gio could not tell if there was a difference because half of Joseph's face was cut off; however, there was another detail in the photo that caught Gio's attention. The Joseph in this photo was severely overweight, not in tip top shape as Joseph is today. Could this be another Joseph M in the photo or was it the same person? Gio knew he would have to wait until his father came home, but he didn't know if he would be able to.

To pass the time, Gio played more of *Phoenix Wright*. He was getting quite good at the game and was even learning quite a bit of legal jargon that he hoped would impress his father. As his sixth case of the day was about to begin, Molly called him downstairs. He didn't want to go, but knew he really didn't have a choice in the matter.

"What do you want?" Gio asked, annoyed.

"First of all, how about knocking off the attitude. I don't know what I did to you, but I don't deserve to be talked to that way," Molly responded.

"Fine. I'm sorry."

"Better. Your father just called. He is coming home early because he could not sit in the courtroom anymore, so I need your help getting the house ready for him. Can you please help your sister clean up?"

"Sure, no problem. And Molly…I really am sorry for the way I acted today," Gio said with remorse.

"It's ok Gio, but thank you."

Gio wanted to make sure his father was able to relax when he came home so he would be able to talk shop with him. He wanted to wow him with all he had learned from *Phoenix Wright* and what he saw in the photo. In order to make this happen, he needed to do an extra special job cleaning up. He grabbed all of Angela's toys and moved them back into her play area. He then went upstairs and put his video games away, made his bed, and even vacuumed his floor. Just as he finished cleaning his room, Sal came through the front door, looking more tired than Gio had ever seen him before. Sal plopped on the couch and immediately fell asleep. Gio knew he would be out for a few hours, so he decided to join him in a mid-afternoon nap. When they woke up, Gio was sure he would impress his father with all he learned during the day.

82

Chapter 29

With Sal having left for the day, Kelly Esteves knew she was on her own to handle the forensic witnesses that were about to be called. Sal is not a forensic expert so he would not have been much help anyway, but she would miss his presence and direction for sure.

"You better know what you are doing with the scientists honey," Joseph said to Kelly.

"I wouldn't be here if I didn't so pipe down there. And don't call me honey."

Joseph gave Kelly a pat on the shoulder and reassured her she had this as Bryce called his next witness. Without any warning, Kelly began to feel her heartbeat a little faster and she became a little lightheaded. She was prone to panic attacks but had not had one in a few months. The Buspar she had been taking was working wonders, so she was wondering why she was having a panic attack now.

"Your Honor. Can I have a fifteen-minute recess?" Kelly asked Judge Santino as Bryce's witness entered the witness stand.

"Request denied. You may proceed, counselor," Judge Santino ruled.

"May I approach the bench Your Honor?" Kelly asked.

"Yes, you may," Judge Santino said, annoyed.

Walking from the defense table to the judge's bench proved to be a difficult task for Kelly. Her legs were wobbly, she felt like she was in a fog, and sweat began to pour down the side of her face. As she approached the bench, Judge Santino clearly took notice of her worsening condition.

"Ms. Esteves, are you ok?" Judge Santino asked.

"No, Your Honor. I feel like I am going to faint." Those were the last words Kelly remembered before she fell to the floor. Panic ensued immediately after Kelly passed out; however, Judge Santino restored order by calling for a thirty-minute recess, having the bailiff call for medical attention, and asking for assistance in moving Kelly to her chambers.

For the next few minutes Kelly laid still, causing concern from everyone. Finally, after five minutes had passed since her collapse, Kelly began to wake up and come to her senses. By the time she woke up, there were two EMTs assisting her, along with a doctor that was in the audience in the courtroom.

"Ms. Esteves, how do you feel?" asked one of the EMTs.

"What happened? Where am I? "Kelly asked, confused.

"You passed out a little while ago. Your heart rate is still elevated. I would suggest going to the emergency room to get looked at," the EMT said.

"No, I will be ok. I just need to take something to calm me down," Kelly said. "So Your Honor, about that recess?"

Judge Santino chuckled at Kelly's joke. "Ms. Esteves, nice to see you have your sense of humor back. We will adjourn until tomorrow morning. Boy, you sure know how to make a case."

"Thank you, Your Honor," Kelly said as she rose to her feet, still a little wobbly.

When she was able to calm down a little more and was alone, she called Alan Lowery.

"It happened again," Kelly said.

"I thought you had it under control," Alan asked. "How bad was it?"

"Bad. It lasted about five to six minutes this time. What should I do?"

"That's not good. Each time is getting longer and longer. Where is Sal?"

"He went home. He was wiped out from sitting in the courtroom," Kelly answered.

"Alright. Do you think you can drive or do you need me to send someone to get you?"

"You better send someone. I don't want to risk driving and this happening again."

"Ok, but Kelly, if you can't get this under control, then you know what will happen," Alan said.

"I know, I know. I promise I will get checked out again. Hopefully this time, the doctor can give me something stronger."

"Let's hope so. I will see you back at your place in an hour."

"Ok Grandpa, I will see you then."

Chapter 30

Sean Lancaster sat at his office desk looking over the photos he received from his contact inside Bedford Hills Correctional Facility. The photos were of inmates in the yard, the cafeteria, and the prison cells. He was particularly interested in the woman who threatened Danielle a few weeks ago. He needed to get an identification on that woman so he would know who was potentially after him and eliminate them. After hours of on and off investigating, he was no closer to finding out who this mystery woman was. In order to progress his investigation, he decided to call Danielle to see if she found anything else out.

"Hi baby. I was wondering if I would hear from you again," Danielle said with great excitement.

"Hey you. Of course I was going to come back around. One little argument wasn't going to derail that," Sean said reassuringly. "I do have a question for you though. Did you find out any more information on our mystery woman?

"No. I haven't even seen her around here after that day. You think maybe she isn't an inmate?"

"It's possible, but I doubt it. Have you asked your contacts about her?"

"Sean, what do you take me for?" Danielle said annoyed.

"I know, I'm sorry. I get irritated when I can't control things."

"No shit. Anyway, I have asked around and nobody knows who she is," Danielle said.

"Ok, well keep your eyes open and let me know if you see or hear anything," Sean told Danielle. "How are you?"

"Angry. I haven't been here that long and I am already tired of this place. I get so angry sometimes, I don't even want any visitors, not even from my lawyer.

"Is that why you haven't set up a meeting with Sal and the kids like I asked you?"

"Excuse me?" Danielle answered, annoyed.

Sean was beginning to lose his patience with Danielle. He knew she was under a lot of stress and that her head was not all there, but he also needed her to do what he asked if he was going to succeed with his plans for Sal.

"You heard me," Sean retorted. "Danielle, you know how important I need this meeting to happen."

"Yeah, but I don't know any details. I am not endangering my children for your sick and demented game," Danielle yelled and then slammed the phone down.

Sean pulled the phone away from his ear and stared at it in shock for a few seconds. He could not believe that Danielle had hung up on him. In that moment, he knew he was losing his grip on Danielle. He would need to do something to put a scare into her to remind her of who she was dealing with.

As Sean sat at his desk and stared at the photos of Bedford again, an idea suddenly popped in his head. He would have to turn to someone he knew would never go for what he was about to propose. Someone that would push back with everything they had. Someone that he would have a hard time getting in touch with. To Sean's surprise, his call was answered on the second ring.

"Hey, it's me," Sean said.

"What are you doing calling me on this line? You know how much trouble I could get into," the person said.

"Then why did you pick up an unknown number you moron?"

"What do you want?" the person asked.

"I need your help. Danielle is becoming a problem and I need your expertise in setting her straight," Sean said.

"I don't do that anymore Sean. I am as straight as an arrow now."

"Bullshit. You and I both know you can't just walk away from the lifestyle, especially not after I know what you have done"

"Is that a threat?" the person asked, suddenly getting nervous.

"You damn straight it is. Can you meet me at the 48 Lounge tonight at ten?"

"Sean, get real. I am not going to meet you in public. Now if there is nothing else…"

"Poor Roland. Never knows when to keep his mouth shut. Need I remind you of what I am capable of?"

"Ok Sean, I understand. I'll be there," Roland said nervously.

"Good. Smart decision. Be prepared to have your socks blown off."

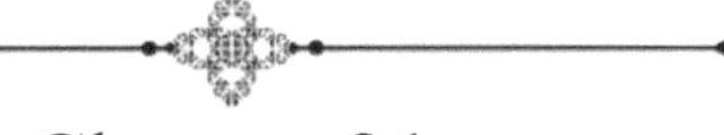

Chapter 31

Having fallen asleep after a long morning in court, I woke up around five in the afternoon and needed a few minutes to gather myself to know where I was. When I finally got my bearings, I picked up my phone from the coffee table and saw I had thirteen missed calls, three voicemails, and fifty-two text messages. Right away, I knew something was wrong but did not know what it was. I also was amazed that I was able to sleep through all the notifications.

After I finished reading my text messages and listening to my voicemails, I called Kelly to see if she was alright. She did not pick up so I left her a voicemail and sent her a text message as well. I felt guilty about what she was going through because I couldn't stay the whole day in court. I wanted to let her know I was sorry and that I would be there for her all the time moving forward.

Once I worked up the energy to get off of the couch, I went into the kitchen to see if I could find the origin of the terrific smell that was traveling throughout the house. To my surprise, Nicole was standing over the stove mixing something in a saucepot.

"You're up and moving around. That is a good sign. How do you feel?" Nicole asked.

"Uh, Nicole. What's going on? Don't get me wrong, I am happy to see you, I am just confused as to why you are here."

"Gio texted me about what happened in court today. I wanted to see if you were ok" Nicole responded.

"How did Gio know about what happened in court?" I asked, annoyed.

"I read your text messages while you were asleep," Gio yelled from the other room.

"We will discuss this later son," I said back to Gio. "I am ok, I guess. Are you here as my therapist or?"

"I am here for you Sal. I am sorry I acted the way I did when you needed me. It was a shitty thing to do, especially to someone who I care deeply for."

"That's ok Nicole. It's not a big deal. I am just glad you are here," I said and gave her a kiss.

When Nicole was done cooking, we all sat down for dinner. Angela's eyes were wide open at the baked ziti Nicole had just made from scratch. Gio took the first portion and barely put it on his plate before digging in. I took the next portion and couldn't wait to taste what was sure to be heaven. I took my first bite and immediately all my problems went away, albeit for a brief moment. I have been eating Italian food my entire life and had the fortunate opportunity to taste authentic Italian cooking from my grandmother, yet I had never tasted a baked ziti like this. Before I knew it, I was digging in for seconds, something I rarely do.

"Nicole, what did you use to make this? It is absolutely amazing," I asked.

"It's all in the sauce and meat. I used my family's special ingredients" Nicole answered.

"What are they? You have to tell me," I pushed.

"Nope. You have to earn that answer."

"Is she talking about sex dad?" Gio blurted out.

I spat out my food all over the table after what Gio said. Even though I knew he was right and it was a hilarious moment that was sure to be retold for years to come, I had to avoid the question to ease the awkwardness that Gio had created.

"Not the place for that son." That was all I could think of. "Anyway, Nicole, this is truly amazing. Thank you."

"You're welcome, I am glad you like it," Nicole said with a big smile.

As I was about to finish up my last bite of my second helping, my phone began to ring. I normally will not answer my phone while we are having dinner as a family, but I was just about done, so I took the call and went into the living room.

"Sal Amici," I answered.

"Sal, it's me," Danielle said.

"Danielle what do you want?" I asked.

"Sal, we need to talk. It is urgent. I know you don't want to see me, but I need you to come here as soon as you can."

"Why?" I asked, as I sighed.

"Because I need your help with something, that is why."

"What number are you calling me from?"

"It is from a cell phone that gets passed around the prison. Why?" Danielle asked.

"Because if you are on a line that is not recorded or traced, you can tell me over the phone what you need me for," I replied.

"Fine. I need your help with Sean. I need him gone."

I stood frozen in my living room, much like the way I was when Sean and David Flores were here last year telling me their tale.

"Excuse me? You need what?" I said confused and still shaking.

"Sal, he has threatened Gio and Angela if I don't do what he wants."

"He did what? I swear. If he puts a finger on those kids…" I screamed, drawing the attention of Nicole in the kitchen.

"That is what I need to talk to you about. I have a way to handle this, but I need your help. Do you think you can bring the kids to see me tomorrow?"

"Danielle, we agreed not to let them see you locked up."

"I know, but Sean told me to bring them along with you. He didn't say why, just that I had to do it."

"There is no way I am bringing the kids to see you Danielle. It's not going to happen."

"SAL, will you for once in your pathetic life think of someone else besides yourself. You think I want to put my kids' lives in danger? All I know is if you don't come with them, he will hurt them. That much you can take to the bank," Danielle pleaded.

"So help me Danielle. If you are playing me…" I said as I gritted my teeth.

"Sal, I'm not playing you. Not about this. I promise."

Something about her voice at that moment told me she was not joking. Having realized she was serious, I began to get worried. Why did Sean want me and the kids to visit Danielle? What could he possibly do to us in that setting? Against my better judgment, I gave in.

"Alright Danielle. When do you want us to come?" I asked.

"Tomorrow, after your court session."

"Fine. I'll see you then," I replied and hung up the phone.

Nicole could see I was upset and there was no better person to talk to than her. I told her what Danielle had told me and the issues I had with bringing my kids to see her in prison, especially knowing that Sean requested it. Without hesitation, Nicole leaned in and gave me one of the most passionate kisses I have ever received. She was so warm and gentle it almost made me forget about what I just went through.

"It will be ok Sal. I am here for you," Nicole said as she gave another kiss.

"I know you are. I need you Nicole. I can't do this alone."

"You don't have to. I promise, I am not going anywhere," Nicole reassured me.

Chapter 32

As Sean entered the 48 lounge, he took a long hard look around to see if anything was out of the ordinary. Roland Crenshaw was a very dangerous man and there is no telling what kind of traps or surveillance he might have set up. After a few glances around the room, Sean felt safe enough to enter. He requested the same booth he had used to meet Sal when he told him about what he did to Sal's brother Peter.

Sean ordered himself and Roland a Glenfiddich 12 on the rocks. He figured it would be a nice touch to ease the tension between the two. Roland used to be a heavy drinker, but if he did indeed clean his act up like he claimed he did, he might not appreciate the drink ordered for him. Sean was hoping that was the case because he wanted Roland angry in order to agree what he needed him to do.

"Well, well. If it isn't mister I don't give a shit himself," Roland said as he approached the table. "Taking an awfully big chance of being seen in public, aren't you Sean?"

"That should tell you how important what I need to talk to you about is," Sean answered.

"Alright. So what is this big favor you have to ask of me?"

"Well, there are two things actually. The first is Danielle Amici. She is becoming a real nuisance and I need your help to set her straight. She is too argumentative and doesn't think about the consequences of her actions."

"And why exactly is this my problem?" Roland asked.

"It is not your problem, I never said it was. I am simply asking an old acquaintance for help in solving my problem."

"Yeah, but I told you, I don't do that stuff anymore."

"Who says you have to actually do anything? All I need you to do is put me in contact with someone who does that stuff. Of course, you will be rewarded very handsomely," Sean said as he sipped his scotch.

"What do you need done?" Roland reluctantly said.

"I just want her scared. To realize she needs to watch what she says and to think about her actions. Nothing more than that. She is still very important to me."

"Ok. I know the perfect person for this. Do you want him to contact you or do you want me to set it up?"

"You set it up. I trust your judgment," Sean replied. "By the way, don't insult me by not drinking your scotch."

"I don't drink anymore, but I will make an exception to celebrate our reunion," Roland said as he took three big swigs of the scotch. "What is the other thing you need?"

"Danielle said that someone approached her saying I was in trouble. She claims to be the fiancé of Titus Baxter and is out for revenge."

"Revenge for what?"

"Well, I may have gone a little overboard and killed the bastard in jail," Sean said as he shrugged his shoulders.

"Damn boy, you are ruthless."

"What are you gonna do?" Sean replied and let out a chuckle. "Anyway, I have no idea who this woman is or how she knows, but I need her found and dealt with."

"Price just tripled Sean."

"You think money is an issue for me?" Sean asked angrily.

Sean had to do his best to control the anger that was building up inside of him. He usually will have a level head and a calm demeanor when negotiating, but one thing that has always set him off was when people questioned his ability to afford what he was asking for. He took this as an insult because he felt everyone should know who he is and how much he is worth.

"I know it is not, I am just letting you know. When do you need this done by?" Roland asked.

"ASAP. I have no idea what that crazy bitch has planned and I am tired of looking over my shoulder."

"You got it. I will be in touch," Roland said as he finished the last of his scotch. "Thanks for the drink."

Before Sean could say anything else, Roland was already on his way to the exit. Sean liked that Roland was on board with helping him, but was also concerned that he gave in so easily. For someone who vehemently claimed he was out of the game, Roland did not put up much of a resistance. Feeling a bit disturbed, Sean needed to make one more phone call before he left for the evening.

"Hey, it's me. Do me a favor, will ya? I need you to follow Roland Crenshaw. I have a feeling there is more to him than he is letting on."

93

Chapter 33

The next morning, I was as prepared for court as I had been in a long time. Things with Nicole were better, I felt more rested than I had been in recent memory, and Kelly was fully recovered for her episode the previous day. As I walked into the courtroom, I felt a sense of peace that had not been present in my life since before Sean Lancaster sent it upside down.

When I made it to our table, Kelly already had her case file open and was preparing for the day. She looked determined to put the previous day behind her and get back to work. I knew it was not going to be easy for her and I wanted to help her with this as much as I could.'

"Hey Kelly. How are you?" I asked.

"UGH! I wish everyone would stop asking me that," Kelly replied back. "I am sorry Sal. I am just fed up with this whole situation."

"I understand. No need to apologize. Why don't you let me handle some of the cross examinations today."

"You sure you are up for it, Sal?" Kelly asked.

"I am sure. Tell me what you got."

Kelly and I spent the next fifteen minutes catching me up on anything I may have missed, discussing the case, preparing our strategy, and who would handle what. It felt great to be back in action after everything I had gone through. It had only been one day since I had to excuse myself because of exhaustion, but I felt like a different person. One that exuded confidence and determination. I was anticipating some bumps in the road, but hoped I would be able to manage them to make it through the day. Just as Kelly and I wrapped up our huddle, Bryce called his first witness.

"You Honor, the state would like to call Lucy Newton," Bryce said.

Lucy Newton was as gorgeous as a woman could get. She had free flowing blonde hair, deep sea blue eyes, a perfect frame, and curves to die for. If a dream girl could be brought to life, she would look like Lucy Newton. I had seen her name on the witness list, but did not know the exact reason Bryce would be calling her. It would not take long for me to find out.

After Lucy was sworn in, Bryce began his questioning.

"Thank you for coming today Ms. Newton. I know this cannot be easy for you. Can you please state how you know the defendant?" Bryce asked.

"I am his ex-fiancé," Lucy answered curtly.

"How long were you engaged to the defendant?"

"About two years."

"And how would you describe your relationship with the defendant?"

"It sucked," Lucy said and got a laugh from the courtroom.

"Order. Order. NOW!" Judge Santino yelled as she banged her gavel.

The courtroom quickly became silent and everyone became as still as statues. With order now restored, Bryce continued his examination of Lucy Newton.

"Ms. Newton, can you please elaborate on what sucked in your relationship with the defendant?"

"I was constantly abused, both physically and emotionally. He would berate me every day by telling me I was no good and I would never amount to anything," Lucy said, holding back tears.

"How long did this go on for?"

"The whole time. I was lucky to get one or two days free from his abuse."

I was looking for a reason to object because this testimony was damaging to my client's case, but as I had noticed yesterday, Bryce has gotten a lot better at examining witnesses. I knew he would mess up at some point, and when he did, I would be there to pounce on it.

"In that time, did you ever report the abuse to the police?"

"Objection! Alleged abuse your honor," I yelled finally getting my chance.

"Sustained," Judge Santino ruled.

"Ms. Newton, did you ever report the alleged abuse to the police?" Bryce asked, looking back at me.

"No," Lucy responded.

"Why not?"

"I was terrified of Joseph. I never knew what he was going to do and I didn't want to take a chance."

"Can you tell the court what you mean by you never knew what he was going to do?" Bryce asked.

"Well, he would often come home early in the morning, usually around two or three and be in a bad mood. Most of the time I would not hear him come home but he would wake me up just to yell at me about something that was out of place or if he didn't have anything to eat, stupid stuff like that."

"What would happen after that?"

"He would call me names and throw stuff around the house," Lucy answered, tearing up again.

"Did he ever throw things at you?"

"Yes."

"Did any of those objects ever hit you?"

"Yes" Lucy replied while keeping her head down, ashamed of what she was admitting to.

"Were you ever hurt when these objects hit you?"

"Yes."

I glanced over at the jury and saw the disgust on their faces. If I wasn't defending this scumbag, I would have the same look on my face. It was an awful experience seeing this woman recount her ordeal, but I also knew that I had to counter most of what she was saying, in order to win the case.

"I am assuming these incidents were not reported to the police either, correct?" Bryce asked.

"Objection!" Kelly yelled. "Leading the witness."

"Withdrawn," Bryce said. "Did you ever report these incidents to the police?"

"No."

"Why not?" Bryce asked.

"Because I was afraid, same as the last reason."

"Thank you Ms. Newton. No further questions."

"Mr. Amici/Ms. Esteves, do you care to cross?" Judge Santino asked.

I looked at Kelly to see if she wanted to do the cross examination but she waved her right hand in the direction of the witness, signaling to me that she wanted me to take the lead on this.

"Yes, Your Honor," I replied and made my way to the witness stand very gingerly.

"Ms. Newton, would you like a recess or a glass of water?" I asked.

"No, thank you. I am good," Lucy answered.

"Ok. You mentioned earlier that your relationship with Mr. Millstone sucked because he was constantly abusing you. Can you recall any good times the two of you had?"

"Yes. They are easy to remember because there were not a lot of them."

"Can you please recall one of those times for the court?"

"They mostly happened when we first got together. He was sweet in the beginning. He always paid for meals, held doors open for me, and bought me presents. He was almost too good to be true. Turns out he was."

"I see. You also mentioned you are his ex-fiancé. When did your engagement end?"

"Well, we never officially ended it, but when he was arrested for murder."

"Alleged murder, Ms. Newton. I would appreciate it if you did not assume guilt based on your opinion of Mr. Millstone," I said cutting her off.

"Yes, sir. I'm sorry," Lucy said, playing the part of victim very well.

"No need for apologies. So technically, you are still engaged?"

"Yeah, I guess so," Lucy said. "Joey, it's over. There. Now we are not engaged anymore."

The courtroom burst into laughter and I have to admit, I chuckled as well. When I looked at Judge Santino to see if she would try to regain order, she had her head turned to the left. It looked as though she was trying to hide her amusement as well. After a few minutes, the laughter died down and I continued my cross examination.

"Well, I am glad we got that covered, "I said, trying to move on. "Ms. Newton, do you recall the night of June 26, 2021?"

Lucy paused a few seconds before looking at me with disgust, but answered in the affirmative. She could tell I was about to confront her with something she did not want to talk about; however, being under oath, she understood she did not have a say in the matter.

"Can you describe to the court what happened that night?"

"I was alone in our apartment, when I received a disturbing phone call about Joseph," Lucy said not wanting to divulge more detail.

"What was said on the phone call?"

"The caller said that Joseph committed a series of crimes earlier in the night and to be careful because he was coming for me next."

"What was your reaction to that call?" I asked, leading up to my ultimate question.

"I was scared."

"Just like anyone would be scared in that situation, right?"

"Objection!" Bryce screamed. "The witness cannot testify as to how others would react in her situation."

"Sustained."

I knew that I would get an objection, but I had also planned that. By having Bryce object to that statement, I was then able to redirect my questioning toward where I wanted it to go. I needed to set up the questioning this way so when I asked my follow up questions, it would seem as if I was reacting to the objection and was not asking these questions in an apparent desperate measure to turn the case.

"What made you scared about the call?"

"It was everything. The caller's tone, message, and timing."

"I am sorry, timing?" I asked, confused.

"Yes. Joseph had been questioned by the police a week earlier about a home invasion that resulted in the death of an entire family," Lucy said.

I was not aware of this fact and had to take a step back from my cross examination to collect myself. This had happened to me a few times before and each time I was able to recover enough that it did not affect me. This time, however, seemed different. This was such a big detail that I had missed, it could possibly do much more damage than the other mistakes combined.

"I see. Did the caller say anything else?" I asked, regaining my composure.

"Yes. He said that Joseph was still out there and to lock the doors. After that, he hung up."

"And you are sure it was a man?"

"Well, no I couldn't tell for sure because he was using one of those voice scramblers, but I assumed it was."

"Why?" I asked, feeling I was getting somewhere.

"Natural instinct is to associate men with serial murders Mr. Amici."

"Who said anything about serial murders? We were talking about a phone call."

"Well, I just assumed that because those murders and now these constitute a serial killer."

"Ms. Newton, do you understand that Mr. Millstone is on trial for his life and that using unproven facts to smear his reputation is unethical and immoral?"

"Objection! Counsel is badgering the witness," Bryce yelled.

"Overruled," Judge Santino said.

Bryce slumped back into his chair with disappointment. I was getting to him and it was great to see.

"Well, Ms. Newton?"

"Yes, I understand and apologize."

"I have one more question for you. After the phone call ended, what did you do?"

"I went into my bedroom to try to sleep off the anxiety."

"Please excuse me, I have some follow up to that," I said to clear any confusion about why my questioning wasn't over like I said it was. "What happened when you went into your room?"

"Joseph was there. He was sound asleep. I knew from the fact that he was wearing his work clothes, that he had been there a while."

"How did that make you feel about what the caller said?"

"I felt it was someone trying to scare me and had no truth to it whatsoever."

"Thank you, Ms. Newton. I have no more questions."

"Ms. Newton, you may stand down," Judge Santino ordered. "Court will be in recess for one hour for lunch."

I asked Kelly what she thought and she said she was in awe at how I attacked the witness without attacking her. She learned a lot and felt ready to take over the afternoon session if I was ok with that. I told her I was and would be there if she needed me. It would soon be our turn to call witnesses and I felt good about that because in my mind, we were winning this case.

Chapter 34

The rest of the afternoon in court was uneventful, other than the fact that Kelly shined again when cross examining Bryce's witnesses. At five o'clock in the afternoon, Judge Santino ended the session for the day, relieving us all from a long day. I was tired from being in court all day and wanted to go home. Nicole said she was making something special for us, and I could not wait to get home to find out what it was.

When I walked in the front door, it was as if I walked into Gordon Ramsay's kitchen. The aroma in my house was so amazing, I wanted to bottle it up and use it as a car air freshener. I couldn't quite place what Nicole was cooking, but I knew my taste buds would be thanking her for it.

When I walked into the kitchen, Nicole was showing Angela how to stir the sauce properly. Angela having to stand on a stepstool to reach the pot was one of the cutest things I had ever seen. At that moment, there was nothing that could damper the atmosphere. It was perfect.

"You cooking angel?" I asked Angela.

"Hi daddy! Yeah, Nicole is showing me how to stir the sauce," Angela answered with pride.

"Is she now? Well then I expect an extra special meal tonight if you made it."

"I am just stirring the sauce daddy. Nicole made the food," Angela joked.

"House smells terrific, Nicole. What are you making?" I asked, as I kissed her on the cheek.

"It is my homemade Bolognese sauce. My mother passed this one to me before she died and I am carrying on the tradition. I am also making some capellini to go along with it" Nicole said.

"Well, whatever it is, it needs to get into my stomach soon. How much longer?"

"About twenty minutes or so."

"Sounds good. Gio, come in here," I yelled, walking into the living room.

"Hey, dad. What's up?" Gio asked as he came into the living room.

"Nothing much. Want to watch some hockey with me?"

"Dad, you know I don't like hockey, but did you hear who the Yankees signed today?"

Just as Gio asked me that question my cell phone rang. I looked at the caller ID and it said unavailable. Once again, I had a funny feeling about this call, but as I had felt a few times before, I somehow wanted to pick it up.

"Hang on to that thought Gio," I said as I went into my office space. "Sal speaking."

"Hey, Sal, it's Joseph."

"Everything ok?" I asked, concerned.

"Yeah, yeah. Everything is fine. I want to know if you and I can chat before court tomorrow. There are a few things I want to discuss with you."

"Uh, yeah. Not a problem. I will be there around six. Are you sure everything is ok?"

"Yeah, fine. That is perfect. See you then," Joseph said and then hung up.

I was not looking forward to waking up earlier than I had to, in order to travel to Rikers Island before court in Brooklyn, but I figured it must be important if Joseph called me to ask me personally. Once I collected my thoughts, I turned around to ask Gio about the Yankees signing, but he wasn't there.

I spent the next twenty-five minutes watching the news, all the while, wondering what Joseph could possibly want. Was this a trap? Was he going to do something to me? Or was it simply something he wanted to discuss and I was worrying about nothing. The more I thought about it, the more nervous I got. Thankfully, Nicole called everyone to the table as her meal was finally ready to be enjoyed.

"Nicole, WOW! This is the best meal I have ever had," I said as a party was developing in my mouth.

"Thank you, but if it is, then you have seriously been deprived," Nicole joked.

"He's right Nicole, this is amazing," Gio said.

"Thank you Gio, I appreciate it. How is the investigation going?"

"I haven't found anything new yet, but I promise I will soon," Gio said as he looked in my direction.

"Don't put too much pressure on yourself son, you will do just fine."

The next ten minutes was spent in complete silence as everyone was busy devouring the delicious meal prepared by Nicole. Once we were all done, I asked Gio to help with the dishes so I could go to my office and look over some files. Truth is, I was going to the bedroom to set up what I hoped was going to be a very special evening.

After helping with the dishes, Gio went to his room to play video games. I will usually ask him to do his homework after dinner, but on this night, I did not mind him being distracted. Once I heard the water shut off from the kitchen, I called Nicole to the bedroom. As she was making her way up the stairs, I lit the last candle and went to lay down on the bed. I was surprised at how nervous I was and how quickly things had escalated with Nicole. I was just over a year removed from what I thought was a good marriage, and here I was about to commit myself to another woman.

When Nicole entered the bedroom, she had the biggest smile on her face. I could tell she was surprised by the candles in the room, low lighting, and music playing in the background. I wasn't sure how she would take it, so my nerves got even more intense when her smile disappeared and she struggled to speak.

"Everything ok?" I asked Nicole.

"Yeah, why?"

"You seem a bit distant. If this is too much let me know, I can…"

"No, no. It's not that. I am flattered and quite honestly surprised," Nicole said.

"So what is it then?"

"If we do this, take this step, then you know I can no longer be your therapist."

"Is that what is bothering you? Our professional relationship?" I asked. "Nicole, you are the best thing in my life right now and the last thing on my mind is who my therapist will be. I would much rather have you as my partner than my therapist. But like I said, if this is too much…"

Nicole didn't let me finish my sentence, as she ran toward me and gave me the deepest, most passionate kiss I have had in quite some time. It was just the reaction I was hoping for, which is why I suddenly felt something I had not felt in what seemed like forever. I began to feel tranquility and got a warm, comforting feeling that coursed through my body. I held Nicole in my arms so tightly, she almost couldn't breathe. I did not want to let her go because I wanted to stay in the moment forever.

"You sure you want to do this?" Nicole asked me.

"Yes. Are you sure?" I asked her.

"Absolutely," Nicole replied.

We spent the next hour or so making passionate love to each other, all the while embracing what we knew was going to change our relationship moving forward. Even though I felt happy at that moment, it was more than just us sleeping together. It was a sign of moving on from Danielle. I had struggled to put that whole experience behind me and was beginning to wonder if I ever would. I was waiting for that moment when I could finally admit to myself that I had let go. *This* was that moment.

Chapter 35

Waking up at five o'clock in the morning is not something anybody can embrace. The sun was not due to rise for another two hours, the house was cold, everyone was sleeping, and there is usually no sign of life. I am a morning person, but not this early. I tend to be very grumpy and irritable when I wake up this early; however, that did not happen on this day. I woke up at five o'clock in the morning with a huge smile on my face and the warm feeling from the previous night still flowing through my body. I looked to my right, and there sleeping peacefully, was Nicole. She looked so beautiful in the moonlight, that I wanted to wake her up just to tell her that.

I knew that I had a meeting with Joseph Millstone at six o'clock; therefore, I only had one more hour of peace before the real world hit again. As I was getting ready to shut the bedroom door behind me, I heard Nicole whisper something. I walked over to her and asked her what she said. She looked me straight in the eye and said, "I love you."

I was taken back a bit because that was the last thing I expected her to say. It was a relief though because I felt the same way. I told her that I loved her as well and we kissed each other goodbye.

On the way to Rikers Island, I kept replaying the previous night in my mind. It brought me so much joy to recount the incredible evening Nicole and I had. I knew I was going to meet my client and that he was probably going to tell me something I do not want to hear, but I was determined not to let that ruin the wonderful mood I was in.

When I arrived at Rikers Island, I was ushered to a room I had never been in before. All of the times I met with Sean Lancaster and Joseph Millstone to this point have been in the visitation room or a private area. I was a bit nervous because all that was in this room was a table bolted to the floor and tiny metal loops that came up from the floor. I sat in the chair the guard told me to and waited for Joseph to be brought in. My mind at this point had put aside the evening with Nicole and was focused on what was about to happen. I was not sure what to expect, but to be called to this meeting by Joseph himself and then brought to this room, was a little unsettling.

Joseph was finally brought into the room by three guards. He was shackled at his feet and waist, which I thought was completely unnecessary. After the door behind them was slammed shut, the guards unlocked the shackles and wrapped them around the loops in the floor. They then attached the shackles to the table that was bolted into the floor. Joseph sat done and gestured for me to sit down as well; a signal that our conversation was about to begin.

"Thanks for coming in so early, Sal. I know it is not easy to get up this early," Joseph said.

"No problem. Just tell me what I am doing here so early and why this couldn't wait until later."

"Ok. I want to tell you everything about me, but I need to be sure it falls under attorney-client privilege," Joseph explained.

"Yes, it does. Unless you tell me something that can lead to bodily harm or death in the future, you are protected."

"Good. Well you know I am from Sarasota and went to NYU right?"

"Yes, I know that," I said, wondering where this was going.

"Have you heard of the NYU slayings and Sarasota slashings?" Joseph said with an evil grin.

"The NYU slayings yes, not the other one. Are you saying those were done by you?" I asked, beginning to get concerned.

"Oh yeah!" Joseph said with pride. "My first victim was in Sarasota when I was moving around foster homes. It was some random girl I met at an amusement park. We were smoking weed together and for some reason I just took my pocket knife out and stabbed her in the chest. She was gasping for air and begging me to help her. I just sat there and laughed and smiled. I was enjoying seeing the life being sucked out of her."

I didn't know how to react to what Joseph was telling me. I had come into this meeting expecting something bad, but nothing like this. I knew that he was caught leaving the King's home, and that he was most likely guilty of killing them, but I never thought he was a serial killer. He had hinted at this to me in prior meetings, but I never believed him. I was so conflicted on how to proceed, I just sat in front of him with my mouth wide open. What I didn't know at that time, was that this was just the tip of the iceberg.

"You are silent. Good, I have your attention. Then I will continue. Once I got to NYU, all I could think about was which one of the sorority girls would be my next victim. I know it is a cliché, sorority girls getting murdered and all, but I also could not control my urges. I studied and followed each one to know their patterns, when they had classes, when they met with their sister, all of that. It was hard for me at first to find the right place and time, but then I got into a groove and killing became second nature."

It is an indescribable feeling hearing someone talk about killing another human being as second nature. I was in the presence of pure evil and hate. Someone, who by definition, was a psychopath. All of the good feelings I had from last night were gone. I tried to think of how wonderful the evening was with Nicole, but all I could think of was how the man in front of me had taken so many lives and seemed proud of it. How can I continue to defend someone so vial and dangerous? I tried to put an end to his tale, but I could not speak. Nothing came out of my mouth except the air I was breathing out.

"Then I decided to stay in New York City," Joseph continued. "This place lit a fire under me that I was lacking when I finished college. I needed to kill again, but did not have the accessibility to easy targets like sorority girls. So I decided to do the next best thing to make life easy; target people while they are sleeping at night."

"So you are the night slasher then?" I asked, finally able to get some words out.

"I hate that name," Joseph said as his face showed intense disgust. "It is so boring and unappealing. Richard Ramirez got the night stalker. John Wayne Gacy was dubbed the killer clown. Dennis Rader was the BTK killer. I get the night slasher? Yuck!"

"Joseph, why are you telling me all of this now when the trial is still going on?" I asked.

"No reason. Just needed to get it off my chest."

"What am I supposed to do with this info?"

"Whatever you want I guess. Doesn't matter who you tell cuz I am going away for the rest of my life anyway, it just depends for which murder."

My head began to pound like someone was taking a jackhammer and digging into my skull. I also was beginning to feel lightheaded. I did not want to hear anymore, so I told Joseph to stop. For the first time in my career, I honestly didn't know what to do. Do I continue to defend him?

Do I report him to the police? Do I mention anything to Nicole? I hated the position Joseph put me in, but I also knew I needed to get a hold of the situation before it got any worse. There were only two people I could go to with this information, Alan and Steven.

"Listen Joseph, I am going to skip court today. Kelly will take the lead on cross examinations. I will be back tomorrow when we get ready to call our first witness. Do not tell anyone about this conversation. You hear? Nobody."

"I got it, Sal. I hope I didn't want to upset you too much," Joseph said.

I gave him a glance that clearly showed I was annoyed with him and made my way out of Rikers Island as fast as I could.

Chapter 36

"Did you find anything out?" Sean asked Roland.

"Not yet. Either this woman doesn't exist or she is the best I have ever seen at hiding," Roland responded.

"Ok, well please keep trying to find her. What about the other thing?"

"I have someone who is going to rough her up a little bit. Nothing too bad, just enough to make her think twice about annoying you again."

"Who is it?" Sean asked.

"Better if I don't tell you. You know how it is," Roland answered.

"You are right. Thanks Roland. I appreciate the work."

"No problem. I will let you know when I have more," Roland said and hung up.

Sean was getting impatient and frustrated that he might be losing control of the situation. He was never one to panic, but he hated when he wasn't in control. He had been planning his revenge for the better part of a year and now someone was trying to take that away from him. Worse than that was that he did not know who this person was.

As the morning went on, Sean continued to look through his files, photographs, and other documents to see if he missed something. Even though it was January, the temperature was in the lower forties, which gave Sean the opportunity to sit outside and enjoy the brisk morning air. He grabbed a few files and photos and sat down on the balcony just outside of his bedroom window.

For the next fifteen minutes, Sean did nothing but reread his files and stare at photos. When he finally picked his head up to look at the street below, he noticed something out of place. The was a black car with tinted windows and a side mirror with a magnifier on it. This was not a car he had seen before, which made him curious right away about what it was doing there. He then looked across the street from that car and saw a man, dressed in street clothes, reading a newspaper while leaning against a street sign pole. Sean immediately thought to himself why someone would be reading a newspaper outside in January?

Without thinking, Sean grabbed his files and photos and went back inside his apartment. He knew something was going on but needed to get more information on what it was. He went to the lobby of the apartment building and made his way around back, where he could get a closer look at the car and the man without being seen. When he reached the rear exit of the lobby, he opened the door and saw another person standing on the corner with what looked like an earpiece in his ear. Panic began to set in as Sean realized that he had been found and these men were here to take him down.

Instinctively, Sean took off running. He was very much in shape and felt he could outrun anyone. He did not have a plan on which way he would go, but he also knew that he could use the crowded streets to his advantage and disappear. His first turn was a disaster as he plowed right into a woman holding two grocery bags. He immediately got up and turned around to see if anyone was following him. To his shock, he saw four people chasing after him with guns drawn.

"Suspect is fleeing on foot down Second Avenue toward Seventy Second Street. We are in pursuit," one of the police officers said over his radio.

"You will never catch me, but try if you must," Sean yelled back.

Sean continued to race down Second Avenue, weaving in and out between the traffic that was coming his way. He was not tired at all and felt he could run five miles before getting winded. He made a sharp left turn down East Seventy Sixth Street, went three blocks, and turned right onto Park Avenue. He slowed down a bit to look behind him and saw that there was nobody there chasing him. He turned back around and continued his sprint toward freedom when he saw one of the police officers directly in front of him, gun drawn, and pointed right at his chest.

"Give it up, Lancaster. We have you surrounded," the police officer said.

"Never. You may think you do, but you don't. Good luck though," Sean said.

Quick to think on his feet, Sean dropped the ground, rolled under the stopped cars in traffic, then made his way under the parked cars. When he got back to his feet, there was an alley right in front of him. He raced down the alley and came to a fence with barbed wire, which he was not going to let stop him. He climbed the fence and tried to jump over the barbed wire, but his shoelace got caught on the spikes, and his leg fell right on top and was sliced open. After a bit of a struggle to get loose,

Sean finally made it over the fence; however, he now had a severe limp and could not run anymore.

Adrenaline fueled Sean at this point as he made his way to a row of parked cars. Sean did not know how to hotwire a car, so he knew he would have to wait for one to come down the street and then steal it. Eight minutes passed before Sean heard a car turn down the street where he was. He could barely walk at this point but knew he had to try his best to get the car to stop. When the car was close enough, Sean threw his hands up and yelled for the driver to stop and help him.

"Oh thank you. I need help. Please. I sliced my leg open when I fell back there and I need an ambulance. Can you call one for me please?" Sean asked.

"You don't have a cell phone?" asked the driver.

"No, I went for a run and left it in my apartment."

"Ok. Hang on. I will call for help," the driver said.

"Thank you, sir. Thank you."

When the driver leaned over to grab his cell phone from the passenger seat, Sean hit him in the head with a rock he had picked up earlier, knocking him out. Sean then grabbed the driver, took his cell phone and threw him out of the car onto the street. He jumped in the car and sped away, hoping he had left the police behind.

"I need you to meet me at our rendezvous point," Sean yelled into the speakerphone.

"Everything ok? What's going on?" Roland asked.

"They found me, those fuckers. I have no clue how," Sean said.

"Who?"

"The police. They were casing my apartment and chased me down Second Avenue. Just meet me in twenty minutes. I need your help."

"Ok, I will be there," Roland said.

Sean pulled the car over to the side of the road and looked around to see if anyone was still after him. He couldn't see or hear anyone who resembled a cop, which made him a bit more relaxed. In order to avoid suspicion, Sean drove to the rendezvous point to meet Roland with extreme caution. He stopped at every yellow light, went under the speed limit, and kept two hands on the wheel. Although he was now past this crisis, Sean still could not rest knowing that someone out there had informed the police where he was. His plans for Sal would need to wait; it was time to catch a rat.

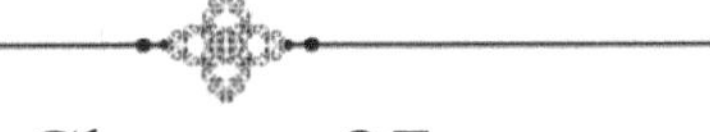

Chapter 37

I did not want to bring the kids to see Danielle, in fact, I was having second thoughts the whole car ride there. I had prepped the kids beforehand of what to expect and that they did not need to say anything if they did not want to. Gio said he wanted to ask her why, which I was more than willing to let him do. Angela said she wasn't going to look at Danielle, which I told her if that is what she wants to do, I support it.

Once we reached Bedford Hills Correctional Facility, I again asked the kids if they are ok with this. They both said yes and also said they wanted to get this over with. We made the long walk to the entrance of the facility, went through security, and made our way to the visitor area.

"I am here to see Danielle Amici," I said to the guard.

"Sign in here," the guard told me.

After I signed in, I checked in with Gio and Angela to see if they were ok. To this point they both were, so we proceeded to enter the visitor area and wait for them to bring Danielle to us.

"Daddy, I don't know what to say," Angela said.

"I know angel. I don't either. You don't have to say anything if you do not want to," I reassured Angela.

"Dad, this is awkward," Gio said.

"Why is that?" I asked.

"Cuz mom is in prison and I am the only person in school who has a mother in prison. I mean what do I say to her or how do I act around her? It's weird."

"I know son, just do the best you can. There is no right or wrong in this situation. Just act natural and don't try to be someone you are not," I said.

"Thanks dad. That helps. Hopefully I can remember that," Gio said.

I felt bad for my kids because they should not have to go through this at their age, or any age for that matter. Danielle had us all believing she was one person for so many years, and never once thought of what the fallout would be if she was caught. That is the part that bothers me the most. I can handle her misleading me, but my kids should never have been put through this torture.

After what seemed like an eternity, Danielle was finally ushered into the visitation area to meet with us. She was wearing a beige jumpsuit with Bedford Hills Correctional Facility printed on the back. She was not shackled like Joseph Millstone when I went to see him, but she was handcuffed. As soon as she saw Gio and Angela, she began to cry. I wanted to feel bad for her, but I kept reminding myself that we were there because of her and that she didn't deserve my empathy.

"Oh my, you both have grown so much!" Danielle said as she went to hug Gio and Angela. "Come on, come here, please."

Both of my kids stood in front of her like statues and did not move. They were so still, it looked like they were turned to stone by Medusa. They still didn't move, even when I tried to talk to them. I didn't know what to do, so I decided it was best to let the situation play itself out.

"I don't want to. I want to go home," Angela cried, then ran into my arms.

"Hi mom," Gio said backing away from her.

"Kids don't be scared. I know what you think of me, but I would never do anything to you," Danielle said, crying.

"Alright, everyone sit down. Let's get this over with," I said, trying to move the awkwardness along.

I could tell by the body language of both Gio and Angela that they did not want to be there. They were trying their best to hide that fact, but after a few minutes, they were not doing a very good job. I wanted to grab them both and take them away from this awful situation; something a father is supposed to do, but I knew I couldn't do that because Danielle had requested I bring the children to see her because they had been threatened by Sean.

"Ok Danielle, what is this about?" I asked.

"Not in front of them," Danielle said, tilting her head toward the kids.

"They aren't going anywhere so this is your one and only chance. "I said, getting angry. "And I am not waiting long."

"Ok, fine. Sean said that I needed to have you bring the kids to see me, but didn't tell me why. All he said was that if I didn't, he would do something to them."

"What?"

"He didn't say."

"You are a piece of work Danielle. The one person who is as sick and demented as you doesn't even like you anymore. What did you do to him?" I asked, chuckling.

"That's the thing I didn't do anything to him. He just got pissed one day and started making threats."

Danielle then told the kids to go to the table behind her and Sal because she needed to discuss something private with me. Neither Gio nor Angela wanted to leave me, but I told them it would only be for a few minutes and the sooner they went, the sooner we would be able to leave. I gave Angela my phone to play games on and Gio took his out as well.

"Sal, listen. I know you hate me and there is no reason you will agree to do what I am about to ask you, but I have been backed into a corner and have no other way out."

"Would you stop stalling and get to it already?" I said, slamming my fist on the table.

"I need your help taking out Sean," Danielle said.

"WHAT?" I yelled, drawing the attention of the guards. "Are you insane? What the hell are you thinking?"

"Calm down, will ya. Let me explain."

"No Danielle. Don't explain. The answer is no. I don't even know how I could help anyway. Unbelievable," I said and stood up to leave.

"Joseph Millstone. That is how."

I froze for a second or two, then sat back down. What did she know about Joseph and does she think I could use him to help her? As much as I didn't want to ask for more details, I had to know to protect myself and my kids.

"How exactly would that work?" I asked.

"Well, you are defending him, aren't you?"

"Yes, but why does that matter?"

"He and Sean have a long history together, some of which is not so good."

"And how do you know this?"

"Sal, come on. Do you know who you are talking to? I know everything."

"Ok. I am done. I'm not gonna sit here and listen to this shit again," I said getting up to leave again.

"Sal, it is not for me, it is for our children. I do not know what Sean has planned and despite what you may think, I love our kids and would do anything to protect them."

I knew she was playing a game with me, but I also could not jeopardize the lives of my children. I had no intention of getting involved in her plans, but I needed to make it seem like I would be willing to do anything as well.

"Alright. What do you need me to do?"

"Thank you Sal. Just talk to Joseph and see what connections he still has. Ask him if he can set something up that will arouse suspicion and be quick."

"I'll see what I can do. I'll let you know," I said and went to get Gio and Angela.

Danielle tried to say goodbye to them but neither one looked in her direction. I was proud of my kids for not giving into her or making a scene. They handled themselves in a very grown-up way in an intense grown-up situation. They had been put through a gamut of emotions and I promised them that they would never have to do this again. As far as I was concerned, this would be the last time Danielle would ever see her kids.

Chapter 38

"How the hell in good conscience am I supposed to continue defending him?" I asked Alan and Steven.

"Sometimes you need to leave your feelings behind you and do what you were hired to do," Alan said. "It sucks, but sometimes that is the only way to handle things."

"I get that Alan, but I also have a conscience and right now it is telling me to get as far away from this guy as possible."

"Look Sal, I don't have words of wisdom like Thomas had, but I can tell you that I know you will do the right thing, because that's who you are. We made you a partner of this firm for a reason; we believe in your ability to defend our clients with the utmost integrity and professionalism. If Joseph Millstone is causing a conflict within yourself, then maybe you should recuse yourself from this case," Alan said.

I knew Alan was right but I also knew that if I did recuse myself, it would send the wrong message to the firm, especially Kelly. She is a definite up and comer and I did not want her to see that it is acceptable behavior to walk away when things get rough.

"No, I will not do that. I will not let Joseph Millstone dictate what I do in my professional life. I was more or less venting and have no intention of walking away," I said, trying to convince myself.

"Good. Now get your ass to court and win this case," Steven said.

On my way to the courthouse, I could only think of two things. One was how I was going to proceed in this case without showing how repulsed I am by Joseph. The other was about what Danielle had asked me to do. Not only did she want me to help her deal with Sean, but she also wanted me to talk to Joseph to help her do it. I didn't have a choice in the matter because Sean had threatened my children and I would go to any length to make sure nothing happened to them. The more I thought about what she asked, the more I found myself inclined to do what was necessary to keep my family safe.

As I pulled into the parking lot at the courthouse, Kelly pulled up next to me. The timing was odd because she should have been at the courthouse already. I was curious to find out why she wasn't there already, yet at the same time, afraid that something might be wrong.

"Hey Kelly. I thought you would be here already," I said.

"I overslept. I have been so tired lately that I didn't hear my alarm," Kelly explained, trying to gather her things in a hurry.

"No worries. We are still on time," I reassured her. "So Bryce has one more witness, then it is our turn huh?"

"Looks that way. Sal, I gotta make up some time, so I will catch you in the courtroom, ok?"

"Ok. See you there," I responded.

Kelly's behavior was very concerning to say the least. She was never late to anything, in fact, she was usually the first to arrive. Additionally, the fact that she was in such a rush to get away from me was also a red flag that I didn't care to have to investigate. I would certainly need to find out what was going on with her, but first, I had to mentally prepare myself for the day ahead.

When I walked into the courtroom, Kelly was at our table looking over her notes for the witness that Bryce would call in a matter of moments. If one were to look at her in that moment, it would be impossible to tell just how flustered she had been not ten minutes ago. She seemed to have the ability to block out everything around her and focus on the task at hand. Most superstar athletes like Derek Jeter and Kobe Bryant have this ability, but it is rarely seen in a first-year attorney.

I sat down next to Kelly and asked if everything was ok. She turned to me and gave me a smile that said yes, but please don't ask me anything else, then went back to her notes. I knew something was definitely wrong and wanted to help, but this was not the place for it. Just as I was about to tell her I was there for her if she needed anything, Bryce called his final witness.

"The State would like to call Timothy King" Bryce said, causing a stir from the crowd in attendance.

As Timothy King walked to the witness stand, he stared at Joseph with one of the evilest looks I have ever seen. It was easy to see both the physical and emotional pain, anger, and disgust that Joseph had caused him. Tim wore a turtleneck sweatshirt to cover up the huge scar left by Joseph's attack. I was sure Bryce was going to ask him to show it to the jury but I couldn't blame Tim for wanting to hide it.

"Can you please state your name for the court please?" Bryce asked.

"Timothy King, but call me Tim," Tim said, in a raspy voice.

"Thank you for coming today, Tim. I know this can't be easy for you."

"No problem. I want to put that son of a bitch away forever."

"Objection Your Honor," I said.

"Sustained," Judge Santino ruled. "Tim, please refrain from adding comments not relevant to the question being asked."

"Yes Ma'am. I apologize," Tim said, still staring at Joseph.

"Tim, can you explain what happened to you on the night of January 16, 2022?" Bryce asked.

Tim had to take a deep breath before answering. It was gut wrenching to see him have to recall the horror of the night his family was murdered. I wanted to tell him he didn't need to be on the witness stand and that his memory of that night was not necessary to tell, but I had a job to do and I was going to see it through, no matter what.

"I was playing a video game," Tim began with nerves in his voice. "And I must have fallen asleep because I don't remember shutting the game off. In fact, the last thing I remember before being attacked was scoring a touchdown to win the game I was playing."

"Then what happened?"

"I felt someone cover my mouth and press my head down into my pillow so hard that I couldn't move."

"Objection Your Honor. How could the witness tell if the attacker was male or female?" Kelly shouted.

"I didn't hear Mr. Weatherford ask for a gender description. Overruled."

"Please continue, Tim," Bryce said gently.

"I tried to get his hand off of my mouth, but I couldn't. He was much too strong for me. Then I felt a sharp pain go across my throat, followed by a sudden feeling of being wet. I knew what had happened to me, yet I could not react. At that moment, I thought it would be best to act as if he killed me so he would just leave."

"Did you think about the rest of your family while you were lying in your bed bleeding out?"

"Yes."

"Did you attempt to do anything to help them?"

"I couldn't. I was frozen. Partly because I was scared, but mostly because of the amount of blood I was losing."

"What did you do next?"

"Once he left my room, I was able to take a blanket and tie it around my neck to hopefully stop the bleeding," Tim recalled. "Once I did that, I didn't know how time I had left, so I grabbed my cell phone and dialed 911."

"Your Honor, the State would like to admit into evidence the 911 tape recording from that night as exhibit F," Bryce asked.

"Mr. Amici, any objections?" Judge Santino asked me.

"No objection, Your Honor," I replied.

Joseph became agitated that I didn't object to the tape being played in court and didn't shy away from letting me know how he felt.

"What the hell, Sal. How could you let them do this?" Joseph begged.

"Look Joseph, I have no grounds to object to this recording from being played. If I object to it, it looks like I am panicking and my defense goes to shit. Got it?" I snarled back at Joseph.

"Got it," Joseph said and fell back into his chair.

I had not heard the 911 tape so this was going to be a challenge for me to hide my reaction, which I knew was going to be near impossible. I looked at Kelly and gave her a look that said *do not react to this tape in any way.* She seemed to understand me because she gave me a head nod right before the court clerk pressed play.

"911, where is your emergency?" the dispatcher asked.

"I... I... I've been stabbed. Please help," Tim struggled to say.

"Did you say you were stabbed?" the dispatcher asked.

"Yes. My throat...it hurts"

"Was your throat cut?" the dispatcher asked.

"I can't...can't" Timothy tried to say.

"Can't what sir? Are you still with me?"

"He's still here. Pl…please come quick."

"Ok sir, hang on. Help is on the way. Are you alone in the house?"

"No, my f…f…" Tim said before he went silent.

The courtroom was dead silent. Almost everyone had their hands over their mouths. There were tears galore and there was also no shortage of sniffling throughout the courtroom. There was an awkward ten to fifteen second pause from the time the recording was over until Bryce continued his examination. I was truly unsure at that point how I would cross exam Tim after hearing what he went through.

"I am terribly sorry you had to go through that, Tim. How are you doing now?" Bryce asked.

"Every day is a struggle. I am going to speech therapy to try and regain the full strength of my voice. I am living with my uncle, which isn't so bad, but I miss my family every day. I often ask myself, why us? What did we do to deserve this? All I can do is keep moving forward and live in honor of my family," Tim said as he began to cry.

"Do you need a break Tim?" Bryce asked.

"No, I am good," Tim said through his tears.

"Can you describe the next thing you remember after you called 911?"

"There were three or four cops and two EMT workers surrounding me. I could barely make out what they were saying, but I was hopeful that they were there to help."

"Did you see or hear anyone being arrested by the police?"

"Yes. I heard someone scream 'I want Sal Amici.'"

"Thank you Tim. You are very brave to be here today. No further questions."

"Mr. Amici, your witness," Judge Santino said.

"Thank you, Your Honor," I said, as I rose slowly.

"Tim, first let me say how awful we all feel about what you have been through. It takes great courage to do what you are doing."

"Thank you, Mr. Amici," Tim replied.

"I have just a few questions for you," I began. "When you were attacked, were you awake or asleep?"

"Most likely asleep."

"Do you remember hearing anyone come into your room?"

"No."

"Did you *see* anyone coming into your room?"

"No."

"During your attack, did you get a look at who was attacking you?"

"No, because he was wearing a ski mask."

"Did the perpetrator say anything to you during the attack?"

"No."

"Did you hear the perpetrator say anything to anyone else once they left your room?"

"No."

"You said earlier that you heard someone yell, 'I want Sal Amici.' Is that correct?"

"Yes, I heard it very clearly."

"Do you know if it was Mr. Millstone for sure?"

"Objection. The witness has already stated that he did not hear the defendant's voice. Is there a need to keep asking the same questions?" Bryce said.

Once again, I had trapped Bryce into an objection. I knew he would object to my question, but it was a necessary objection because I needed him to say that Tim had not heard Joseph's voice at all.

"Withdrawn," I said. "Tim, if you did not hear any voices at any point before, during, or after the attack, how can you be sure that the voice you heard ask for me is Mr. Millstone's"

"I can't," Tim said as his head fell downward.

"You also testified earlier that the assailant was wearing a ski mask. Is *that* correct?"

"Yes."

"Then is it fair to say that you cannot, with one hundred percent certainty, identify Mr. Millstone as your attacker?"

"I guess so, but I know it's him," Tim said with desperation.

"No more questions Your Honor."

"Mr. King, you may step down," Judge Santino ordered.

I felt like a dirty piece of shit cross examining Timothy King the way I did. One of the first things they teach you in law school is never let emotion get in the way of an examination. I had practiced that in every case, and this case was no different. I knew Joseph slashed Tim's throat and butchered his family. I knew that Joseph was a serial killer that needs to be stopped by any means necessary. But how do I do it without raising suspicion?

"Your Honor, while I hold the right to recall a witness to rebut future testimony, the State rests," Bryce said.

"Very well. We will adjourn for lunch and return for the defense's first witness in ninety minutes," Judge Santino said as she slammed her gavel down.

"You ready for this Sal?" Kelly asked me.

"As ready as I will ever be. What about you?"

"Sal," Kelly said nervously. "We need to talk."

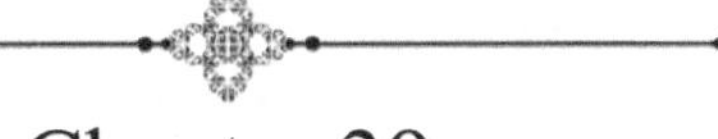

Chapter 39

Having narrowly escaped the police the day before, Sean was understandably on edge. He looked over both shoulders when leaving a building. He was very cautious about going out in public and wore layers of clothing to make himself look larger than he really was. He dyed his hair blond and pierced both of his ears.

He had spent the night going over the plan he put together with Roland Crenshaw to see if there were any details he may have overlooked. The plan was simple. Sean needed to get out of New York City as quickly as possible, but without being seen. That task would prove to be a gargantuan one because every exit in and out of the city was being watched. All the tunnels and bridges were being patrolled by the police and the coast guard. The plan to get him out was going to take a few days, so he decided to stay with Roland to keep a low profile.

"How do you think they found you?" Roland asked.

"I have no idea. Maybe it was Danielle," Sean answered.

"But she doesn't know where you live, does she?"

"Yes, she does. I told her when she was first locked up. "

"You really think she would rat you out? Isn't she in there because she wanted to be with you?"

"Who knows what that bitch thinks. We have had some rough times lately and I wouldn't put it past her to sell me out," Sean said.

He hoped that wasn't true. Although he and Danielle were fighting a lot, Sean really cared for her. She understood him and didn't judge him by his actions. Even though he had told Sal that Danielle was the one that set the murder plot of his family up, he still wanted the best for her and hoped one day she would win in appellate court. .

"I can't see it, Sean. Sorry, but I don't think she would do that to you. Not after all you guys have been through," Roland said.

"Well, you may be right, but I can't rule it out. If not her, who?

"No idea Sean, but we can't waste time worrying about it. Nor can we speculate who might be after you about Titus. We have to get you out of the city. Pronto," Roland said.

Sean's eyes went wide and he swung around very slowly. He looked at Roland with a confused expression on his face.

"What did you just say?" Sean asked.

"I said we need to get you out of the city pronto."

"No before that."

"Oh. It doesn't matter who ratted you out or is after you, we don't have time to worry about it."

"Why the sudden interest in helping me. A few days ago, you wanted no part of me," Sean asked suspiciously.

"The last few days have brought back some memories and reminded me how much I enjoy working with you. Are you ok? You are acting weird."

"See Roland, the thing is, I never told you about Titus. I never once mentioned that I was threatened because of what I did to him. So how did you know about that?" Sean asked.

"Uh," Roland said with a frightened look on his face. "Are you sure you never told me because I distinctly remember you did."

"No I didn't Roland. Cut the shit. What is going on? How did you know about that?"

"Well, see Sean..." Roland said, as he lowered his head and charged into Sean's mid-section. The force of his charge drove Sean into the wall behind him. Roland followed up his bull charge with a one-two combination to Sean's ribs and followed that up with a kick to the groin.

Sean was on the floor, writhing in pain, but Roland kept attacking him. Finally, Sean was able to grab Roland's foot and twist it enough to make Roland off balance and fall to the ground. Sean was then able to muster up enough energy to crawl over to Roland and began pounding on his chest. Sean was relentless in his attack, landing blow after blow to Roland's chest, mid-section, and face. Once he had subdued Roland, he looked around the room for something to tie Roland up with. Luckily for him, Roland had some string on the kitchen counter that he was using to tie up newspapers to recycle. Sean used the string to tie Roland's hands behind his back. Once he was able to stand, Sean then kicked Roland in the back to wake him up. It was time to get some answers.

"What the hell was that about?" Sean asked while still trying to catch his breath.

Roland did not answer. Instead, he just stared at Sean.

"I asked you a question you fuck. What the hell was that?" Sean asked again.

"Fuck you!" Roland answered.

Sean kicked Roland two more times in the back and once in the chest. He was not going to stop until he found out what was going on.

"Wrong answer pal. I can do this all day and all night. The question is, how much can you take?" Sean said.

"You want to know what's going on, I'll tell you what's going on. I have been waiting to see the look on your face anyway," Roland said as he tried to stand. "You killed my future brother-in-law. That's what is going on."

"Roland, I have killed so many people, you are going to have to be more specific than that."

"Titus Baxter, you prick. He was engaged to my sister. I believe Danielle met her a little while ago," Roland said with a smirk.

Sean was taken aback at what he just heard. How did he not know that Roland's sister was in prison and was the one that threatened me through Danielle? He could not believe that Roland would do this to him, but had to put his shock aside to find out what the ultimate goal was that Roland had.

"You're kidding me right?" Sean said.

"No. I was sent to take you out and that is exactly what I intend to do," Roland said as he continued to try and break free.

Sean thought about that for a moment and came to a harrowing conclusion. On one hand he was glad he knew had threatened him but on the other hand, he felt a sense of pain having been betrayed by someone he trusted.

"It was you, wasn't it? The one that ratted me out to the police," Sean said with a snarl.

"Took you long enough. Geez, for someone who claims to be a mastermind, you sure don't look at the things right in front of you, do you?" Roland responded laughing.

A feeling came over Sean, similar to the one he had when he was smashing Titus Baxter's head against the bars in jail. He ran toward Roland with the force of a Mack Truck and tackled him to the ground. Sean began to pummel Roland with punch after punch and showed no signs of slowing down. While he was hammering away at Roland, Sean kept asking, "How could you do this to me? I trusted you." He wasn't really looking for an answer, he just needed Roland to know how much he was hurt. After one solid minute of a non-stop assault, Sean began to tire. When he finally stopped, he looked at Roland and saw blood all over his face. Sean was breathing very heavily, trying to catch his breath, when he noticed Roland was not moving. Sean checked for a pulse and found none. He then put his ear to Roland's chest to see if there was a heartbeat. There was none. Realizing that Roland was dead, Sean spat in his face as a final insult. Not only did he just eliminate the threat against him, but he could now let Danielle know who the woman was that confronted her and tell her to take proper precautions to protect herself.

Although he was glad he took care of his problem, Sean now had another one. How was he going to clean up the mess he just made? He would need to get rid of the body, clean the apartment, get rid of the rugs, and do all of this without anyone noticing. There was a lot of planning to do and Sean knew he would not be able to do it feeling the way he felt at that moment. He decided to take a nap on the couch and deal with everything when he woke up. As he went to close his eyes, he saw that Roland's phone had fallen out of his pocket. Sean went to pick it up and saw that a call had been placed five minutes prior to a number with a New Jersey area code. Someone out there had heard the entire altercation with Sean and Roland.

Chapter 40

I knew something was wrong with Kelly and I was hoping she was about to tell me. I hated being left out in the dark on anything, but it was worse when it directly involved my partner. I did not know Kelly all that well, but we had built a solid working relationship over the past few weeks, something I hoped she thought highly enough of to tell me what was bothering her.

We entered the nearest sushi restaurant and placed our order at the counter. Afterward, we sat down in a booth that was far away from both the entrance and counter. I wanted a space that Kelly would feel comfortable telling me whatever it was that she had to tell me. As soon as we sat down, I began the quest of finding out what was wrong.

"Kelly, what did you want to talk about?" I asked.

"Sal, I am just so nervous to tell you, I do not know if I can," Kelly replied.

"You can tell me anything. For right now, I am a friend, not a partner at the law firm. Just tell me so I can help you."

"Ok, I will try," Kelly said, as she wiped sweat away from her forehead. "I was late this morning because I went to see my grandfather about how I feel."

"Ok?" I said, confused.

"Sal, my grandfather is Alan," Kelly told me.

I am usually pretty good at reading people and expecting surprises. It is difficult to be a successful defense attorney and *not* possess that skill; however, I was completely caught off guard with that.

"What? How come nobody ever told me?"

"I wanted you and everyone else to view me as a colleague and someone who earned her way to where she is, not Alan's granddaughter."

"I can understand that. Well, you have certainly accomplished your goal. You are very well respected in the office. So what is it that you spoke to him about?"

"Sal, I don't know how to say it so I will just blurt it out. I don't think I am cut out to be a lawyer," Kelly answered.

"Uh-huh. I see," I said smiling. "Look, Kelly, every lawyer at some point doubts his/her abilities. Thomas used to tell me all the time, 'if you don't doubt yourself once in a while, you aren't human.' In this profession, there is so much pressure to always get it right, to always do the right thing. We have to know so many rules and regulations that it can become overwhelming at times. It is natural to begin to think that you are not cut out for this, but I will tell you this. You are one hell of a lawyer and you have a bright future. You have all the traits necessary to be successful. You are smart, gritty, determined, and most of all you have talent. Not everyone is meant to be a lawyer. You were born to do this."

"I appreciate the sentiment Sal, but I just am not feeling it. Seeing you cross exam Tim King earlier made me realize, I can never do that. There is too much emotion for me to be able to put it aside."

"Kelly, again, I understand where you are coming from. I truly do, but you have to realize that you are only in your first year out of law school. You are not expected to have all the tools necessary to be successful yet, that is why we pair people up with senior associates. It takes time to develop your style and how you approach each case. I have been doing this for seven years, so I have developed my style. While that style works for me, it may not work for you. In time, you will come to realize what works best for you, and when you do, I will be right here to help guide you," I said hoping to reassure Kelly.

"I don't know Sal. It makes sense what you are saying. I just can't seem to get rid of this feeling that I am not supposed to be doing this."

"Ok. I'll tell you what. Finish this trial with me and after it is over, we can debrief and talk about your future. It is hard to decide your future in the middle of a case because as you said, there is too much emotion involved. I hated cross examining Tim like I did. It ate at my soul to have him look vulnerable and admit that he is not positive it was Joseph who was there. I know Joseph was there, you know Joseph was there, hell most of the jury probably believes that too. But it is my job to create doubt and in order to do that, I have to sometimes do things that are uncomfortable. That is part of the job. If that is something you have a hard time dealing with, then we can help you with that."

"Ok, Sal. I will ride this one out with you. I owe you that much," Kelly said unsure.

"You don't owe me anything. You should do this for you. Nobody else. Only you are going to know what the right thing to do is. I am here to guide you, that's all."

"Sounds good, Sal. Man, you really are a good talker," Kelly said smiling.

"Yeah, it does get me in trouble occasionally though," I responded laughing.

Kelly and I finished our lunch, told some jokes, packed our things up, and headed back to the courthouse to begin our case. I was confident we were winning this case and was filled with excitement about calling our first witness.

"I have one more thing to say to you Kelly and then it's go time," I said and paused for dramatic effect. "This trial starts *NOW!*"

Chapter 41

When we returned from lunch, Kelly and I met at our table to go over our strategy for the upcoming witnesses we were going to call. We both agreed that we needed to remind Joseph of our prep meetings with him and also to remind him to stay calm. Joseph had a hard time understanding that our job was to provide doubt, not prove his innocence. After an intense lunch together, Kelly and I were ready to let loose.

"Mr. Amici, are you ready to call your first witness?" Judge Santino asked me.

"Yes, Your Honor. The defense calls Julie Rossi," I answered.

"This ought to be interesting," whispered Joseph.

"Shut up. What did we talk about Joseph?" Kelly reprimanded.

"Sorry. I will keep quiet," Joseph said with a slight smirk.

After Julie was sworn in by the bailiff, my opportunity to shine and show Kelly how the job is done, finally arrived.

"Good afternoon, Ms. Rossi. Thank you for joining us today. Can you please state your full name and how you know Mr. Millstone for the court please?" I asked.

"Julie Rossi and I had a long-term relationship with Joey."

"Had? Does that mean you two are no longer together?"

"That is correct," Julie answered.

"When did your relationship begin?"

"About eleven years ago. We met at the bar he worked at," Julie answered.

"I heard he was quite the bartender," I said, trying to lighten the mood. "Can you describe your relationship?"

"It was great. Joey would always surprise me with flowers or a gift for no reason. When he took me out to dinner, he would always open the door for me and pull out my seat for me. He was such a gentleman."

"Sounds like a dream come true. What type of things did the two of you do together?" I asked.

"Objection. Relevance?" Bryce interjected.

"Establishing a personality trend Your Honor," I replied.

"Overruled. Please continue Ms. Rossi," Judge Santino said.

"We would often take trips to the countryside, go hiking, camping, things like that."

"How were those trips?"

"They were so much fun. Joey had a way of making me feel like each trip was our first together," Julie said with a smile.

"Ms. Rossi, you seem to really love Mr. Millstone and your time together. If that is the case, what went wrong?" I asked, hoping for nothing too damning.

"Well, we each wanted different things. At first, we were happy just being together, but then I wanted more. I wanted to get married and have kids, but Joey didn't. This went on for a number of years. Finally, I gave him an ultimatum. We decided to end things mutually."

"How did Mr. Millstone take the news?"

"He was upset, just as I was, but we both understood that it was the best thing for both of us."

"Was Mr. Millstone ever violent toward you?" I asked.

"Oh no. Joey would never do something like that. He was the sweetest man I have ever met."

"Thank you Ms. Rossi. No more questions," I concluded.

"Mr. Weatherford," Judge Santino said.

"Thank you. Ms. Rossi, it certainly seems like you have fond memories of the defendant. Does it surprise you at all that he is facing these charges?" Bryce asked.

"Yes, it does. My Joey would never do these horrible things. He doesn't have it in him."

"Doesn't have it in him? And you would know this after spending several years with him?"

"That's right."

"Tell me Ms. Rossi, when you went on these camping trips with the defendant, where were you going?" Bryce asked, causing me to raise my eyebrows.

"We mostly went to Update New York," Julie answered, getting uncomfortable.

"Where specifically?"

"Usually the Catskills or Adirondack Park."

"Do you remember when you went camping?"

I could tell where Bryce was going with this and I felt helpless because there was nothing I could do to stop it. The questions he was asking were legitimate and I had no reason to object. If I did object, it would show panic and certainly cause the jury to wonder what I was hiding.

"Mainly in the summer," Julie answered.

"During your camping trips, was there ever a time when you and the defendant were separated?"

"Not that I recall."

"What about when you went to sleep? Did you ever wake up in the middle of the night and he wasn't there?" Bryce asked.

"Objection!" Kelly said, jumping up. "Relevance?"

"Overruled. Continue," Judge Santino said annoyed at Kelly.

I looked at Kelly after her objection was overruled and she looked defeated. She was trying to overcome her feelings, I could clearly see that, but it did not seem to be working. Maybe she wasn't cut out for this after all. I knew I had to have a discussion with her at a later time, but for now, I had to remain focused on the case.

"Not that I recall," Julie said.

"Do you recall the time period in which you would take these camping trips?"

"They were every summer between 2010 and 2017."

"Uh huh," Bryce said as if a light bulb just went off. "Would it surprise you, Ms. Rossi, to know that a series of murders remain unsolved from the Catskill and Adirondack areas and that these murders took place between 2005 and 2017?"

"I wouldn't know anything about that," Julie said uneasily.

"Would it also surprise you to know that *all* of these murders were stabbings?"

Julie was silent and motionless. She had connected the dots in her head and it was evident that she was disturbed by what just unfolded. She did her best to compose herself, but couldn't hold back the anger she had. She erupted in rage that nobody saw coming.

"No it doesn't. I am not surprised at all. The Catskills and Adirondack Park are prime areas for crime to occur. This is common knowledge. To sit there and infer that my ex is responsible for those crimes is preposterous. He would not hurt a fly and would give the shirt off of his back for anyone. You need to reexamine your facts counselor because Joey Millstone did not commit any other those crimes, nor did he commit these crimes. You should be ashamed of yourself for making such an accusation."

If it was possible to print out an image from one's mind, I would certainly have chosen to print the look on Bryce's face. He had set up his questioning about as smoothly as an Olympic Beach Volleyball player sets up a spike. I could not have done a better job myself, and I was sure the entire courtroom knew what he was doing. Either Julie Rossi really believed that Joseph was innocent or she loved him so much that she was willing to look past what was right in front of her. Either way, I looked like a genius putting her on the stand.

"No more questions," Bryce said dejectedly.

When Julie left the stand, she gave me a wink and blew a kiss to Joey. I turned to Kelly to see how she was doing and she was ferociously writing notes on her pad, like she did in law school.

"What are you doing Kelly?" I asked her.

"I am taking notes on how to become a superstar because that is what you are Sal. You are a superstar and I can learn a lot from you," Kelly answered.

"Glad to see you are back, Kelly," I said and patted her on the shoulder.

"Good to be back. Now let's continue with our masterpiece."

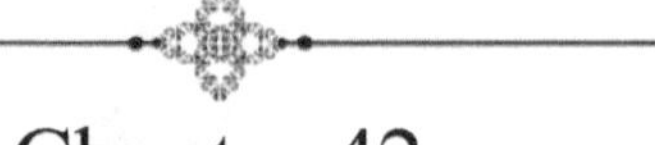

Chapter 42

I called only two more witnesses the rest of the afternoon, both of which testified to the character of Joseph Millstone. There were no fireworks like Julie's testimony, but they served their purpose in establishing the personality of Joseph. Once the court session was over, I headed straight home for a home cooked meal that Nicole was making for everyone.

There is nothing like coming home to a warm house in the dead of winter. The coziness of the fireplace, the comfort of the couch while sipping on a glass of wine, and the presence of family all around make for a relaxing evening. What makes this experience even better, is walking into the house and immediately being hit with the smell of a delicious meal being cooked in the kitchen. I cannot cook to save my life, in fact, one time I attempted to make baked mac and cheese and forgot to cook the macaroni before putting the dish in the oven. This is how I came to be known as an expert in making rock mac and cheese. Fortunately for me, I have been blessed that most of my partners are terrific cooks. For all of her flaws, Danielle was an outstanding cook, but Nicole may be just a bit better. Tonight, she was making Chicken Sorrentino with her special homemade sauce.

"How is school going Angela?" I asked as I sat down to eat.

"Good Daddy. We are making a special project in art class. I can't wait for you to see it," Angela answered.

"That's great angel. I am really looking forward to seeing it," I responded. "How about you Gio? How's school?"

"Fine," Gio answered.

"That's it? Fine? No details?" I prodded.

"No. Can I have the bread please?" Gio asked.

"What is wrong with you?" I asked, getting angry.

"Nothing dad. I just had a rough day."

"Why? What happened?"

Gio turned toward Nicole and gave her a look that begged her to tell me instead of him. She gave him a look back that said it will be alright and that I will understand. I didn't want to interrupt the moment the two of them had, but I needed answers before I lost my cool.

"Whatever it is son, you can tell me," I said as a put my hand on Gio's shoulder.

"I got into a fight at school today," Gio told me.

"What happened?"

"Some kids were making fun of me about mom so I hit two of them. I know I shouldn't have but they deserved it," Gio said, holding back tears.

"What were they saying?" I asked. "You know what, never mind that. What happened afterward?"

"The principal called the house and I went to get him at school," Nicole said.

"Why didn't anyone call me?"

"You were in court and it wasn't a big deal. All I was doing was watching TV and working on my patient notes."

There are certain moments when you know as a father, you must instill both wisdom and empathy toward your children. There are other times that you must do the opposite and give them discipline. This was a time for the former.

"I'm sorry this happened to you Gio. It is not fair and you shouldn't have to go through this. I wish there was something I can do to make this go away, but there isn't. What I can do though is help you through this by being there for you and supporting you in any way I can. What do you need from me?"

After a few seconds of thinking, Gio uttered a phrase that shook the entire table.

"I wish mom would die," Gio said and ran upstairs.

I turned to Nicole to see what I should do since this was more her area than mine. She gave me a motion with her hand to calm down and then told me to let him be, as we both would go up and talk to him later. My concern at that point turned to Angela because she was seven and I wasn't sure how she was processing what just happened.

"Why would Gio say that daddy?" Angela asked with puppy dog eyes.

"I'm sure he doesn't mean it angel. Sometimes when people are upset, they say mean things that they don't mean," I answered.

"Angela, do you want to talk about it?" Nicole asked.

"No, I just want to eat this delicious food."

"Ok, angel. But you let me know the second you want to ok?"

"Yes, Daddy."

The three of us finished our dinner in silence. I kept looking at Angela to see if she was ok and to my amazement, she didn't show any signs of being bothered by what just happened. I gave Nicole a few glances as well and in return, got the I'm sorry head tilt from her. I was debating on whether I should go and talk to Gio when he came storming downstairs with a bag on his shoulder.

"Where are you going?" I asked Gio.

"I am going to Jim's house. His mom will be here any minute to get me," Gio replied.

"Did you ask?" I questioned.

"No and I don't need to."

"Excuse me?"

"You heard me dad. I'm not staying a minute more in this house."

"Gio, put the bag down now and come over here and talk with us," I said getting frustrated.

"No. I told you I am going to Jim's. That's it."

"GIO PUT THE FUCKING BAG DOWN NOW!"

The only way to describe the look on everyone's face, especially Gio's was terror. They all knew me as a calm person at home and that I would occasionally raise my voice if needed. I had never spoken like that before to Gio and it caught them by surprise. I did not regret what I did because I needed to let Gio know that he was not in charge and that I commanded respect.

"Don't you ever talk to me like that again. Do you got it? DO YOU?" I yelled. "Who the hell do you think you are? Get your ass upstairs and don't come down until I say it's ok. MOVE!"

After Gio went upstairs and slammed his door, I apologized to Angela and Nicole for my outburst and went to my office. I needed some alone time after what happened to cool down. The first thing I thought of was how I was going to deal with the aftermath and the second thing I thought of was how would I explain my tirade to Nicole. I sat in my office for five minutes thinking of what to do next. Ultimately, I decided that I was not in any mood to deal with either situation now, so I left my office, sat on the couch, and turned on the TV. Nicole joined me on the couch and didn't say a word. All she did was pat me on leg two times and rest her head on my chest. It was exactly what I needed at that moment, and she knew it. After a few minutes of stroking her hair, we both fell asleep on the couch without a care in the world.

Chapter 43

Danielle was getting nervous because she had not heard from Sean in a while and she didn't know when she would. He was supposed to get back to her when he found out who the woman that threatened him was, but to this point, she heard nothing. She began to think that this woman would become a threat to her as well, given her relationship with Sean. Trying to keep her mind busy, Danielle decided it was time to reorganize the prison kitchen.

She began to take everything out of the cabinets and drawers and throw out anything she did not need. She also felt it was necessary to put stickers where each item should go, which would let others know where to put things back when they were done. After finishing the cabinets and drawers, she went into the walk-in fridge to reorganize all of the meats and cheeses. As she was checking the dates on the meat, she heard the door close behind her.

"Got you now bitch, don't I?" a woman said.

Danielle turned around slowly not knowing if the woman had a weapon on her or if she was with a group of prisoners. To her delight, the woman was alone; however, she was brandishing a shiny, sharp shiv that seemed to be calling for Danielle's blood.

"Who are you and what do you want?" Danielle asked. "What a minute. You're the one who threatened me. You're Titus's ex-finance."

"That's right and I'm here to settle the score," the woman said.

"What do you mean, settle the score? What happened?"

"Don't act like you don't know."

"I don't. Why don't you enlighten me?" Danielle said.

"My brother Roland is missing and I think, no better yet, I *know* your boyfriend has something to do with it."

"Whoa! First of all, back up. Second, who the hell are you?

"My name is Tiana Crenshaw. Why do you want to know?"

"No reason," Danielle said, staring Tiana up and down. "What makes you think Sean has anything to do with Roland's disappearance?"

"Cuz they were together the last time I spoke to Roland. Roland always calls me in the morning and he didn't call this morning. If he didn't call, then something happened to him and since Sean was the last one with him, that makes him suspect number one."

"You're a crazy girl. Now get out of my way so I can finish cleaning out the fridge unless you want to eat expired food," Danielle said as she pushed Tiana out of the way.

"I don't think so missy," Tiana said as she swung the shiv in Danielle's direction.

Tiana had landed a clean swipe on Danielle's side, piercing her liver. Immediately, Danielle crumbled to the floor, desperately trying to stop the bleeding. Without regard for what she had done, Tiana plunged the shiv into Danielle's upper thigh, just missing her femoral artery. Danielle begged Tiana to stop, but Tiana drove the shiv into her shoulder.

Feeling she had made her point, Tiana ended her brutal attack and wiped off the shiv with a towel that Danielle once held. She looked down at Danielle, who was barely conscious, and felt no remorse at all. She had done what she wanted to do and now she needed to give Danielle a message before Danielle passed out.

"Now you listen here bitch," Tiana said in her most intimidating voice. "If I find out that Roland is dead and Sean killed him, this is gonna seem like a fairytale compared to what I will do to you. By the way, the ham is moldy."

Danielle tried to utter something back to Tiana, but nothing came out of her mouth. She was having an extremely difficult time breathing and everything around her was blurry. When Tiana left the walk-in fridge, she closed the door and placed a chair under the handle so Danielle could not get out. Lying on the floor bleeding out, Danielle struggled to make noise, hoping someone would hear her. It was to no avail. Nobody was coming to save her. She thought to herself at that moment that she needed to conserve as much energy as she could because she did not have much left.

As the minutes went by, the more Danielle began to slip away. The pain was so intense she almost did not feel it anymore. Everything around her continued to get fuzzier and darker and she felt herself breathing slower and slower. Eventually, after a few more minutes of struggling, Danielle decided to give in and let go. She closed her eyes, concentrated on her breathing and resigned herself to the fact that she was going to die.

Chapter 44

Not having all the resources he was used to, Sean was having a difficult time finding out who the phone number belonged to that Roland had dialed before their altercation. He had to be careful of who he called because the police were surely canvasing all possible areas Sean could turn to in order to get out of the city.

He called his contact at the phone company, but the number could not be traced to anyone. He called his tech guy, Theo, who put MacGyver to shame, and even he could not figure out who the number belonged to. He even went to a pay phone and called the number himself, only to get a generic voicemail message. Running out of options, Sean turned to the one person who he knew would not help him in a million years, but was the one person who could.

"Hey, it's Sean."

"No, it can't be, because the Sean Lancaster I know, doesn't make mistakes like calling someone he should have no business calling."

"I know, but I have nowhere else to turn," Sean said.

"Wait, wait, wait. Sean Lancaster is stuck? What is this world coming to?"

"Joe, knock it off. You gonna help me or not?"

"Depends on what it is you need help with," Joseph Millstone said.

"Not over the phone. I need to tell you in person," Sean answered.

"Nah," Joseph said. "That won't happen. I don't want to see you because you know what will happen if I do."

"I know, but I'm desperate. Please Joe. Help out an old friend," Sean begged.

"You can tell me right now or not at all. Your choice."

Sean thought it over for a few seconds and realizing what he was about to say was going to be recorded and played back eventually for a jury to hear, he still felt he had no other option but to move forward.

"I met with Roland Crenshaw yesterday and things got out of hand and well, he is no longer with us. When I went to take a nap, I noticed his cell phone had fallen out of his pocket during our scuffle. When I looked at the phone, I noticed he had dialed a number before our disagreement and I cannot find out who the number belongs to. This is where I need your help," Sean explained.

"Why don't you go to Theo?" Joseph asked.

"I did. He couldn't figure it out. I tried calling it also and nothing."

"And what makes you think I will be able to find out who it belongs to?"

"Come on Joe. You and I both know you can," Sean said getting frustrated with Joseph's games.

"Alright. What makes you think I want to? What is in it for me?"

"How about freedom?" Sean replied.

"Fair enough, "Joseph replied. "What do you need?"

"I need you to ask around inside. See if anyone wants to see me hurt or dead. That call came from Roland's phone and it wasn't in his contacts, so I'm thinking the call was made to someone he did not want any record of. The only people Roland dealt with that he didn't want anyone to know about were inmates. He said he was out of the game, but I know that was bullshit. Someone like Roland Crenshaw does not one day decide to go straight."

"Ok, I like where your thinking is. Who should I be looking out for?" Joseph inquired.

"Someone who was there when I was there. We hang around the same people, so it should not be too difficult to find a few that fit the bill. Also look for any guards that may still hold a grudge against me. I am sure there are plenty of those out there."

"Alright Sean. I will get to work. How will I reach you after I finish digging?"

"Use our old method," Sean told Joseph.

"Sounds good. Anything else?"

"No, that's it for now. And Joe…" Sean said.

"Yeah?"

"Thank you."

"You bet."

Sean hung the phone and had conflicting feelings. He felt good that Joseph was on his side and was willing to help him. He knew that Joseph had a high status in jail, so he would be able to produce results. Yet, he also knew that everything he just said was recorded and would be listened to at any moment. He knew he couldn't stay in Manhattan much longer, so he decided he would wait another day or two until the heat died down and the exits out of the city opened up. What Sean didn't know was that he was about to receive news that would alter his plan.

Chapter 45

When I woke up the next morning, I had a feeling of guilt the way I spoke to Gio. I knew he was going through a rough time and was having an extremely difficult time handling what happened with Danielle, but I also thought that does not give him the right to speak to me the way he did or act like the way he did. Before I started my day, I realized I needed to talk to him.

As I approached Gio's room, I thought about what I would say to him. Do I just apologize or do I explain why I reacted the way I did? Do I even need to apologize? I am the parent and should not have to justify myself to my children.

Unsure of how I was going to proceed, I knocked on Gio's door. He did not answer right away, so I knocked again. Once again, no answer. I tried knocking one more time and finally, I got an answer.

"Yeah?" Gio asked.

"It's me Gio. Open the door."

"No. I don't want to talk to you. Go away," Gio responded.

At that moment, I had a choice. I could either respect his wishes and walk away or just enter the room. I chose the latter.

"Look, I know you don't want to talk to me and I respect that, but you need to hear what I have to say," I said.

"Fine. What," Gio said, as he turned away from me.

"Sometimes, adults act in ways that children find hard to understand. When you get older, you will see how much stress you will have in your life and it will make you do things that are out of the norm for you. Trust me on that. I am sure you understand that a little now because of the fight you got into at school, but son, you cannot talk to me or any other adult that way. It is very disrespectful and it will not be tolerated in this house. Is that understood?"

"Yes," Gio said, still facing away from me.

"Gio, look at me," I said, twisting his shoulders to help him turn around. "I am sorry for yelling at you the way I did. I truly am. You are my son and I love you very much and you did not deserve that."

"Thank you, dad. That means a lot," Gio responded.

"But that doesn't mean I don't regret the message it sent because I don't."

While I was speaking to Gio, my cell phone kept going off. It was a frantic pattern of phone call, text message, phone call, text message. All the messages were from my office, so I knew they were important, but I needed to finish the conversation with Gio first. As I was about to finish my speech to Gio, I happened to glance at the last text message sent to me.

Sal I need you to answer me ASAP. Drop what you are doing because It Is not as Important as this. I mean It Sal. Call me ASAP. NOW!!! - Jill

Jill never acts that way so I knew something big was going on. I had to find a way to stop short the most important talk I have ever had with my son to call Jill to handle what was undoubtedly a major crisis.

"Gio, I am sorry, but I have to call my office. Something big is going on and they need to speak to me now. I promise this won't take long. I will be right back, ok?" I said to Gio hoping he would understand.

"Sure dad, no problem," Gio said.

I was relieved to hear Gio was understanding and in a better mood. The stress of not knowing how he would react to our talk and its subsequent end was gone. I felt a sense of calm come over me that I wanted to enjoy for a few seconds because I did know what to expect when I called Jill back.

"Jill, it's Sal. What's going on? I was talk—"

"Sal!" Jill said, interrupting me. "It's Danielle."

"*Danielle?* Who gives a fuck about her?" I said.

"Sal, she is at New York Presbyterian. She was brutally stabbed in prison. She is in surgery right now."

I can't describe the feeling I had at that moment. Part of me was numb because she was after all the mother of my children and I didn't want this for them. Another part of me didn't care because of what she did to me and my family. Yet another part of me was happy because she finally got what she deserved.

"How is she?" I asked Jill.

"I don't have any other news. Apparently you are still her emergency contact and the HIPAA form she signed is still valid. We got a call a little while ago asking for you, which is when we were told what happened."

"So much for HIPAA regulations. Alright, thank you Jill. I am going to head over to the hospital so tell Kelly I will not be in court today."

"I will. Sal, I am sorry," Jill said.

"Yeah, me too."

A morning that had started out with such promise, suddenly turned into a nightmare. Yes, Danielle and I were divorced and I despised her for what she did, but I did not want this for her. Now, I had to tell both Gio and Angela what happened and I had no idea how to do it. The only thing I could think of was to wake up Nicole and ask her for advice.

Before I had the chance to wake up Nicole, my phone rang again. This time, it was a number I did not recognize. Given everything that was going, I decided to pick it up.

"Sal Amici here," I answered.

"Is this Sal Amici?" a voice asked.

"Yes it is. Who is this?"

"My name is Dr. Richards and I am a trauma surgeon at New York Presbyterian Hospital."

"Yes, what can I do for you doctor?" I asked, confused.

"Your ex-wife, Danielle, was brutally stabbed in prison and sustained a significant amount of blood loss. I was able to stop the bleeding and repair the wounds to her shoulder and upper thigh; however, the laceration to the liver is a major cause for concern. Fortunately for her, the knife missed any major arteries in the liver, but the amount of blood loss has been catastrophic. Because we do not know when the stabbing occurred, it is hard to say how much longer she can hold on, but typically, a patient can last up to about two hours with a moderate laceration."

"So what happens next?" I asked, unable to think of anything else.

"Well, we will continue to monitor her in the ICU and keep her as comfortable as possible, but there is a slim chance of survival."

"Ok, thank you doctor. I appreciate your candor," I said and hung up.

I sat at the edge of my bed watching Nicole sleep, wondering if I should wake her up to tell her. I would certainly need her help telling the kids, but I wasn't sure I wanted to tell them yet. I decided to not wake up Nicole and go to the hospital to visit Danielle. On my way out, Gio asked me if we could finish our talk. I let him know that we would later that evening and that I had to go to my office to help with something. He gave me a high-five and went back to his room. I needed that moment of happiness because I knew what was ahead of me was going to be anything but joyful.

Chapter 46

Kelly Esteves did not always want to be a lawyer. In fact, she wanted to be a teacher. Her mother was an eighth-grade science teacher and her father was a tenth-grade math teacher. She would enjoy helping both of her parents' grade exams and homework assignments, as well as help them plan their lessons. She would often pretend she was teaching a group of students in her room and would also grade fake exams.

When Kelly graduated high school, she attended Vanderbilt University in Nashville, Tennessee, which is one of the top colleges to earn a teaching degree. During her second semester at Vanderbilt, her grandfather, Alan Lowery, paid her a visit to try and convince her to become a lawyer. Alan knew that she had the talent to be an excellent lawyer and the grades to be successful in law school. Kelly had never considered being a lawyer because all she ever wanted to was to be a teacher, so she didn't give the visit much thought. However, as time passed by and the more Alan spoke with her, a career in law was becoming more and more appealing. Finally, in her second year at Vanderbilt, Kelly decided she wanted to change career paths and pursue a career as a lawyer. When asked by her parents why the change, she told them because she wanted to be a voice for those who need it. Kelly would go on to attend Columbia Law school and graduated near the top of her class. She was awarded a position at Alan's firm, Lowery, Hill, and Greenwood when she finished law school and was thrust into the Joseph Millstone case after just one year of service. Now, because of Sal's absence, she was alone in calling the defense's next witness.

"The defense would like to call Vincent Castellano," Kelly said.

As Vincent made his way to the witness stand, Bryce Weatherford looked at Kelly to gauge how nervous she was. He knew not having Sal with her was going to make a difference because there was no net for her to fall back on, in the event she struggled. To his amazement, she looked focused and not at all bothered by the situation. Before beginning her examination of Vincent, Kelly looked over at Bryce and winked at him, as if to say, "bring it."

"Would you please state your name and how you know Joseph please," Kelly said.

"Vincent Castellano. I do not know Joseph all that well, having only met him a few weeks ago," Vincent replied.

"Under what circumstances did you meet Joseph?"

"We were brought together by your office to discuss a mutual problem we had."

"What problem was that Mr. Castellano?" Kelly asked.

"Detective Timothy Landis," Vincent replied.

A not so quiet sigh went through the crowd on hand. There are usually one or two of these reactions in a murder trial and the key to using them to one's advantage is to follow it up with an intelligible question.

"Who is Detective Landis to you, Mr. Castellano?"

"He was my arresting officer six years ago."

"What were you arrested for?"

"Solicitation of a prostitute," Vincent replied.

"I see. How did Detective Landis catch you?"

"He didn't. I was caught by an off-duty cop across the street. He then called in Detective Landis."

"So Detective Landis did not actually see you commit the alleged crime?" Kelly asked.

"No he did not," Vincent replied.

"When you were arrested, was Detective Landis present for questioning?"

"No he was not."

"Do you know why?" Kelly asked.

"Objection!" Bryce yelled. "The witness is not an expert on police procedure.

"Sustained," Judge Santino ruled.

"I'll rephrase. Were you provided an explanation as to why Detective Landis was not at the questioning."

"No."

"Have you seen or come in contact with Detective Landis since he arrested you?"

"No I have not."

"I would like to switch now to your meeting with Joseph Millstone. What was the purpose of that meeting?" Kelly asked.

"To discuss Detective Landis."

"What about Detective Landis?"

"We were comparing the strange circumstances surrounding Detective Landis's methods," Vincent answered.

Kelly fully expected an objection from Bryce, but was surprised when none came. Sal had told her to expect an objection anytime she asks a question that tried to discredit a witness for the state. Bryce Weatherford had a reputation of over-objecting, which would usually play into the defense's hand; however, as noted before by Sal, Bryce has sharpened his courtroom skills considerably over the last year.

"And what was the result of that meeting?" Kelly asked.

"We figured out that our arrests were made in the presence or by Detective Landis, yet he never actually witnessed any crime."

"Interesting. What does that mean to you?"

"Objection! Witness is not a legal expert," Bryce screamed.

"I didn't hear her ask for an expert opinion. Overruled," Judge Santino said.

"Mr. Castellano?" Kelly said.

"Well, to me, it means that Detective Landis is a hotshot and others do his work for him. It also means that he can't definitively say whether I or Joseph are guilty," Vincent answered with a smug look on his face.

"Thank you Mr. Castellano. No more questions."

"Mr. Weatherford?" Judge Santino stated.

"Thank you, Your Honor," Bryce said. "Mr. Castellano, since you claim to be an expert in how to read people…"

"Objection Your Honor!" Kelly said, jumping out of her seat. "The witness never made such a claim and the state's sarcastic questioning is not appreciated."

"Sustained. Watch yourself Mr. Weatherford" Judge Santino ruled.

"My apologies to you and the court ma'am," Bryce replied. "Mr. Castellano, what is your current profession?"

"I own a landscaping company."

"How is business?"

"It is ok. Not our season so we have time on our hands to prepare for the spring."

"What do you do for money in your offseason?"

"Oh you know a little of this and a little of that," Vincent said, chuckling.

"No, I don't know. That is why I am asking. Can you be a little more specific please?"

"I do side jobs for neighbors and friends."

"What type of side jobs?"

"Objection! Relevance?" Kelly asked.

"Establishing a base Your Honor," Bryce responded.

"Overruled. Continue."

"Snow plowing and snow removal, gutter cleaning, driveway repairs, things like that."

"So in keeping yourself busy, have you been able to keep up with your finances?"

"Objection! Again, relevance?"

"Ms. Esteves. Your objection was heard and overruled. If you object again to the relevance of this questioning, I will hold you in contempt. Is that understood?" Judge Santino yelled.

"Yes, Your Honor."

It was the first time Kelly showed her amateur status in this case. She had been told by Sal when the trial began to make sure that any of our witnesses are not badgered or backed into a corner. Kelly knew this line of questioning was leading up to something Bryce had up his sleeve and she wanted to put an end to it; however, she did not expect the judge to react like that. She turned to her right to look for answers, but there was nobody there. She had momentarily forgotten Sal wasn't there. In that moment, she felt more alone than she had at any point in her law career to that point.

"Mr. Castellano, please answer the question," Judge Santino said.

"Yes, Your Honor. No, my bills are behind."

"I see," Bryce said. "You testified earlier that you met the defendant just a few weeks ago, is that correct?"

"Yes, that is correct," Vincent said, sitting up in his seat.

"Well, we both know that is not true, right?" Bryce said.

"Objection! Prosecution is leading the witness," Kelly said.

"Overruled."

"In fact, Mr. Castellano, you met the defendant in jail before meeting with the defense team. Isn't that correct?"

"I, uh," Vincent said clearly shaken.

Kelly did not know what to do. Her witness was about to be exposed by something she was unaware of. What did Bryce mean Vincent met Joseph in jail? She turned to Joseph, but he did not look back at her. All he did was stare at Vincent with squinted eyes, like he was planning his next murder.

"Joseph, what is he talking about?" Kelly whispered.

"Not now. Focus," Joseph replied.

"Your Honor, I would like to ask for a recess to confer with my client," Kelly asked.

"Request denied. You have had ample time to speak with your client Ms. Esteves."

"Mr. Castellano, please answer the question," Bryce instructed.

"Yes, that is correct," Vincent replied.

"Can you describe the circumstances in which you met the defendant?"

"I was visiting a friend and Joe was at the table next to us speaking to someone. I am not sure who the person was, but the conversation was heated."

"Go on," Bryce said, knowing there is more.

"After a few minutes, Joe turned to me and said, 'Do you know Detective Landis Vincent?' Of course I said yes because I was curious how Joe would know that. Anyway, we continued to talk discreetly for the next few minutes. When I asked him how he knew who I was and how Detective Landis had investigated the scene the night I was arrested, all he said was a name."

"What was the name he gave you Mr. Castellano?"

"Sean Lancaster."

The second sound of shock of the trial traveled through the crowd like wind in a tornado. Everyone in attendance gasped at the news that Sean Lancaster and Joseph Millstone knew each other.

"Order!" Judge Santino yelled while banging her gavel. "*I said ORDER!*"

The crowd quickly quieted down, still in a state of shock.

"You mean *the* Sean Lancaster?" Bryce asked.

"Yes, him."

"Did the defendant explain how he knew Sean Lancaster or what he wanted from you?"

"Not at that meeting, but in subsequent meetings, he mentioned that I could help him with his defense and get rich at the same time."

"By doing what?"

"Discrediting the work of Detective Landis. We compared stories and evidence from both of our arrests and began to plot how to pin it all on Detective Landis."

"I'm sorry, I don't understand. Pin what on Detective Landis?" Bryce asked, confused.

"False arrest, breaking protocol, things like that. We figured if we showed Detective Landis violated protocol, then we would both make out."

"Well, that plan went to hell now didn't it? No more questions."

After Vincent was excused from the witness stand, Judge Santino adjourned for the rest of the day. It was quite a shock to Kelly, as she had another two witnesses prepared for the rest of the day. However, she was also relieved at the abrupt end to the day, because now she had time to recover from the beating she just took at the hands of Bryce Weatherford. Right before Joseph was about to be taken away by the bailiff, he leaned into Kelly and whispered something that shook her to her core.

"Make sure you are looking over both shoulders from now on."

Chapter 47

While I was driving to the hospital, I had a million thoughts running through my head. What would I say to Danielle? How was I going to tell my kids? What type of retribution would she want to get? All of these thoughts kept playing over and over like a CCTV video feed on a loop. Just when I thought I had everything figured out, another problem came to mind. The biggest question I kept asking myself was why was I rushing to see my ex-wife who was the mastermind behind one of the biggest murder for hire plots in New York City history?

When I entered the hospital, I was hit with a sudden feeling of sadness that I had not expected. Why was I feeling this way for someone I now loathed? I was beginning to feel angry with myself for feeling this way when I realized why I was having this feeling. I had not been to New York Presbyterian since Thomas died a little over a year ago. All of the feelings I had on that night in his hospital room came flooding back to me like a tsunami. I missed Thomas more as each day passed, even after all this time. He was like a second father to me and always believed in me. He was also the only person I could go to in situations like this.

As I made my way through the halls of New York Presbyterian toward the ICU, all I could think of was Thomas Greenwood. I had been there when he passed away, along with his wife, Alan, and Steven. His room was in the ICU and I was afraid I would have an emotional reaction remembering the last time I was there. I did not want that to happen in front of Danielle because then she would think I cared and start in with her apology shit again. When I got to the nurse station, I asked where Danielle was and when they gave me the room number, I nearly passed out. It was the same room as Thomas had been in when he passed away. I began to rethink whether I should go into her room, but decided that I needed to get this over with.

I approached the room slowly, trying to suppress all of the memories I had of Thomas's last moments, but it was no use. I could not control my tears from falling down like waterfalls as soon as I looked into the room. I saw Danielle hooked up to wire after wire and all I saw was Thomas lying in that same bed, clinging to life. The only thing I could think of at that moment was Evelyn, Thomas's now widow, and how devastated she was that she was about to lose her husband.

After a few minutes, I was able to pull myself together and focus on Danielle. She had a breathing tube in and her eyes were closed. I was not expecting her to be in this condition and was caught severely off-guard. I stared intently for about a minute or so before I realized the doctor was standing behind me calling my name.

"Mr. Amici, I would say it is nice to see you again, but given the circumstances…?" Dr. James said.

Dr. James had been Thomas's doctor last year up until the moment Thomas passed. I admired Dr. James for his attention to detail but mostly because of his frankness. He had told me everything that was wrong with Thomas and how dire his situation was. It is understandable that a doctor withholds some information from family members in an effort to make them more comfortable, but Dr. James was a different kind of breed. He believed that family members should know the truth and have all the facts so they can make an informed decision on patient care.

"Hi Dr. James. How are you?" I asked.

"Can't complain. We need to stop meeting under these circumstances," Dr. James said.

"True, but this is not like last year. I'm sure you know about Danielle and why I don't really care what happens to her," I said, shocking Dr. James.

"Yes, I understand, but would you like to hear what is going on anyway?"

"Yes, but only for my kids. That needs to be understood from the beginning."

"Of course.," Dr. James said, confused. "Mrs. Amici has a lacerated liver that is causing internal bleeding. We cannot stop the bleeding for some reason, but have managed to slow it down. She is unable to breath on her own and has not shown to be aware of what is going on."

"So what happens? Does she just lay here until she dies?" I asked.

"No. We have already tried to seal the blood vessels without surgery by passing a thin plastic catheter into the blood vessels in the groin and then up to the liver. That was followed by injecting a few medicines to help seal off the blood vessels. It did not work. We then went in and tried to seal the vessels manually. That did not work either. The last option now is to perform a hepatectomy, which is removing part of the liver. We are not entirely sure if she will be able to tolerate this procedure, so we have called in a specialist to consult. We are waiting for her arrival shortly."

"So basically, if she can't withstand part of her liver being taken out, she will die," I asked sarcastically.

"Essentially yes," Dr. James said as his pager went off. "Uh, please excuse me for a moment. The specialist has arrived. I will consult with you after our meeting."

When Dr. James left the room, I immediately began to think of what the best option was moving forward. I was Danielle's medical proxy; therefore, had complete say over her care. If I were the only other person involved, I would absolutely refuse treatment and let her die; however, I am not the only one involved. Danielle was the mother of my kids and I had to put their needs in front of mine. My decision would also depend on what the prognosis was and what kind of quality of life Danielle would have. After all, she would be going back to prison once she was better.

While I sat in Danielle's room pondering what the right choice would be, the machines that Danielle was connected to began to make loud beeping noises. I knew something was obviously wrong, but I did not have it in me to seek help. I was frozen at Danielle's bedside just staring at the monitors. I did not have one instinct to get a nurse or interrupt Dr. James's meeting so he could help her. Instead, I just watched and listened as the chaos seemed to intensify.

After what seemed like hours, when in reality it was only a few seconds, two nurses came running into Danielle's room and began to work on her. Within another few seconds, Dr. James came sprinting into her room as well. There was medical jargon being tossed around, people moving quickly to get supplies to try to save Danielle, and the whole time, all I did was stare at the monitors. My gaze had not shifted for several minutes. I began to hear something faint over the beeping of the machines, but could not make out what it was. The more I tried to listen, the harder it was to hear.

"SAL! Do we have your consent?" Dr. James screamed at me.

"Huh?" I answered.

"SAL. WAKE UP! Do we have your consent to the surgery?" Dr. James repeated.

"What surgery?" I answered confused.

"We need to take Danielle to the OR *NOW!* You hear me *NOW!* Do you consent?"

Here was my chance to put Danielle out of her misery and at the same time, end my suffering as well. She had caused so much pain and heartache over the past year, I wanted her to pay for what she did. A life sentence to me did not suffice. She needed to die and this was my chance to make it happen. I had finally made up my mind on what I should do. Not knowing if it was the right decision, I answered, "Take her."

Chapter 48

Sean sat in the car he had stolen in shock. Anger coursed through his body like a free-flowing river. He could hardly see straight and was having trouble breathing. How could this have happened? Was this all his fault? Why hadn't he been able to protect her? Feeling lost for the first time in a long time, Sean decided to drive around and blow off some steam; however, he was too distracted trying to wrap his head around who could have done this. He had not set the plan in motion with Roland, so he knew it wasn't him, not to mention that Roland was now dead.

Feeling like someone ripped out his heart and stepped on it, Sean began thinking of a way that he could see Danielle without getting caught. This would be extremely difficult and risky, given that almost every NYPD officer was looking for him, but Sean did not care. He was determined to see Danielle and let her know that he was there for her.

When he pulled up to the hospital, he immediately saw two police officers stationed at the main entrance and one in the parking attendant stand. It had not occurred to him that police presence would be increased at the hospital because Danielle was a patient there. He thought the best chance for him was to use the valet parking service and try to slip past the officers, while wearing a semi-disguise. He put on his New York Mets baseball hat and his Gucci sunglasses, then pulled up to the valet stand. Almost immediately, he was greeted by an attendant.

"Hello sir," the attendant said.

"Hi. Please take care of her. She means a lot to me," Sean said as he handed the valet the keys.

"With pleasure sir."

Sean gave the attendant a twenty-dollar bill and made his move toward the main entrance. He didn't want to arouse suspicion so he had to find a way not to walk too fast but at the same time, not walk too slow. As he found the right pace at which to walk, he took out a cell phone and pretended to look up something on the internet. Looking down at his phone, he slithered past the two officers at the entrance and breathed a sigh of relief when he finally entered the hospital.

"Excuse me, sir," one of the officers yelled.

Sean kept walking hoping that the officer wasn't calling him, but he soon realized he was at a crossroads. If he turned around, the officer would surely recognize and arrest him, thus his plan for Sal would never happen. If he ran, he could certainly escape, but he would not get to see Danielle.

"Sir, stop!" he yelled once more.

Sean decided to play it cool and see what the officer wanted before running. He was mentally preparing himself for a long chase, although his leg still hurt from being cut on the barbed wire from his previous chase with the police. With his heart racing a mile a minute, Sean slowly turned around to face his fate.

"Sorry officer, I didn't know you meant me," Sean said in a disguised southern accent.

"No problem. You dropped this at the door," the officer said, handing Sean one of his gloves.

"Oh. Thank you. These were a gift from my wife and she would kill me if I lost them."

"I know how that is. Have a good day sir," the officer said, turning to go back to his post.

"You as well."

Although he felt a huge sense of relief, Sean needed to calm himself down before he continued making his way through the hospital. He spotted a nearby chair in the lobby that looked like the perfect spot to cool off; however, he would be in a wide-open space and did not want to run the risk of someone identifying him. As tired and rattled as he was, Sean found hidden energy and pressed on.

At the information desk, he used his fake southern accent again to find out what room Danielle was in and how to get there. He was amazed at how easy it was to fool people into thinking he was from the south, especially since he had never practiced it before. Anytime he asked for something, he was greeted with kindness and hospitality, which was something he was certainly not used to. When he reached the elevator, there was nobody else waiting for the next ride. He felt a sense of calmness come over him as he realized he would not have to contend with the idea of being in a confined space with other people. When the elevator door opened, he stepped in, he pressed the button that had an eight on it and then pressed the close door button so nobody else had the chance to get on. Right before the doors closed, someone stuck their arm in between the doors, stopping them.

"Sorry about that. I don't feel like waiting for another one to come," the stranger said.

Sean said nothing in return, hoping this person did not want to engage in a conversation.

"You have someone in the ICU as well?" the stranger asked.

Sean had no choice but to respond. When he looked up to see who was ruining his moment of calmness, he saw one of the most beautiful women he had ever seen. She had curly black hair, deep blue eyes, and was wearing a pencil skirt that if it was any tighter would suffocated her.

"Yeah, my friend. She isn't doing too well," Sean replied.

"I'm sorry to hear that. What's wrong with her?" the woman asked.

Sean was beginning to feel uncomfortable and was doing everything in his power to remain calm, but he felt a rage coming on that he was afraid he would not be able to control.

"She had an accident. I do not know much more," Sean said curtly.

"Well I hope she feels better. Have a great day," the woman said as she got off on the sixth floor.

When the elevator door closed, Sean began to doubt whether this was a good idea. He had been stopped by a cop to hand him a glove he dropped, stared at by numerous people throughout the hospital, and was forced into a conversation in an elevator with a gorgeous woman. Ordinarily, these events would not even be a blip on his radar, but given the circumstances and who he is visiting, they became magnified and caused Sean more anxiety than he had had in quite some time. If he had any thoughts of taking the elevator back down, they were erased once he reached the eighth floor and saw Danielle's room straight ahead.

Sean stepped off the elevator in stunned disbelief. He expected Danielle to be in the bed, but when he saw that she was not there, he did not know what to do. Why was she not there? Was she taken for a test? Did something go wrong? He wanted to ask the nurse at the nurse's station but was afraid she would ask how he knew Danielle. To avoid further risk to himself, Sean turned around to go back on the elevator, when he saw something that sent his nerves into another stratosphere.

Of all the things and people to account for, this was most certainly not on his list. Thinking quickly on his feet, Sean dropped his phone and bent down to get it so he would not be seen. While low to the ground, he moved forward toward the elevator but had to stand up when one of the doctors asked if he was ok. Once he stood up, the inevitable happened. He was spotted.

Chapter 49

After realizing that there was not much more I could do, I decided to leave the hospital and go home to rest for the following day in court. My emotions had been put through the ringer and I needed Nicole and the kids to help me make it through the night. As I approached the elevator, I got a phone call from an unknown number. Unlike the previous days, I did not pick up and I let it go to voicemail. When I looked up to see what floor the elevator was on, I caught a glimpse of a strange man wearing sunglasses and a Mets hat. He seemed nervous and out of place, but I assumed he had just visited someone and was upset.

The elevator door opened and as soon as the chime went off and me and the strange man got in. I do not like talking in elevators because it creates an even more uncomfortable environment than just standing there with a stranger in silence. For some reason, I felt the need to ask the man if he was ok because I was genuinely concerned for him based on how lost he looked.

"Are you ok sir?" I asked.

The man nodded his head and turned his body away from me. He clearly did not want to talk about what was bothering him, but me being me, I persisted on knowing if he was alright.

"Sir, I can help you if you need," I said reassuringly.

"I'm ok, but thank you," the man responded in a thick southern accent.

I felt the urge to keep pressing but I didn't want to start an unnecessary argument. As the elevator continued its descent, the man continued to cower in the corner. The more he cowered, the more nervous I got. Something seemed off with the man and he did not seem entirely stable. I began to think less and less that he had just visited someone and more and more that he felt uncomfortable with me. I tried to get a peak at the man's face using the stainless-steel wall of the elevator, but the sunglasses prevented me from seeing his eyes. I did, however, spot something on his neck that caught my attention. It was a tattoo of a barcode. That is a very unique design to get tattooed on one's body and I knew of only one person that had such a tattoo, but there was no way that it was possible for *him* to be here. I moved a bit closer to the man to get a closer look and saw the numbers 48795 under the barcode. It was at that moment, I got a massive head rush that was accompanied by a sudden rapid increase in heart rate. I was standing in an elevator alone with *Sean Lancaster!*

I tried to remain as calm as I could and think of what to do next. I was not sure if he knew I knew it was him, but I had a feeling he didn't because he continued to stay silent in the corner and not look at me. When the elevator finally reached the lobby, Sean exited without saying a word to me and took off like he was running the 100m sprint at the Olympics. I tried to keep pace while remaining inconspicuous, but he was too fast for me. I had no other choice but to do the one thing I did not want to do.

"SEAN!" I yelled at the top of my lungs.

He turned back, saw me running toward him, and took off again. He lost his sunglasses and hat and went into a full sprint for the exit. I could tell he was hobbled by what looked like a leg injury, but he was still much quicker than I was. I took off as fast as I could weaving my way in and out of the busy crowd in the lobby. I still had Sean in my sights, but once he was out on the streets, it would be near impossible for me to keep up.

"Stop that man! Stop him!" I yelled at the police officers at the door while pointing to Sean.

Sean, with no regard for authority, barreled into both cops, knocking them over. He exited the hospital and made a sharp right to go down One Hundred Sixty Eighth Street toward Broadway. He was running in between the cars stuck in traffic to avoid the packed sidewalks. I did my best to keep up with him and to my amazement, I was able to do so with relative ease.

I continued to chase Sean down Broadway as he made his way to the Washington Heights subway station. Was he really going to go into a subway station? His escape route would be limited and he would have a better chance of getting caught. It was not like Sean to make such a big mistake. Despite my rationale, Sean ran down the stairs of the subway station as I remained in hot pursuit of him.

Sean hopped over the turnstile and continued running as fast as he could through the crowd. I was beginning to lose ground so I yelled for any police officer in the subway to stop him. I could not see too far ahead because of all the people waiting to buy tickets for the subway trains, but I was sure I saw at least two police officers respond. Regardless if I was going to get help or not, I kicked it into overdrive and ran as fast as I could, trying not to barrel into someone as well. In order to gain ground, I would need a stroke of good fortune.

As I approached the staircase leading down to the trains, I heard a train begin to approach. Surely Sean would get on one of those trains and complete his escape. I grabbed the handrail and swung myself toward the stairs to save seconds I did not have. I then ran down the stairs, skipping three steps at a time. When I made it to the bottom of the stairs, I bolted toward the train with speed that would rival The Flash. I was within one foot of the door, when it began to close. I tried to stick my arm in between the door so it would remain open, but my attempt was futile.

When the train began to move away from me on the platform, I saw Sean smile and wave goodbye to me. Then he pointed to his eyes as if to say I'll see you again. I was breathing so heavily from all the running I had done, I had to sit down on the platform right at the edge to prevent myself from passing out. A few strangers asked me if I was ok and I answered in the affirmative to all of them. However, the truth was, I was not ok. I had just encountered someone I didn't even know was in the country, let alone New York City. He had beat me once again and then taunted me to make matters worse. I knew that I would need to plan my next move quickly, but I would need some help in doing so. I did not know who I could turn to, but I knew someone I could start with.

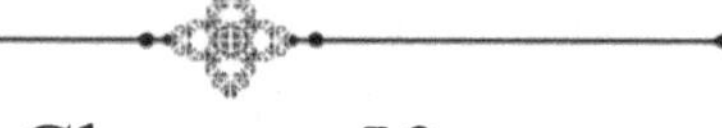

Chapter 50

By the time I got home that evening, I was completely drained both emotionally and physically. I had gone from seeing Danielle and making the decision to allow life-saving surgery to encountering Sean Lancaster and then chasing him into a subway station, only to have him escape. All I wanted to do was take a shower, have a cold beer, and go to sleep but with a house full of people, that would not be in my immediate future.

I made my way to the kitchen where Nicole was again, making something magical. She was almost done preparing whatever it was that she was cooking, which was a good thing because I wanted to go to sleep as soon as I could. I felt like I had not eaten in weeks, but at the same time, did not have much of an appetite.

"Are you ok? You look exhausted," Nicole said.

"Have you not watched the news?" I responded sarcastically. "Sorry, I did not mean for it to come out that way."

"That's ok. No I haven't. What happened?"

"I went to see Danielle in the hospital because I got a call this morning from Jill that she was stabbed in prison and was in the hospital. I then spoke with the doctor who said he didn't expect her to make it. That is why I went to the hospital. It turns out, I am still her medical proxy and had to make a decision on a life-saving procedure. Once that ended, I went to leave and got into the elevator. Nicole, Sean Lancaster was there."

"WHAT?" Nicole screamed.

"Yeah. He was in the elevator disguised as some bum off the street. He ran once I called out his name and I chased him down Broadway and into a subway station. He ended up getting away but I think he got spooked."

"Oh my God Sal. Are you ok?"

"Yeah. Now on top of the case with Joseph, I gotta deal with this shit," I said, slamming my fist down on the table.

"Anything I can do?" Nicole asked sweetly.

"I don't think so, but thank you."

"Wow. I can't believe it. So, what are you going to do?"

"Well, first I need to come up with a plan on how to find him again. For that, I am going to need help."

"I thought you said you didn't need help," Nicole said curiously.

"I meant there is nothing you can do to help me right now, but I do need someone."

"Who?"

"After dinner. Let's eat first. I am starving."

For the next thirty minutes, I enjoyed the company of my family along with some excellent food. It is sometimes hard to understand the value of eating a meal with my family when things are so chaotic. I relished in the laughter and banter we shared, as well as the love and support we have for each other. Nicole has been a wonderful addition to our home and I was hopeful she would stick around for the long haul. Not only was she an amazing cook, but she cared for Gio and Angela as if they were her own children. They adored her as well, which made for a much easier time accepting her into our family. She also understands me very well, mostly because she is a therapist, but also because she cares for me as much as I care for her.

When we finished eating and cleaning up, Nicole gave me a look like you better tell me now or else. I smiled back at her and then nodded my head in acknowledgment of her threat. For me, the fun was about to begin.

"Gio, can you come downstairs for a moment please?" I yelled.

Gio came running down the stairs like it was Christmas morning. His demeanor had completely changed since we ironed things out earlier that morning. He seemed much more energetic and jovial, which was a warm welcome for me. It is not often a pre-teen is happy like he was, so I was not going to waste my chance to speak with him.

"Yeah dad. What's up?" Gio asked.

"Son, sit down," I said and motioned my hand to a chair at the kitchen table.

"Something wrong?" Gio asked, scared.

"Not really. I want to ask you something," I said feeling anxiety come over me for what seemed like the one millionth time. "Do you know who Sean Lancaster is?"

"Yeah. He's the man that mom got into trouble with and the one in the photo I showed you, right?"

"Yes, that is correct."

Nicole looked at me and when we made eye contact, she enlarged her eyes so I knew she disagreed with what I was about to do. She then motioned her head to the left to tell me she wanted to talk to me, but I didn't listen. I needed to get this out, regardless of what anyone else thought.

"What about him?" Gio asked.

"I need your help catching him. The last time I spoke to him was last year and he was in Italy. I did not know he was back in the United States until today. I ended up chasing him into a subway, but he got away."

"That was you?" Gio said with excitement.

"What do you mean?"

"I heard about that on the news. Oh man. That is so cool."

I was beginning to think I made a mistake asking Gio for help. As much as I wanted my son to help me, I had forgotten that he was twelve years old and most likely way too immature to handle such a request. Even if I was able to calm him down and let him know my plan now, there was no guarantee he would not act this way again in the future.

"Gio, I need you to calm down, ok?" I said as I put my hands on both of his shoulders. "This is something very important and complicated I am asking of you. If you can't handle it, you need to let me know now."

"Sorry, dad. I can handle it. What can I do to help?"

Faith restored.

For the next twenty minutes, I laid out the plan with Gio. He seemed to be understanding what I was saying and did not have a childish outburst like he did before. I knew Nicole did not agree with what I was doing, but to be frank, I did not care. This was my situation and my son; therefore, I was going to do whatever I wanted. Sean Lancaster needed to be caught at all costs and the best option to accomplish that was to enlist the help of my twelve-year old Giovanni. It was shaping up to be one hell of a ride.

Chapter 51

Walking into the courtroom the next morning felt different than it ever had before. The courtroom was my sanctuary and the place I went to to escape everything that was going on in my life. However, this morning, I had so many things racing through my mind and so many things that needed my attention that it was hard for me to focus on what was right in front of me.

Kelly and I had been preparing to call this witness ever since the trial began. This was going to be the person to put the doubt of all doubts into the state's case. We had been over the questioning a thousand times and prepared the witness for almost anything Bryce could throw at him. Kelly knew her role, I knew mine, and the witness knew his. This was going to be the star witness everyone would speak of when the trial ended. It was all lined up to be a glorious victory for Kelly and myself. All we had to do was follow the script and we would be home free.

"You remember what to do?" I asked Kelly.

"Yes, sir. This should be fun."

"It will be but just stay calm and act like everything that happens is what we expected."

"I know Sal. I'll be fine," Kelly said.

"Is the defense ready to call their next witness?" Judge Santino asked.

"Yes, Your Honor. The defense calls Joel Matheson."

When the courtroom audience looked around to see who Joel Matheson was, nobody appeared. Five…ten…fifteen seconds went by and nary a person stood up to walk to the witness stand. The audience began to make small mumbling noises and exchanged glances with each other in confusion. I looked at Kelly and saw a terrified expression on her face that told me she was not prepared for this possibility. We had been over everything together and with all that had happened to that point, I began to question if I discussed with her what happens if a witness does not show up.

"Mr. Amici, where is your witness?" Judge Santino asked.

"Um, I...I don't know Your Honor," I said. "May I please have a ten minute recess?"

"Five minutes Mr. Amici. You hear me? Five minutes," Judge Santino scolded.

"Come with me," I whispered to Kelly.

Kelly and I left the courtroom in earnest to find our witness. I had told Joel to be at the courthouse at nine in the morning sharp and he had promised me he would be there. I looked in the men's restroom and Kelly looked in the women's restroom. Joel was not there. I called his cellphone and landline. No answer. I even went back to the parking lot to see if he was outside the building and was getting cold feet. He was not there. Panic began to set in because without Joel, my entire strategy would be foiled. He was the key to everything Kelly and I had set up so far in this case. I sat down on the bench outside of the courtroom without a clue on what to do.

"Sal, please tell me you have a plan. Please tell me that this happens all the time and you have some fancy lawyer trick planned," Kelly said, nervously.

"There is no playbook for this Kelly. None. The son of a bitch told me he would be here. I trusted him. I don't have a backup," I said as I punched the concrete wall.

"Sal, what are we going to do?" Kelly asked, hopelessly.

"I...I don't know Kelly. I honestly don't know."

Standing in the hallway just outside of the courtroom, I felt the weight of the world on my shoulders. I was hoping that Judge Santino would grant me a continuance until the next morning, but was not expecting it. My hunch was proven right when I Kelly and were summoned back into the courtroom.

"Mr. Amici, time is up. Judge Santino has ordered you back into the courtroom," the bailiff said.

"Be right there," I replied holding up one finger.

The past twenty-four hours had really taken its toll on me. I was tired, hungry, confused, and angry. All I wanted was for this to be over and then be able to take a vacation. I wanted to go somewhere far away where nobody knew me and I could relax in peace. I had done the exact same thing after the Sean Lancaster trial last year and came back a new person. This time, I would go for a much longer period.

Kelly and I walked back into the courtroom dejected. I preached to her and my other colleagues never to show emotion in the courtroom. Never let anyone see how you truly feel and to always act as if you expected what was happening. At that moment, I did not have the ability to take my own advice. Right away, Joseph asked me what was wrong and when I told him I lost the witness, he gave me a chilling smile. I looked at him with curiosity in my eyes and all he said to me was, "I will explain later."

"Mr. Amici, were you able to locate your witness?" Judge Santino asked me.

"No, Your Honor," I said, as I hung my head.

"Then proceed."

"Your Honor, we do not have any more witnesses."

"Then the defense rests?".

"Yes, Your Honor. The defense rests.

"Very well. I will now offer each attorney the opportunity to make a closing argument. Mr. Weatherford, you can go first," Judge Santino stated.

For the next twenty minutes, Bryce Weatherford presented a magnificent closing argument. He clearly had taken a lot of time to prepare what he wanted to say and how he was going to say it. He touched on every point he promised he would and then summarized his case to paint Joseph Millstone as The Night Slasher. Everything he said was true and when I looked at the jury at the end of his statement, almost every single person was nodding his/her head.

"Mr. Amici, your closing statement please," Judge Santino said.

As I stood up, my legs began to weaken, as they had not yet totally healed from the car accident. I was not prepared for a closing statement at this time because I had anticipated having Joel Matheson as a witness. I had to use all of my skills to piece together what was surely going to be an incoherent closing statement. My only hope was that I would be able to mesmerize the jury enough that they could not see it.

"Ladies and gentlemen of the jury. As you can probably tell, I am not prepared. My last witness did not show up, which has caused a bit of panic from myself and my team. It is a shame you will not get to hear what he had to say but that does not mean that you have not already heard enough. You heard Detective Landis state that the front door was unguarded the night of my client's arrest. You heard Ms. Newton testify that she believed the phone call she received about Mr. Millstone committing these murders was false because he was in bed. You heard Ms. Rossi testify how highly she thought of Mr. Millstone. What does all that mean though? Does it mean that my client is a saint? I would say not at all. Does it mean that my client is immune to aggressive behavior? Of course not. Does it mean Mr. Millstone was set up? Well that is for another day; however, I can tell you what it does mean. It means that there is *doubt* as to whether my client is guilty of these crimes against the King family. As I stated in my opening statement, the facts of this case were never to be disputed. My client was caught by the police covered in blood at the rear entrance of the King's home. Although damning, being covered in blood at a crime scene does not automatically make someone guilty. The state failed to provide any evidence that Mr. Millstone actually committed these crimes. Moreover, the fact that the police failed to secure the front entrance to the King's home, leads to the possibility of someone else possibly having committed these crimes. Is that likely? Who knows. But the fact is, the opportunity was there for the real murderer to escape. And *THAT* ladies and gentlemen, is doubt. Thank you."

When I returned to the defense table, Kelly gave me a pat on the leg and a quick half smile. Joseph gave me a thumbs up and said he was proud of the job I did. My closing statement was certainly not my best, but it also went much better than I thought it would. For a split second, I felt relaxed and confident that we had done enough to get Joseph acquitted. All that went away when Judge Santino began to talk to the jury and put the case in their hands.

Chapter 52

I left the courthouse not knowing what to expect from the jury. I usually have a good idea as to how the case will play out in deliberations, but this time, I was convinced it could go one way or the other. My star witness had not shown up and that threw my entire strategy out the window. Kelly and I did a good job putting a case together to create doubt but was it enough? I felt guilty I had missed some time due to personal issues, but Kelly had done an admirable job filling in for me. My hope was that the jury was going to be able to look past our last hiccup and judge the case based on what was argued in court, not what wasn't.

As soon as I stepped outside into the bitter cold winter air, my phone rang. I looked at the caller ID and saw it was Alan Lowery. I found it odd that Alan would call me in the middle of the day knowing that I was supposed to be in court. When I picked up the phone, I did not get a chance to say anything. All I heard was panic.

"Sal, I need you and Kelly to meet me at the office in one hour. No excuses, just be here."

Alan hung up immediately after that and left me wondering what was wrong. I found Kelly in the lobby and told her we needed to leave for the office right away. To make things a bit simpler, Kelly offered to drive to the office instead of taking public transportation with me. Neither one of us said a word on the way to the car but I could tell she wanted to ask what was going on.

Before Kelly would turn the car on, she finally asked me the question that had been weighing on her mind since I grabbed her from the courthouse lobby.

"What's going on Sal? Why are we rushing to get back to the office?"

"Alan called me and said he needs to meet with us in one hour. There was something in his voice that told me he was panicking. I never hear him like that so something must be wrong."

"He didn't elaborate?"

"No. He hung up immediately after telling me he wants us at the office," I explained.

"I'm gonna call him to see what's up," Kelly responded.

"NO! Let it be. We will find out when we get to the office," I yelled.

The rest of the car ride was in complete silence. No talking, no radio, no loud breathing. Nothing. It gave me time to collect my thoughts on what could possibly be so important that Alan had to whisk us away from the courthouse as soon as the jury began their deliberations. I went over the case and everything else that had been going on and came up with nothing. I had no choice but to wait until we met with Alan.

As soon as Kelly and I entered the lobby, we were told to go straight to the boardroom and nowhere else. The urgency in the voice and on the face of the security guard caused me to become more paranoid than I already was. When we got in the elevator, I glanced over at Kelly and she appeared to be feeling the same way.

"I'm sure everything is fine. No need to worry," I said, trying to reassure Kelly.

"Yeah, keep telling yourself that," Kelly said.

"Yeah, I know. Whatever it is, we need to stick together. Ok?"

"Ok Sal. We stick together."

When we finally reached the boardroom, both Kelly and I took a deep breath before opening the double solid oak doors. Inside was not just Alan; he was accompanied by Steven and Jill. I found it odd that Jill was in the room and that she was seated on the side of the table with Alan and Steven. Alan motioned for us to sit down, which we did very nervously.

"I am sure you are wondering what is going on. I know this was unusual but we had to make sure to speak to you both before the verdict comes in," Alan said, easing us into whatever was wrong. "Well, here it is. I, no, *we*, want to know what happened today."

I looked at Alan with a confused look on my face before I realized what he was talking about.

"Look Alan," I began. "I can sit here and lie to you or make up some crazy story to buy some time, but the truth is, I don't know. I spoke with Joel this morning about an hour before he was set to testify and then he didn't show up. I don't know where he is or why he didn't show up but I intend to find out."

"Sal, Joel is dead," Alan told me.

"Huh?" Kelly asked.

"Yeah, he was found in an alley near the courthouse with his throat sliced from ear to ear," Steven said.

"Well, now we know why he didn't show up," I joked.

"Sal, seriously? At a time like this?" Alan scolded.

"Alan, what else am I supposed to say? You want me to feel bad for the guy? I didn't even know him. I can tell you this though. He fucked up my case royally."

"How bad is it?" Steven asked.

"Well, it can go either way. Without Joel's testimony, the jury has been deprived of some vital information," Kelly answered.

"What information is that Kelly?" Alan asked.

"Joel was going to testify that on the night of the King family murders, he was also in their house," I told everyone.

"Why would he do that? That would also put him in jeopardy of being arrested and charged with their murders as well," Jill asked.

"Excellent question Jill. Joel was leading a destitute life. He had nothing. No car. No home. No job. No money. He figured if he could get locked up for life, then he would at least get shelter and three meals a day."

"So he was never actually there?"

"According to him, he was. He provided me with details that he could not have gotten anywhere else."

"Do you think he got that information from Joseph?" Alan asked.

"That is very possible," I responded. "In fact, that very well might be the case. When Joseph found out that Joel was missing, he gave me a weird smirk. I didn't know what to make of it at the time, but now it makes sense."

"How?" Kelly asked.

"Because if Joel does not show up, then Joseph can take full credit for the murders. He thrives on recognition and doesn't seem like the kind of person who is willing to share it."

"So what are your plans if it doesn't go our way?" Alan asked.

"We will cross that bridge when we get to it," I said, as my text tone went off. "Holy Shit!"

"What is it?" Steven asked.

"The verdict is in already."

Chapter 53

Waking up from a drug induced sleep, Danielle was confused as to where she was and what was going on. She had intense pain on her side, something stuck in her nose, and wires laying all over her body. She also noticed that her left hand was handcuffed to the bed. She tried to adjust her position in the bed, but was unable to due to the amount of pain she was in. She pressed the button to call the nurse and got no response. She waited another fifteen minutes before pressing it again, and again, got no response. With no other option, she yelled for help as loud as she could. Finally a nurse came in to see what she needed, with an attitude that would make The Grinch proud.

"What do you want?" the nurse asked.

"Why am I here? What happened?" Danielle said.

"What do you mean why are you here? You got stabbed in prison. You honestly don't remember that?"

Danielle looked at the nurse with a confused look on her face. She could not remember what had happened and that she had been in prison as well. After thinking for a few more minutes, her memory began to come back and she could now picture herself back in prison being attacked by the person who had threatened her once before. Even though she now knew why she was there, she did not know what the extent of the damage was.

"What type of injuries do I have? How long will I be here?"

"Look honey, I am not the doctor, ok? I did not go to school for that precisely for this reason. I am just here to make sure you are checked on every so often and you are given your medications. If you want answers to how badly you are hurt, ask the doctor," the nurse replied and then walked out of the room.

Danielle wondered why she was being treated this way when she did nothing wrong. Then she looked at her handcuffed hand and realized why the nurse was so nasty. Danielle thought that might be a reason why, but that didn't mean she was going to accept it. She pressed the call button at least twenty times in a row to make sure the nurse came back into her room. When the nurse failed to show up, Danielle began screaming loud enough that the patients on another floor could hear her. After two minutes of yelling, the nurse finally came back into Danielle's room. This time, she was ready to let Danielle know what she thought of her.

"WHAT?" the nurse yelled.

"Listen bitch. Do you know who I am? Do you know what I did? If you did, then you would think twice about treating me like this. In case you don't know, let me tell you. I am Danielle Amici. Yes, *that* Danielle Amici. The one that murdered her entire family for money and then when I wanted more, convinced my lover to have his family killed as well. All the while pretending to be the sweet, innocent mother and wife everyone envied. So if you value your life and the lives of your family, you will apologize and show me some fucking respect."

The nurse stood in front of Danielle more terrified than she ever had been before. She knew who Danielle was and what she was convicted of, but hearing it from her mouth and then being threatened brought her fear to another level. She did not know what to say or what to do, which is why she remained frozen for a good thirty to forty seconds. She tried to talk, but nothing came out. She also tried to smile at Danielle, but her face muscles were paralyzed. Once she was able to get her bearings and compose herself, she apologized to Danielle and told her she would help her with anything she needed from that moment on.

"Good," Danielle replied. "Don't you ever forget what we talked about here today. You got that? *EVER!*"

"You got it Mrs. Amici. Let me know if you need anything else," the nurse said and darted out of the room.

Danielle laid in her bed with a smile on her face that had been missing for quite some time. She felt good that she was able to exert her dominance over someone else, while injecting fear at the same time. Even though she was in a hospital bed and handcuffed to the railing, she still felt she had the upper hand on the nurse. She knew escaping was not a possibility given her condition; however, she felt it might be possible to manipulate the nurse into undoing the handcuffs. Before she could put a plan together, the nurse came back into her room.

"Excuse me, Mrs. Amici. I do not want to disturb you, but there is a Terence Callahan here to see you. I told him you are not having visitors at the moment, but he insisted."

"You can send him in, it is fine. Thank you," Danielle said, trying to control her excitement.

"Hey baby! How are you?" Sean asked.

"Better, now that you are here. What took you so long?"

"I came to see you before, but your asshole ex-husband was here and spotted me. I had to run for my life to get away from him," Sean replied.

"So he knows you are back in NYC?"

"Uh, yeah. He saw me and called me by name."

"Sean, that is not good. Now we do not have our tactical advantage anymore. He is going to be on high alert," Danielle said with anger.

"You honestly think I am going to let Sal Amici dictate what happens to me?" Sean said as he began to laugh. "Our plan for him is still going to happen. There will just need to be some adjustments. Forget about that for a moment, how do you feel?"

"Ugh. I am in so much pain but I keep refusing painkillers because I want to remain coherent, in case, you know, I need to handle any business."

"That is smart, but do you really think it is wise to be in this much pain? You might not be able to function while being in such great pain."

"I will manage. I am stronger than you think," Danielle replied and grabbed Sean's hand.

"I know you are strong, but it is your lack of restraint that concerns me," Sean said.

"Lack of restraint? What does that mean?"

"Danielle, you and I both know that you can't keep your mouth shut. You take the first opportunity to show someone how bad you can be or how dominant you can be. I often worry that you may let something slip one day and the effects will be irreversible," Sean said, as he closed the door to Danielle's room.

Sensing a disturbing tone in Sean's voice, Danielle attempted to sit up and find out what was going on. As it turned out, she was not able to. She was in too much pain to move and could not catch her breath once she put her hands down to try and lift herself up.

"Sean, what is going on and why are you closing the door?"

"What do you mean?" Sean asked, as he moved closer to her.

"You are acting funny. What's wrong?" Danielle asked, nervously.

Sean did not reply. He did not move. All he did was stare at her, as if he were in a trance. His eyes began to become more narrow and his breathing a bit heavier. He then began to rub his right hand over his chin, which concerned Danielle even more. Sean had never acted this way in front of her and she did not know what to make of it.

"Sean, you are really scaring me. Stop it or I will call the nurse in to remove you."

"Yeah, that's not going to work," Sean said as he showed her the disconnected nurse call button. "See Danielle, I have put up with your arrogance and sloppiness for a while now. To be honest, it really has not been an issue. I actually like cleaning up some of your messes. What I can't stand, what I can't tolerate, is that big fucking mouth of yours. You just don't know when to stop. I bet you are wondering what I am talking about. Well, I will tell you. I know it was you that Roland called. I know it was you who heard everything. At first I could not understand why Roland called you because the two of you had nothing in common. But then I did a little digging and voilà. You met his sister in prison, Tatiana. She was the one that threatened me. He needed to keep his contact with you a secret, which is why your number was not under a contact. My only assumption is that he called you in case something happened to him, given that he and I were in a struggle at the time. He wanted someone to be a witness in case I killed him. Roland was always thinking two steps ahead. That doesn't matter. What does matter is that I don't like to be double crossed."

"I have no idea what you are talking about. You have gone completely mad," Danielle said, still trying to sit up.

"Don't bother getting up. In fact, let me make you a little more comfortable."

Sean walked over to Danielle's IV pump and connected a syringe to the line. He glanced at Danielle and saw a terrified look in her eyes that he had never seen before. He got a rush just seeing her like that.

"Sean, what are you doing? Please, whatever it is you are thinking of doing, please don't," Danielle begged in a soft voice.

"This, my dear, is Pancuronium Bromide. It is the second step in carrying out a lethal injection sentence. The purpose of this substance is to induce skeletal muscle relaxation. In other words, it is meant to paralyze you. I am giving you a much higher dose because I don't have time to wait for it to kick in. You should begin to feel the effects real quick. Trust me, it will make things go much more smoothly."

"What things? Sean, please…" Danielle said frightened.

"Oh, you have to wait for that," Sean said, as he squeezed the plunger of the syringe, emptying its contents into Danielle's bloodstream.

Over the next two to four minutes, Danielle went from trying to move as much as she could to try and escape, to becoming completely immobile. Her eyes, however, remained wide open in terror. All she thought of was how could Sean, this man she loved more than anything in the world, do this to her. Where had she gone wrong? She tried to move her arms and legs but nothing happened. She then wondered to herself what was going to happen next. Surely, Sean could not just leave her like this and leave. Thirty seconds later, she got her answer.

"I really didn't want to do this, Danielle. I honestly mean that. I loved you, I still love you. But I love myself more, and I just can't take any risks. See you on the other side," Sean said as he placed a pillow over Danielle's nose and mouth.

Sean knew that suffocating someone did not happen like it does in the movies. It takes much longer than ten seconds for a person to die from suffocation. It also was much more difficult than the movies show it to be, which is why he decided to paralyze Danielle. With Danielle not able to fight back, it would make this process much easier. Sean wanted this to be over as soon as possible; therefore, not only did he smother her face with a pillow, he also knelt on her chest; cutting off the ability of her lungs to contract. Although she couldn't move, Danielle managed to make Sean uneasy by using her eyes to show how desperate she was. Usually Sean can look in the eyes of the person he is killing; however, in this case, because he loved Danielle, he could not bear to see her go through this. He turned away and began to cry. After four minutes of kneeling on her chest and smothering her face with a pillow, Sean began to ease his attack. Danielle's eyes were now closed and there were no signs of life. He got off of the bed and checked the monitors he had muted when he arrived. He saw the flatline representing the sinus rhythm of the heart, the heart rate reading of zero, and the blood pressure reading of 0/0. He calmly put the pillow back under her head and adjusted the blankets to make her look comfortable. Knowing he had to leave before being caught, he took one last look at Danielle and said, "Goodbye my sweet Danielle. I hope you can forgive me."

With that, Sean slipped out of Danielle's room, closed the door behind him, and vanished into the hallways of the hospital without being seen.

Chapter 54

When Kelly and I arrived back at the courthouse, we had a strong feeling of what to expect. The jury had returned a verdict within one hour, which is never a good sign for a defense attorney. I usually like to see a jury take anywhere from one to three days to deliberate, sometimes longer; however, when a verdict is returned this quickly, it almost always comes back guilty.

As soon as I passed through the metal detector, my phone began to ring. I looked at the caller ID and saw it was from New York Presbyterian with what was undoubtedly news about Danielle. I decided to let the call go to voicemail because I had to focus on the case and could not afford any distractions. Kelly urged me to pick it up, but I told her that the most important part of being a lawyer is being there for your client. If I answered the call, I would have to devote some of my attention to Danielle and I was not going to allow that to happen.

For the next three minutes, my phone kept ringing from the same number at New York Presbyterian, signaling something was seriously wrong. I finally relented and stepped out into the hallway to answer the call. The next thing I heard would change my life forever.

"Hello Mr. Amici," the nurse at New York Presbyterian said. "I am afraid I have some terrible news for you. I am so sorry to have to tell you this, but Mrs. Amici has passed. I am so very sorry for your loss. Please let me know if there is anything I can do for you."

I went completely numb and hung up the phone without finding out what happened. My legs gave out from underneath me and I fell to the floor. A fair number of people came rushing over to me to assist me back on my feet. They were all asking me if I was ok, but I could not answer them. All I was able to do was stare ahead into what seemed like an abyss and try and process what I was just told. Instinctively, I put my hand over my mouth and began to tear up.

Why was I so upset over Danielle's death when all I could think of for the past year was this moment. I had wished this on her so many times before, during, and after her trial, that I should have been relishing the moment. Instead, I felt like a part of me died and my world was about to come crashing down. It wasn't until Kelly came looking for me, that I realized the jury had been brought into the courtroom and the verdict was about to be read.

"Sal, what's wrong?" Kelly asked me.

It took me a few seconds to respond and when I did, all I could say was, "nothing."

I did the best I could to mask how upset I was as I walked back into the courtroom. I must have done a decent job because Kelly nor Judge Santino asked me if I was ok. I sat down in my chair and began to ponder how I was going to tell Gio and Angela. Even though Gio despised Danielle and Angela did not have a firm understanding of what she had done, Danielle was still their mother and now she was gone. I was deep in thought when Joseph, Kelly, and myself were asked to rise. I did not hear the judge because of how distracted I was, so Kelly nudged me and motioned for me to get up. My legs were still very wobbly, thus making standing for a verdict I already knew, that much more difficult.

"I understand the jury has reached a verdict," Judge Santino said.

"We have Your Honor," the foreperson stated.

"Very well. Bailiff, please pass me the verdict sheet."

As Judge Santino looked over the verdict sheet to make sure everything was in order, I allowed my mind to once again focus on Danielle. I kept thinking of when we first met at the Yankees game and how I saved her from getting hit with a foul ball. I thought about our wedding and when our kids were born. I also thought about all the Christmases we spent together and how much we loved each other. I then started to feel anger when my mind shifted to what she had done to me and the kids. How everything I thought was real was in fact a lie. I got even madder for allowing myself to get upset over her, even though it was the natural way to react. As I got deeper into thought about Danielle, I felt Kelly's hand grab mine. I turned to her and saw she looked extremely nervous about what was coming. I was so into my own issues, that I failed to realize that this was Kelly's first trial and her first verdict reading. I redirected myself and held her hand to support her and to prepare for the verdict.

"Madam foreperson. On the count of the first-degree murder of Harold King, how does the jury find the defendant?" Judge Santino asked.

"Guilty," the foreperson said.

"On the count of the first-degree murder of Donna King, how does the jury find the defendant?"

"Guilty."

"On the count of the first-degree murder of Karen King, how does the jury find the defendant?"

"Guilty."

"On the count of the first-degree murder of Megan King, how does the jury find the defendant?"

"Guilty."

"On the count of the attempted murder of Tim King, how does the jury find the defendant?"

"Guilty."

Even though I knew the verdict was coming, it was still a shock. I felt bad for Kelly because she had given everything she had into this case and had come up short. I knew I was going to have to give her some words of encouragement, but that was going to be very difficult given the circumstances I was facing. Before I had a chance to speak to her, Joseph erupted in anger.

"YOU WILL PAY FOR THIS AMICI AND ESTEVES! Mark my words. You will pay. This isn't over by a longshot. You both better look over your shoulders the next time you are out in the open. You'll pay!" Joseph screamed.

The police officers that were on duty in the court grabbed Joseph and dragged him out of the courtroom before he could make any more threats. Once he was gone, I took a few deep breaths and turned toward Kelly. She was hyperventilating and I could see the terror in her eyes. She clearly was affected by what had just happened and was not able to calm down. I called for medical assistance and two EMTs came running in. They tended to Kelly and finally convinced her to go to the hospital as a precaution. Before they wheeled her away, I managed to get a few seconds alone with her.

"Kelly, listen. I know that was frightening, but you have to forget about it. I have had many clients make threats to me after losing a case; it is a part of the job. I can arrange for security if that will make you feel better.”

“Sal, he said we would pay and he is a *fucking serial killer!* Why aren’t *you* more scared?” Kelly responded.

“I am scared, but I can’t let him see that,” I said, trying to reassure Kelly. “I want you to know that you did an outstanding job! You really impressed all of us out there. The jury had their minds made up about this trial before it began. It was going to take a miracle to win this case. Go rest and I will come see you tomorrow, ok?”

“Ok Sal. Thank you,” Kelly said, as she was wheeled away.

After Kelly and everyone else were gone, I sat down in my chair and finally lost control. I began to sob uncontrollably, partly because of Danielle and partly because of the threat Joseph had made. If I was going to make it through this, I would need the support and love of my family and Nicole. I knew I was headed for a rough night, but I also knew that the lives of two innocent young children would soon be forever changed. I gathered myself together, packed up my belongings, and headed out the door of the courtroom, trying to think of a way to tell my children that their mother was no longer with us.

Chapter 55

I have driven up to my house and pulled into the driveway hundreds of times before; however, this time was different. I knew I was not going to be able to hide the fact that something was terribly wrong, but I was going to have to try my best. Gio is particularly adept at identifying when something is wrong, which is what makes him such a good detective at the age of twelve. Angela was going to be a little easier because she is a happy go lucky little girl and doesn't seem to have a care in the world. Nicole was going to be just as, if not more, trickier than Gio because she is a psychiatrist and recognizing people's problems is what she does for a living.

I sat in my car for a minute or two pondering what I was going to say. How was I going to tell my kids that their mother is dead? Danielle was an evil person, but she did not deserve to die. I continued to sit in the warmth of my car, drifting away into a deep fog, when my phone rang. At first I did not hear the ringing through the car speakers but then suddenly, I was jolted back into reality and answered the call.

"Hi Daddy! Why are you sitting in the car all by yourself?" Angela asked.

"Sorry angel. I will be right in," I answered, still in a daze.

"Ok! I have something to show you also."

When the call ended, I took a deep breath and exited the car. I made sure to take my time walking to the house, in order to delay what inevitably was going to be the worst conversation of my life. When I approached the front door, Angela opened it before I could put the key in and jumped into my arms. She had a huge smile on her face and something in her left hand. I tried to get a glimpse of what was in her hand, but she put it behind me when she wrapped both her arms around me.

"Daddy, look what I made mommy. Do you think she will love it? Do you?" Angela said with great excitement.

To say that I was at a loss on how to act would be an understatement. I didn't want to lie to Angela, so I did not say anything. I didn't want her to see me happy, yet I did not want her to question why I was sad. I was truly stuck between a rock and hard place and had no way out. The only way to delay the inevitable was to keep hugging Angela and not let go. Apparently, I was squeezing her too tight because she told me to let go and that she couldn't breathe. When I let her go, I felt a sense of fright come over me, as if I knew subconsciously that I had to do this and could no longer delay it.

I put my keys on the table near the door, took off my coat, hung it up, closed the closet door very softly, and held onto the door handle, as if I was going to be saved by an inanimate object. I stood in front of the closet door just staring at the door handle when someone came up behind me and put their hand on my shoulder. The gesture startled me and caused me to bump my head on the closet door. I turned around to see who was behind me and immediately felt comfort when I saw who it was.

"Oh, hey," I said to Nicole.

"Hey yourself. Everything ok? You seem distracted," Nicole said.

"No. Everything is not ok. There is something I need to tell everyone. Can you please ask Gio and Angela to come into the living room?"

"Can it wait until after dinner? The meatloaf is almost done," Nicole said.

"No, it cannot. Living room. *NOW*"

"Sal, you are scaring me. What's wrong?" Nicole asked, concerned.

"Nicole, please. Just come with me," I said, as I grabbed her hand.

I sat on the couch with Nicole and waited for Gio and Angela to arrive. I thought of telling Nicole before the kids but I did not feel that was the right thing to do. I knew she would try to give me advice on how to handle the situation, but I did not want to hear anything from her, even though I knew she would have good intentions. I wanted to handle this in my own way and deal with the fallout as a family, instead of feeling like I was in one of Nicole's sessions. Nicole continued to probe me for the next few minutes, but

I did not say anything. I just stared ahead at the dining room table that Nicole had set so beautifully and waited for Gio and Angela to arrive.

After two or three minutes, my children finally came downstairs and sat on the couch. They both looked so happy and were actually getting along for a change. Angela was brushing her dolls hair, while Gio was playing his Nintendo Switch. I looked at both of them and for a split second thought of not telling them until tomorrow because they looked so happy and content. However, in the end, I felt it was best to tell them now because they would eventually need to deal with this and it was better to deal with this together with the whole night ahead of us instead of rushing through it in the morning.

My heart began to pound and beat faster than it ever had before as I began to tell my children and Nicole what had happened.

"Listen, I need to tell you all something and it is going to be very hard to hear, but I want you all to know that you are free to express yourself in any way that makes you feel better, ok?" I started.

Everyone looked at me with confused eyes and gave me their full attention. Gio put his Switch down. Angela laid her doll on top of one of the throw pillows on the couch. Nicole sat back and crossed her legs. I knew that each of them was hanging on my every word and that I was about to shake up their world forever, but for some reason, I was not able to bring myself to actually say the words. Nicole reached over to grab my hand and to tell me whatever it was they were all there for me. She looked deep into my eyes and gave me a sweet kiss on the cheek. That was all encouragement and support I would need to move forward.

"Gio. Angela. There really is no easy way to say this so I am just going to say it," I said, then took a deep breath. "Your mother passed away this morning. I am so sorry guys."

Both Gio and Angela looked at me confused, yet they were each confused about different things. I was sure Gio understood what I meant and was trying to process it, but Angela seemed to not totally grasp what I had just said. I turned to Nicole for help, hoping she would be able to explain to Angela what death meant better than I could, but she had her hand over her mouth in shock. I was on my own.

"What does that mean daddy? Where did she pass to? Is it somewhere I can give her my drawing?" Angela asked.

"Oh Angel. No honey. Passing away means she died and she is not coming back," I said, fighting back tears.

It was at that moment Gio began hysterically crying and became inconsolable. I asked Nicole to stay with Angela while I tried to calm Gio down. She nodded her head and went over to hug Angela. At the same time, I went over to Gio and attempted to hug him, but he pushed me away, wanting no part of my comfort.

"You did this to her! You hated her and wanted her dead and now she is! I hate you!" Gio yelled, then ran upstairs to his bedroom. I knew he did not mean what he said and he was overflowing with emotion, but that didn't lessen the pain it caused. Tears began falling down my face faster than the waterfalls at Niagara Falls, which did not help ease the pain Angela felt. She had never seen me cry before and knew that something was seriously wrong when she finally did.

"Daddy, are you ok? I know you are sad so here, this will help," Angela said as she handed me her favorite doll.

"Thank you, angel. She will definitely comfort me, but I think she wants to comfort you as well."

"She will, but you need her more now."

"Thank you! How are you doing? Did Nicole answer your questions for you?"

"Yes, she did. I know mommy isn't coming back and that makes me sad," Angela said with a puppy dog face.

"I know angel, me too. But we have each other and that is important now more than ever," I said and gave Angela a big hug.

After a few minutes, Angela left to go play in her playroom. I was glad to see she was ok at the moment and seemed to be processing Danielle's death better than I thought she would. Gio, on the other hand, was a complete mess. I discussed with Nicole if I should try talking to him or if I should leave him alone and we both decided it was best to let him be. She explained that at his age, it is important to allow him some level of independence.

I spent the rest of the evening sitting on the couch watching TV with Nicole. We occasionally talked about Danielle and how I felt, but for the most part, we sat in silence. I appreciated the fact that Nicole allowed me space to be in my thoughts and go through the grieving process. She understood that although Danielle and I were divorced and I hated her for what she did, I *was* still married to her for thirteen years and she was also the mother of my children.

When the news came on at eleven o'clock, I got up to go to bed, but was frozen on the couch when Danielle was the lead story on the newscast. They mentioned how she had died in the hospital under suspicious circumstances and that an investigation was underway. I was certain that detectives would come knocking on my door at any moment to question me; something I was not looking forward to. Once Danielle's news story was over, I got up off the couch, walked up the stairs toward my bedroom, and plopped down on the bed. As soon as I landed on the bed, I received a text message from an unknown number that caused my heart rate to skyrocket.

You will pay Amici! You will pay! You better be looking over your shoulder from now on. You and your kids!

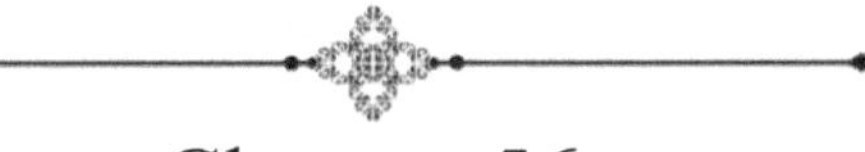

Chapter 56

Sean Lancaster was still grieving over Danielle when he decided it was time to put his final plan into effect. He knew he had to do what he did but he also had more regret than he had ever felt. He loved Danielle and was confident he would have been able to get her out of prison so they could spend the rest of their lives together. He also had visions of possibly starting a family with her; something he never thought would be possible again after his family was murdered. Those dreams were all gone now and Sean was having trouble dealing with the reality of not having someone by his side again.

Despite his depression, Sean was still upbeat on this day because he was going to see Joseph Millstone in prison. This was not going to be an ordinary visit. This was going to be the beginning of the end for Sal Amici. The anticipation of this meeting excited Sean so much that he had a hard time getting rid of the smile on his face and giddy up in his step. He would continue to smile even after being cut off by someone on the Henry Hudson Parkway and nearly getting into a major car accident. He also continued smiling even though he was getting dangerously close to missing the cutoff time for visitation. He did not have a care in the world at that moment because he knew that by the end of his visit, the final plan would be in place.

When Sean arrived at Sing Sing Correctional Facility, he immediately put on his fake mustache, his wig, his eyeglasses, and then donned a jet black fedora. Finally, he grabbed the drivers license for Terence Callahan and exited his car with great anticipation. He felt loose and free walking toward the prison entrance, despite his pain over killing Danielle. Even though his disguise completely changed what he looked like, he was still nervous that someone would spot him. Within thirty seconds of leaving his car, his fear came true.

"Excuse me, sir!" a man behind Sean said.

Sean kept walking, hoping the man was talking to someone else.

"Sir. Wait. *STOP!*" the man yelled.

Reluctantly, Sean slowly turned around after adjusting his mustache.

"Yes? What can I help you with?" Sean asked.

"You dropped this back there. You don't want to lose it," the man said, as he handed Sean the wallet he had dropped by the car.

This had been the second time that Sean dropped something while trying to remain in disguise. It was also the second time someone had stopped him to return the item he had dropped. Both times Sean hoped it was someone else that was being called out and both times he got nervous. Moving forward, he was going to have to pay extra attention to what he is doing because there will come a time when he won't be so lucky and someone will identify him.

"Oh, thank you sir. That is very kind of you. Here take this," Sean replied and took out a twenty dollar bill.

"Oh, no I can't accept that. I am just doing my good deed for the day. Have a nice day."

Sean felt a sense of enormous relief when the man walked away and didn't recognize him. His face and profile was all over the national news, so there was not a person alive that did not know what Sean Lancaster looked like. Even though the man did not recognize him, Sean picked up his pace and speed walked to the entrance to avoid any further confrontations.

After going through the entrance and metal detector, the real test was about to begin. When Sean had visited Danielle at Bedford Hills Correctional Facility, the guards there half assed their jobs and did not fully inspect the ID he had. However, the guards at Sing Sing were like bouncers guarding the entrance to Studio 54. They took their sweet time inspecting and analyzing every single ID presented to them. Sean knew that the one he had was pristine and in no way could be identified as fake, but he also knew that someone might pick up on his nervousness and question who he was.

Nervously, Sean handed his ID to the guard at the visitor's sign-in booth. The guard was around six foot eight and weighed close to three hundred pounds. He had a tattoo of a hammer, similar to the one Thor uses, on each bicep facing each other and another tattoo of those hammers colliding on his neck. As if his appearance wasn't intimidating enough, his voice was deeper than Barry White's.

For the next several seconds, the guard looked back and forth at Sean and the ID. He tilted the ID, turned it over, ran it under a black light, and felt the edges as if he was going to try to peel the laminate cover off. Even though it was only a few seconds, Sean felt like it was an eternity before the guard finished examining the ID. When the guard finished, he told Sean to step aside.

"What for?" Sean asked.

"Mr. Callahan, please step aside. I'm not going to ask you twice."

Not wanting to cause a scene and risk getting caught, Sean did as he was told and moved to the side of the check-in counter. The guard followed him and then ordered him to move toward a door that was just off the side. Sean was getting extremely nervous at this point and almost thought about leaving, but this was too important to him. Sal had ruined his and Joseph's lives and they needed to finalize their plan for revenge now.

"What is this about? I have done nothing wrong," Sean yelled.

"Sir, I am going to ask you to calm down. Don't make me ask twice," the guard replied.

"Ok., but please tell me what this is all about," Sean pleaded.

"Relax Sean," the guard whispered. "Millstone said you were coming."

Shocked, Sean immediately began to think this may be a trap. Does he trust that this guard really was told by Joseph who he was and what name to look for? Or was the guard really that good that he identified Sean through his disguise? Having no other option at that point, Sean decided to play along with the guard, but also to proceed with extreme caution.

"So Joseph told you about me?" Sean asked.

"Yes. He said to make sure you go to see him with no issues or distractions. Millstone and I have an operation here that doesn't work if we do not trust and look out for each other," the guard said.

"What operation?"

"Drugs. I smuggle the drugs in and Joseph sells it. We split the profits seventy/thirty, with Joseph getting the higher share because there is more risk involved."

"What kind of drugs and where do they come from?" Sean asked.

"Meth and heroin. Joseph knows someone on the outside that cooks the meth and can get the heroin in mass quantities for cheap. He doesn't tell me who they are because the less I know, the better."

Sean knew at this point that he could fully trust the guard. All of the answers he gave were true and were given without hesitation. Sean got the feeling that the guard knew he was testing him, which is why he answered all of the questions without any issues. Now knowing that Joseph had set this up, Sean was anxious to know what the plan was to get him to Joseph and how they were going to have all the time they needed to set up their revenge plan.

Chapter 56

I have made the trip to my office hundreds of times and always found it relaxing. Whether I was driving or taking public transportation, I used that time to get deep in thought and reflect on what was happening in my life. This morning, however, I had terrible anxiety and was constantly checking all around me to see if I saw anything suspicious. The only other time I was in shambles going to my office was last year right after David Flores killed his family and I was going to talk to Alan, Steven, and Thomas about it. While I felt high anxiety for both trips, this one felt a little different. I was not going to the office thinking I was going to be fired or taken off a case. I was going into the office to provide an update on Joseph Millstone and to discuss the disturbing text I received the previous night. I knew Alan and Steven could not directly help me, but they had contacts in the NYPD that might be able to help. When I arrived at the office, I was greeted in the lobby by Alan; something he never did. I was caught off guard and did not know what it meant, but I was sure there was a reason for it.

"Sal, how are you?" Alan asked, as he extended his hand to shake mine.

"Doing ok, considering. How are you?" I answered, shaking his hand.

"Same old. You know how it is," Alan said. "Listen, I wanted to prepare you before you go upstairs."

"Prepare me for what?"

"Kelly is here as well. She got the same text that you did. We need to resolve this ASAP."

I had to take a step back to regain my balance. It was one thing for me to receive the text message, but it was quite another for Kelly to also receive it. I had dealt with threats like this before and I was used to knowing how to handle it. Kelly was so young and so inexperienced, I was afraid she might go into a shell and not know how to get herself out. Furthermore, I was worried she would begin to resent me for convincing her to stay with the case when she had doubts about continuing. Not only was I going to have to work with Alan and Steven to figure out what to do, but I would also have to try and calm Kelly down as well. I knew she was still reeling from the jury's decision and what transpired after the verdict was read, but if she was going to get through this, she would need to toughen up.

"Thank you for letting me know Alan. I appreciate the advance notice."

Most of the elevator ride up to Alan's office was silent. We both wanted to say something, but we did not know what that was. I could feel the tension between us, not because of a disagreement or feud, but because of what was going on. The office had not experienced anything like this before, so this was new territory for everyone. For their entire careers, Alan and Steven had steered clear of messes like this one, which is why I felt immense guilt having to put them through a few tough ordeals the past year. I knew they would give the corporate line that they are here to help and we will get through this together, but I also knew that on some level, this had to be bothering both of them beyond words. When we were almost on the fifth floor, I finally broke the silence.

"Alan, look. I know that things over the past year have not been great, mostly because of me. I am truly sorry for everything I have put you and Steven through. I don't know what else to say. You both had faith in me by making me a partner and I feel like I am letting both of you down," I said, hanging my head.

"Let's talk in my office before we go to the conference room," Alan replied.

We exited the elevator and stopped by the conference room so Alan could tell everyone he and I needed to speak before we met with everyone. I was not sure why, but I was getting more tense as we got closer to Alan's office. I knew that I wasn't going to be fired or even reprimanded for that matter, yet something did not sit right with me. The tone in Alan's voice was different than it usually was and he was walking in front of me; something he never did. I do have a tendency to overthink things and draw inaccurate conclusions, but I also like to think I am a good judge of character and can read people well. There was no sense in continuing to dwell on what was wrong with Alan because eventually we made our way to his office, where I was preparing to have yet another difficult conversation.

"Sal, talk to me. What's going on?" Alan asked me.

"Well, I am not sure if you heard, but Danielle passed away yesterday in the hospital. She was put there because she was stabbed in prison. The police think her death is suspicious so I am waiting for them to reach out to talk to me."

"I know about that Sal. I mean what is going on with what you said earlier."

"Oh, that. Look, I know things have been hectic around here the past year and I feel like it is my fault. I do not want to bring any of my issues to the office and I know that I have not done a very good job of that. I want you to know that I give my all to this job and firm, no matter what is going on in my personal life."

"Sal, I want you to listen to me and listen to me good because I am only going to say this once," Alan said sternly. "We made you a partner of this firm not only because of your talent in the courtroom, but also because we believe you are the future of this firm. Let's face it, Steve and I are not getting any younger and with Thomas gone, we have to start thinking about who we can trust to take over when we retire. Right now, you are one of those people. I know that things have not gone well over the past year and now with this latest issue they seem to be getting worse, but you should not feel any guilt about what it may bring to the firm. We can handle it and have people in place if we need help. Got it?"

"Got it. Thank you, Alan. I appreciate it."

"Good. Now let's go meet up with everyone to see what the hell is going on."

Chapter 57

Sean was getting so anxious about his meeting with Joseph Millstone that he failed to notice the guard was trying to tell him something.

"Yo, Sean. You there?" the guard asked.

"Yeah, sorry. I was just thinking about…never mind. What?"

"Millstone is inside," the guard said, pointing to the room directly in front of them. "You have one hour. Not one hour and one minute, *one hour*."

"Got it. Jeez, calm down Deebo," Sean said, referring to the character from the movie *Friday*.

"One hour Sean," the guard said and left.

Sean opened the door to a private meeting room that looked like an executive of some kind occupied the room. It was decorated with diploma frames and achievement awards behind the desk. There were also van Gogh paintings all over the room, which gave the room life, yet also a sense of eeriness. In the back corner of the room, there was a large mahogany desk that was set up on an angle facing the door. Sitting behind the desk was Joseph Millstone. He had his legs on top of the desk and was thumbing through a magazine when Sean approached him.

"Damn Joe, moving up in the world, huh?" Sean said.

"Nah, just asked the warden if I could use his office."

"Looks like you set a record for the shortest time to gain respect and clout. Very impressive," Sean said, admiring Joseph's brashness.

"You could say that," Joseph said with a smile.

"Ok, let's get to it. We only have an hour."

"Sean, why do you continue to let that prick get to you?"

"Joe, it's not about him getting to me. It's about punishing the only person who has been able to outsmart me. He took Danielle away from me and he needs to pay for that. I wasn't done with him last year when he forced me to leave the country after Danielle was arrested. I knew she wouldn't rat on me, but that son a bitch Amici knows everything and would have turned me in without a second thought. I am here to finish the job I started last year. Understand now?"

"Yeah, I understand. We just have to be smart about this. Like you said, he is a smart guy and will be able to sniff out what you are doing if we are not careful."

"He's not as smart as me, remember that Joe."

Sean was beginning to get annoyed at the coy attitude that Joseph was displaying. He knew that Joseph understood the urgency that Sean wanted to operate at, yet still he was enjoying toying with Sean. It was a difficult situation for Sean because he needed Joseph to help him execute his plan, but he also didn't want to give Joseph the satisfaction of knowing that he was getting to him.

"Alright, Joe. Here is what I am thinking," Sean began. "You will lure Sal to see you here in this shithole within the next week or so. I don't care what reason you use, just get him here. Once he is here, I will be hanging around the area and when the time is right, I will pounce on him. He won't know what is coming, which will give me the upper hand. Can you do this for me?"

"Of course I can, Sean. I have two questions though. One is how and the other is why?" Joseph answered.

"What do you mean why?" Sean asked, confused. "I told you why before and the how is what we need to discuss."

"No, I mean why should I help you? I am already in this dump for what will certainly be the rest of my life so I can't possibly improve my situation. In fact, it can only get worse if I am caught helping an international fugitive."

Sean stared at Joseph with a look of both disgust and confusion. He and Joseph had been planning revenge on Sal for a while and now Joseph seemed to either not be interested anymore or he wanted something in return now from Sean. Whatever the reason Joseph had, Sean was going to get to the bottom of it and solve it quickly.

"You're kidding me right? How about the fact that he let that incompetent woman defend you, thus dooming your case from the beginning? Or the fact that you were never his top priority."

"Yeah, but it's over and done with now. There is no sense in continuing to dwell on it. I want to try to behave as well as I can here and not raise any red flags," Joseph replied with a smirk.

"Oh, bullshit," Sean yelled. "You know as well as I do that you have always been and will always be a vindictive son of a bitch. People like you and I do not change Joe. We just don't"

"I guess you are right. Who am I kidding? I can't change. Even if I wanted to, I wouldn't be able to. But I am sorry Sean, I won't be able to help you," Joseph said.

"Joe, what do you mean? Come on. I need you pal," Sean begged.

"No, you don't understand. It's not that I don't want to, I literally will not be able to help you."

Before Sean could say anything in response, Joseph, in one swift motion, reached into his sock, took out a makeshift shiv, and slashed his throat from ear to ear. He immediately fell to the floor, clutching the gaping wound he had created. Sean stood in utter shock, staring at what Joseph had done. There was blood all over him and the warden's desk. It continued to pour out of Joseph's neck like a free flowing river headed toward the ocean. Clearly seeing that Joseph was dead and there was nothing he could do, Sean gathered his things and made a beeline for the prison exit. Even though the temperature outside was below freezing, Sean had to remove his jacket and carry it with him because of all the blood that was on it. He hustled through the hallways, not stopping for anything or anyone. Once he made it to the exit, he lowered his head so he would not be seen and then sprinted toward his car. He felt fortunate that nobody had seen him or had sounded the alarm in the prison during his escape. With no time to spare, Sean sped out of the prison parking lot and was gone before anyone knew what had happened to Joseph.

Chapter 58

When I entered the boardroom to meet up with Steven and Kelly, I could already tell this was going to be a tough meeting. Kelly was tapping her leg rapidly, a clear sign she was nervous. Steven had a look of deep concern on his face, which did not help settle my nerves. Alan sat down next to me and did not say a word as I took my seat. The tension in the room was so tight, you could have cut it with a box cutter instead of a knife.

We sat in silence for what seemed like an eternity; however, in reality, it was only a few seconds. Nobody knew how to begin the conversation, with each of us staring at one another. Kelly's leg tapping picked up in pace and now she was beginning to bite her fingernails. Steven did not look up from the table in front of him and Alan would open his mouth a few times, but nothing came out. Finally, I decided I would break the ice and get this meeting rolling.

"Alright look. Let's just get this out there, ok? Someone, and I think we all know who, sent threatening text messages to Kelly and I. The question is what are we going to do about it? Kelly, what did your text message say?"

"The same as yours did, without the kids part," Kelly answered.

"What do you make of it? Do you think it is a viable threat?" I asked her.

"Well duh. Uh, let's see. Joseph gets convicted of multiple murder one charges, then threatens us in front of everyone in the courtroom. Oh and then as if that wasn't enough, he sends both of us these text messages just to remind us that he can fuck with us anywhere at any time. So yeah, I think they are viable," Kelly answered.

"Look, I know you are upset, so am I, but you better watch how you talk to me. I am still your boss and I demand you show me some respect. Got it?" I yelled back.

"Sorry Sal. I really am. I just don't know what to do. I am scared out of my mind and can't keep going like this," Kelly said, as she began to cry.

I felt guilty yelling at her when she was in such a vulnerable state, but I also needed to establish that she needs to keep her emotions in check. She had shown too much emotion during Joseph's trial and would need to learn to curb those emotions if she was going to be a good attorney. Every opportunity I had, I was going to coach her on how to do that, no matter what the circumstances were. In this case though, I would have to be a little less forceful, given Kelly's current frame of mind.

After being silent for the entire meeting and looking more lost than a deer in headlights, Steven finally spoke up and voiced his opinion on the whole situation.

"Bottom line is someone needs to go visit Joseph and tell that asshole that he needs to stop making threats or we will press charges. Even if he is not the one directly sending these text messages, we all know he is behind it, thus making him equally culpable. I am not going to continue to sit here and waste all of my time over someone who deserves to be put to death. This shit stops now, you hear me? *NOW!*" Steven yelled.

The room was in complete silence after Steve's outburst. We all felt the same way but Steven, like always, was the only one brave enough to actually say what was on his mind. We all knew that Steven was a bit of a hothead and that he could over exaggerate things, but in this case, he was absolutely correct. The question now on my mind, and I am sure on everyone else's, was how do we do this. Before I had a chance to ask, we were interrupted by Jill barging into the boardroom.

"Put on channel four, quick!" Jill said out of breath.

"What is Jill?" I asked.

"Just do it, will you?"

I put on the TV and tuned to channel four and received one of the biggest shocks of my life. I couldn't believe what I was reading at the bottom of the screen.

Convicted serial Killer Joseph Millstone found dead in jail cell.

I would be lying to myself if I said I was not in the least bit satisfied at this outcome. It seemed, for the moment, all of the issues we had been discussing were gone. We no longer had to wonder about how to deal with Joseph or what potential backlash would be. I no longer had to entertain the thought of going to see him in prison. Kelly and I could finally relax and focus on future cases. As good as I may have felt in that moment, I suddenly felt a panic set in. Without knowing how Joseph died, I would need to continue to remain vigilant. It was totally conceivable that someone killed Joseph and was coming after Kelly and I next. However, it was also possible that Joseph took his own life. The uncertainty was beginning to overtake my thoughts and I quickly realized that I needed more information on what happened.

The rest of the newscast offered little to no additional help on what happened to Joseph, only saying that his throat had been slashed and that he died instantly. I thought it was rather ironic that Joseph died in this manner, considering that is how he killed all of his victims. It almost seemed like poetic justice, which temporarily brought a smile to my face.

"How are we going to find out what happened?" I asked everyone in the room.

"Well, I will call my connection at the coroner's office to see what he can tell me. It might be too early because I am sure an autopsy has not been performed yet, but I can let him know to call me the minute he finds out. I guess we can start there," Steven said.

"Good. That will be very good, "Alan added. "I am sure there is more to this than the news is letting on and we need to be informed of any details every step of the way."

"In the meantime, I suggest that Kelly and I receive protective detail outside of our homes until we know what happened. Just in case something is going on that we are unaware of."

"Do you really think that is necessary, Sal?" Kelly asked me.

"I agree, Sal. I don't want my granddaughter to be any more nervous than she already is?" Steven said.

"I understand Steven, but this is just a precaution."

"Ok. I will set it up. Kelly, are you ok with this?" Alan asked.

"Yes, it is fine. But I am not staying home. They are only there to watch over my apartment building. That's it."

We continued to talk about what Joseph's death meant and who might be responsible for the next few hours. When we wrapped up our meeting, I decided to try to get caught up on some work that had been backlogged, but it was no use. All I could think about was my family and if they were safe. I packed up some boxes and headed home for the rest of the day. My intention was to work from home to get caught up, while keeping an eye on my family. Little did I know what a terrible decision that would turn out to be.

Chapter 59

When I got home, I was greeted with a warm hug from Nicole. She had heard on the news what happened to Joseph and knew I would be bothered by it. She always had a way of knowing when to be gentle and caring, which I suppose is due to the fact that she is an excellent therapist. She also knew when to talk and when not to talk, something I greatly appreciated in this case. She continued to hug me at the front door, while telling me everything will be alright without actually dictating the words to me. When we separated, she noticed the black sedan parked across the street.

"What's that?" Nicole asked, pointing to the sedan.

"Protective detail. It is no big deal. Just a precaution," I reassured her.

"For what? Are we in danger?"

"No. Like I said, it is just for precaution. There is nothing to worry about."

"Sal, protective detail is not issued unless there *is* something to worry about. What aren't you telling me?" Nicole asked, getting annoyed.

"Nothing. I promise."

"Sal, I am not going to ask you again. You seem to forget that I saw you when you were at your most vulnerable and I know something is up. Now what is it?"

At that moment, I realized that I could not hide anything from Nicole. She was able to see through me like hardly anyone else had been able to do. I knew I had to tell her about the text message but I did not know how much I would tell her. Did she need to know the whole truth or would I be able to give her just enough that she would back off? Based on how she had just seen through me like I was swiss cheese, I decided it was best to tell her the whole truth.

"Alright, but you have to promise me you won't go all Nicole on me."

"What does that mean?"

"You know what it means. Promise me," I said, giving Nicole a stern look.

"Ok. I promise."

"Good. I got a text message last night from an unknown source telling me I better be looking over my shoulder. It also mentioned Gio and Angela as well."

"What about them?" Nicole asked, trying to keep her promise.

"It just mentioned for me and my kids to look over our shoulders. That is all it said. That is why I asked for the protective detail. Kelly got a similar text and given what happened with Joseph, I thought it best to be safe."

I could tell that Nicole was trying her best to hide her emotions and felt guilty asking her to do so. I wanted to reciprocate the comfort she had just given to me but also had to show her that I was strong and was going to be the rock that this family needed. She continued to look at me with concerned eyes as I detailed everything that was discussed in my meeting with Alan, Steven, and Kelly earlier. Eventually, Nicole could not hold it in anymore and she began to get visibly upset.

"I am sorry, Sal. I know you said not to let it get to me, but this is too much. I care way too much about you and the kids to not let this affect me. I tried to not get too attached but I can't help it. I love you and your kids more than I ever thought was possible. I do not want anything to happen to any of you and if there was a way I could make it all go away, I would."

"Nicole, you don't have to apologize. You know we all love you as well and I am grateful that you are in our lives," I responded, reaching out my arms so I could give her the comforting hug she needed.

While Nicole and I were embracing, Gio and Angela came downstairs to see what was wrong. Once again, I was faced with a difficult decision. I definitely could be more evasive with my children, but I needed to tell them a little bit of what was going on so they could be cognizant of their surroundings.

"Gio, Angela. I need you both to come with me and Nicole on the couch. There is something we need to discuss with you," I said.

"Did someone else die, daddy?" Angela asked.

"No, angel. But it is very important that we talk to you."

Nicole and I spent the next ten minutes explaining what was going on and what to look out for. We explained why the black sedan was parked across the street and not to pay much attention to it. We also let them know that there was no imminent danger and they should not be scared. As usual, Angela just agreed to everything and went about her business, but Gio had questions. We did the best we could answering those questions, giving the respect he deserved for handling this situation so well. It was not until he asked his final question that I began to rethink my position on whether we were in danger.

"So I should not have given any information over the phone?" Gio said.

"What do you mean given information over the phone?" I asked, puzzled.

"This morning, someone called looking for you and I said that you were not home. When they asked me when you would be home, I said I was not sure because you were at work. They then asked me where you work and I told them. Should I not have?" Gio said, now realizing he may have made a mistake.

"Is that all you told the person?" I asked.

"Yes. I swear, I didn't say anything else. I am sorry dad."

"Don't worry. Where I work is public information, so it is not a secret. You didn't do anything wrong," I said, trying to calm Gio down.

Even though I tried my best to make Gio not feel bad, he still got upset and ran back to his room. At twelve years old, he had not yet begun to understand how the world works and took most things to heart. He is an extremely sweet and generous person, but he also needed to toughen up and learn that he is going to make mistakes in life and that it is ok to make those mistakes. I wanted to go after him, but Nicole told me to let him go. She had told me that before when I broke the news about Danielle to Gio and it worked out then, so I decided to trust her again in this instance.

After Gio closed the door to his room, the doorbell rang. I really did not want to answer the door, but whoever it was kept ringing the bell. I asked Nicole to check on dinner and went to answer the door. When I opened the door, I was immediately grabbed by two men in ski masks and dragged outside. I did not have time to call for Nicole because the men put a gag in my mouth before I knew what was happening. The two men continued to drag me along the front lawn as I tried to escape, but it was to no avail. The men were much stronger than me and together, they formed a dominant force. Before long, I was shoved into the back of a van and pistol whipped in the back of my head. The pain was so intense it made me nauseous. After being punched a few times in the stomach, the two men slammed the door to the van shut and got into the front seats. I was trying to look around to see what I was up against and how I might be able to escape when the man sitting in the passenger seat said something that froze me right where I was.

"Cooperate with us or your son dies."

Chapter 60

For the first time since his college days, Sean Lancaster felt like he was losing control. He always had a sense of direction and purpose, especially when it came to his survival. He knew he had to kill Danielle because she would have eventually told someone about their plans for Sal, but he hated doing it. The guilt he felt was unlike anything he had ever experienced before. He was constantly thinking about her and pondering if he did indeed do the right thing. It was obviously too late to change anything, but he felt more regret than he cared to and it was playing games with his mind.

Trying to regain his composure and continue what he and Danielle had started, Sean sat at the desk in his motel room and thought of what to do next. Does he go after Sal now or does he still need to accomplish a few other things first to set the stage. His anxiety and impatience were telling him to go to Sal's house immediately, but his common sense and smarts were telling him to wait it out and be patient. To help him make this decision, Sean decided to enlist the help of his old friend Samuel Porter.

Sean asked Samuel to meet him at the motel he was staying at so he could keep a low profile. Sean advised Samuel to flash his headlights three times when he arrived so Sean would know when he was there. Samuel agreed and said he would be there within the hour. Sean said he needed him there sooner than that but Samuel explained that he was with his lady friend and he would get there when he got there. Knowing that he needed Samuel's help, Sean had no other option but to agree to Samuel's terms.

While he waited for Samuel, Sean decided he would take a shower to pass the time. His anxiety was at an all time high and he was pacing around the motel room at such a frantic pace, he didn't feel any pain when he banged his foot into the metal post of the bed. After tending to his injury, Sean kept thinking that showering would not only pass time, it would also hopefully calm him down. What he failed to realize was that he had spent so much time in thought, he no longer had to pass the time; Samuel would be arriving any minute.

As Sean got up to head to the bathroom, he saw a beam of light flash three times. He was stunned that Samuel had actually shown up, let alone followed directions. Sean quickly grabbed his cell phone and flashed back at the car parked in front of his room to let Samuel know that it was safe to come in. Even though he had been through this dozens of times before, Sean was unusually nervous to meet with Samuel. Maybe it was because he knew that this would be the final meeting to plan Sal Amici's fate or maybe because for the first time, he doubted himself.

When Samuel came to the motel room door, Sean didn't wait for him to knock. Instead, he opened the door just enough so Samuel could squeeze inside and he could not be seen. Once Samuel was inside the room, Sean closed the door and the curtains to ensure nobody would be able to see inside of the room. Paranoia was beginning to take over and it made Sean feel very uncomfortable.

"You ok, Sean?" Samuel asked.

"I just don't want to be seen by anyone Sam," Sean replied.

"I get that but…never mind. So tell me. What's going on?"

"I need this thing with Amici to end and I need your help to make it happen," Sean said, as he motioned to the chair at the desk for Samuel to sit down.

"How can I help? I don't see how that is possible."

"Well, that is not true. You were Sal's first client, correct?" Sean asked.

"Yeah, so?" Samuel responded, confused.

"So, you are going to say you need his services again. I don't care what reason you use, just make it sound convincing."

"And why would I do this? I mean, I like you Sean, you are a cool dude, but I am not exactly itching to get back into bed with Sal Amici."

"Understood but money talks, my friend," Sean said, while taking out three rolled up stacks of one hundred dollar bills.

"Can't argue with that," Samuel said, with a big smile. "How are we going to do this?"

"Well, I was thinking you can reach out to Sal's office and ask for him. I assume they will know who you are and will be more than willing to connect you with him. Once they do, ask him if he is willing to represent you again because you think you are about to be arrested. Again, it does not matter what the reason is, as long as it is believable and easy to remember."

"Sounds like a good plan, but there is just one problem."

"What's that?"

"Danielle's funeral is in two days and I don't think he will be available," Samuel answered.

Sean was taken back a bit by the news. He had not thought about when Danielle's funeral might be and certainly had not thought about that possibly being a factor in his plans. He tried his best to hide his emotions from Samuel, as he was still devastated at what he had done to Danielle. Although he did a good job for the most part, Samuel was still able to detect that something was off with Sean.

"You miss her, don't you?" Samuel asked.

Without missing a beat, Sean simply nodded.

"I had no idea her funeral would be in two days. That actually changes things for me. I may not need you after all," Sean said.

"Wait, what?" Samuel asked, confused.

"Yeah. A new plan has hatched in my brain and as it turns out, your services will no longer be required."

"Just like that?"

"Just like that. Thank you anyway, Sam. I appreciate your willingness to help out. I am sure there will come a time when I will need you," Sean said and turned to open the door for Samuel to leave.

"I don't think so, Sean," Samuel said with a stern voice.

"Put it away, Sam. You don't want to do this," Sean said, using his sixth sense.

Sean always had a way of sensing how things would play out before they escalated. He did not know where that ability came from or why he had it, but it had served him well in the past. It worked for him when he killed David Flores, which was an accident. He had not intended to kill David, but when David demanded more money from Sean for his role in the scheme they ran, the two got into a heated argument and engaged in a tussle. In that struggle, David pulled out his gun and managed to point it at Sean's stomach. Fearing for his life, Sean's adrenaline went into overdrive and he grabbed the gun and discharged it accidently. The bullet had struck David in the back of the head, killing him instantly. Without much choice, Sean set the scene up to look like an execution, in an effort to throw off the ensuing investigation.

"You still don't get it, do you Sean?" Samuel said. "I am tired of you trying to boss me around. I am tired of you thinking you are better than me. I am tired..."

"What was that? I can't hear you. You will need to speak up," Sean said, as he leaned over the slumping body of Samuel Porter. "See Sam, I am smarter than you. I also think three steps ahead of you. I knew you would bring a weapon to this meeting and that you would carelessly flaunt it at some point. I, on the other hand, also brought a weapon, only I know enough to conceal it and use it only if I have to. That sharp pain you feel is the bullet from the Beretta Pico I have in my pocket."

Samuel tried to say something back to Sean, but the blood that was pouring out of his mouth prevented him from doing so. He then tried to raise his gun toward Sean, but could not muster up the strength to do so. With no other options left, Samuel held his gun against the femoral artery and fired. It took a little over two minutes for Samuel to pass out from the blood loss and another five minutes to bleed out and die. All the while, Sean made no effort to save him.

Chapter 61

I had no idea what was going on or who these people were, but for some reason, I was not scared. I kept thinking to myself that if they wanted me dead, they would have killed me already. They clearly wanted something from me and I was eager to find out what it was. The problem was that I had a gag in my mouth and was not able to speak. Rather than cause a scene or exert energy I may have needed later, I decided it was best to simply continue to lay still and wait to see what would happen next.

We had been driving for well over an hour since I was first taken, which led me to believe that we were not in Manhattan anymore. The road was beginning to get bumpy and the street lights were disappearing. I started to get a little worried because my mind began to wander and think of all the places we could be and I kept coming back to one thought. I was being taken out to the woods or some other deserted area. Again, I was not fearful of dying because I did not think these men would go through all this trouble and drive all this way, just to kill me. I began to think of everyone who could have possibly sent these people for me but everyone I thought of was either dead or in prison. For a brief moment, I thought it might be Sean, but he likes to do his own dirty work and would never trust someone else to do it for him.

When we finally reached our destination, I was surprisingly relieved knowing that I would soon find out why this was happening to me. I had been racking my brain the entire time and came up with nothing. What amazed me the most was that I was more concerned about why I was taken rather than the fact that I *was* taken. I have seen these situations on TV all the time and the victim is always panicking and stressing that they will be killed. In reality, it was quite the opposite for me, which I knew would benefit me when I was confronted by the men who took me.

A few minutes after we stopped, the side door to the van opened and I was dragged out and tossed on the ground. I looked around to see I knew where we were, but all I saw was trees, trees, and more trees. The calming feeling I had just a few moments ago about not dying quickly evaporated when I realized people like these men do not take victims out to the woods for no reason and then let them live. As I was being tossed around, I kept thinking to myself that these men do not need to be rough, I was willing to cooperate with them, no matter what. They had to know on some level that I was not the violent type and that they had control of the situation. Once I centered myself, one of the men finally took my gag off and told me to stand against the van. I did as I was told and waited for my fate.

"We are going to make this very easy, Sal," one of the men began. "You are to do as we say. No questions asked. Is that clear?"

I gave a slight nod and waited for further instructions.

"Good. Now, do you know who Paul Trevino is?" the man asked me.

"No," I responded.

"I didn't think you had. Well, Paul is an associate of ours and was a good friend of Joseph Millstone, until Joseph died."

"Ok. What does this have to do with me?"

"I told you no questions. That was your one and only mistake I will allow. Violate my rules again, and you will pay a penalty. Now, Paul is in a little bit of trouble and that is where we need your help. We need you to use your contacts at the NYPD to get information on what evidence they have on Paul and then help us get rid of the information. That is what this has to do with you."

"I can't just ask a cop to give me that information unless..." I said, realizing what they were telling me.

"That's right, Sal. You *and ONLY you* will defend Paul to get access to this information. "

"Why me?

"I warned you, no more questions. Now, you will pay the price."

The other man grabbed me by my neck and spun me around so I was facing a car about twenty feet away. The windows were tinted jet black, so I could not see inside. The man that was holding me nodded to the car and a large, bald man came out of the passenger side door. He gave me a quick look that scared the hell out of me and opened the rear door. When the door was open, he reached in and grabbed someone who had a mask over their face, gagged, and had their hands tied behind their back. When he removed the mask, I felt the pit of my stomach drop like I was on a free falling roller coaster. *It was Kelly!*

"Oh, please. Stop. Whatever you are thinking, please stop!" I begged.

Without any warning or chance to negotiate, the bald man pulled out his pistol and shot Kelly in the head. She fell like a ton of bricks and did not move when she hit the ground. The bald man then calmly put the pistol back in his jacket, closed the rear door, and got back into the car. The car then sped away, leaving Kelly lying dead on the ground for me to look at.

"I told you there would be a penalty. *DO NOT BREAK MY RULES AGAIN.*' the man said and punched me in the stomach.

I was in such a state of shock that I could not yell, cry, or even talk. All I could do in that moment was think of Alan and how he would react to the news that his granddaughter was executed. It was my fault Kelly was dead and that was something I was going to have to deal with for the rest of my life. The guilt began to overwhelm me, causing me to vomit.

"Hey, hey, knock that off," the man said, annoyed. "I need you to pay attention to what I am about to say. There is a car parked about one hundred yards west of here. The keys are in the glove compartment. Take that car and go back home and wait to hear further instructions from me. I think this goes without saying, but do not repeat *DO NOT* mention a word of this to anyone. If you do, your son will suffer the same fate as Kelly, only it will not be as quick. Do I make myself clear?"

I nodded and continued looking at Kelly.

"Can I ask a question please?" I asked.

"Sure, why not."

"What will happen with Kelly's body?"

"Oh I don't know. Maybe the animals will get to her," the man said, as he got into the van chuckling.

Once the van was gone, I did not know what to do. I knew I needed to get home before Nicole and the kids began to worry, but I also did not want to leave Kelly in the woods. If I called the police, I would surely be putting Gio's life in danger, so that was not an option. If I just left her there in the woods, what kind of person would that make me? Despite my desire to let the police know about Kelly, I decided the best thing to do was to go home in the car that was left for me. There was nothing I could do for Kelly at this point and I needed to protect my family.

I began to walk toward the car, constantly looking over both of my shoulders. I was so terrified that a sniper was going to shoot me, that I vomited again and nearly passed out. Even though it was only a football field length walk to the car, it felt much longer because of how much I was exposed. I was able to finally take a few deep breaths and calm myself down enough that I was able to run to the car to get home as soon as I could. I got in the car, found the keys, and sped off, while looking in the rearview mirror at Kelly.

When I finally got home, Nicole was pacing back and forth in the hallway near the front door. She had a look of sheer terror on her face and I could tell she had been crying. When she saw me, she ran to me and wrapped her arms around me so tight, I could not move. I tried to maneuver my way out of her grip, but gave up after it became obvious she was not letting go. I have to admit, it was a great feeling.

"My God, Sal. I was so scared. What happened to you?" Nicole asked me, while pulling away.

"Nicole, you know I love you and don't want to keep anything from you, but you have to just trust me on this. I cannot tell you now. I promise I will when the time is right. Please Nicole, trust me on this."

"Sal, I want to, but you disappeared for hours and came back clearly upset and disheveled and now you are asking me to not ask what happened? Sal, do you know what that is doing to me?"

"I know Nicole, but you will know everything eventually. I promise."

"Does this have anything to do with the protective detail that was outside?" Nicole asked.

"What do you mean *was* outside?"

"They left about two hours ago," Nicole informed me.

I was so traumatized by what happened to Kelly that I didn't even think to look to see if my protective detail was still outside when I got home. I went to the bay window ledge in the living room and peaked behind the curtain. The black sedan was no longer there, just as Nicole had said. I began to wonder who sent them away and why.

I wanted to ask Nicole if she knew more about them leaving but she had been through enough and I didn't want to upset her more.

"Alright, Sal. I am going to trust you. But you promise me, you will tell me everything when the time is right?"

"I promise," I said and gave Nicole a kiss on the cheek.

Needing to rest, I went upstairs and took a shower. The hot water definitely felt good on my head where I had been pistol whipped. There was a large bump on my head and with my short hair, Nicole would be able to spot it right away. I stood under the hot water and thought of what to do. On one hand, I wanted to tell Nicole and quite frankly, I *needed* to tell her. I knew it was going to be hard to go through this alone and I needed her help and support. On the other hand, I was specifically told not to tell anyone or Gio would die. I kept thinking to myself how would these guys know if I told Nicole? The more I thought about it, the more I realized that I needed to tell Nicole because I needed her support. When I finished my shower, I wrapped a towel around my waist and went into the bedroom to speak to Nicole. Sitting on the bed with a box in her hand was Nicole. She looked mortified and was pale as a ghost. She handed me the box and told me to look inside. I was afraid to look inside because of the look on her face, but I knew I had to. When I did, I had to take a few steps back to gain my balance. I thought to myself that I have been able to be scared or rattled way too much the past few days and I needed to toughen up. Once I was stable, I got to the point where I could remove the item in the box. When I got a good look at the item, that feeling in the pit of my stomach made its unwelcome return. In the box was a hand with Kelly's ID taped to it.

Chapter 62

When I woke up the next morning, I was unsure of what was reality and what was fiction. The experience of getting a package like I did last night not only changed my perspective of what was most important to me, but it also made me realize that someone was indeed watching me. After thinking of all the possible people who could have sent that package to me, I still had no idea as to who it was. That led me to change my mind about telling Nicole what happened to me until I was sure we were all safe. We both went to bed without talking about the package or what happened to me. I knew it bothered Nicole and it upset her, but I was doing it this way to protect her; something I hoped she would realize in time.

Each morning, I usually would wake Nicole up, then the kids, then go make breakfast for everyone, but today was going to be a different day. I was headed into the office to meet with Alan and Steven about all that has been going on, which most likely meant dealing with Kelly's death. I was not sure if Alan had heard what happened, but if he had not, then I was going to be the one to break the news to him. In order to be able to do that, I would need to get to the office before him and prepare.

Given that I was on an accelerated timeline, I drove into the office, despite the ice that was on the ground from the previous night's storm. Alan usually arrived at the office between seven-thirty and eight o'clock, so I wanted to get there at six-thirty to be sure I beat him there. To my surprise, traffic was much lighter than what I was used to and I got to the office at six-fifteen. When I pulled into the parking garage, I saw Alan's car parked in his reserved spot. My immediate thought was that there was no way he came in this early unless he knew something was wrong. I prepared myself for all possible scenarios and what they would mean for both my career and personal life. I had spent the entire drive to work thinking of what to say to Alan and each response I came up with sounded fake. Maybe it would be better if I did not know what to say because it would seem more genuine.

When the elevator got to my office floor, I stepped out to complete silence and darkness. It was awkward being the first to arrive, but I was also looking forward to being in my thoughts without interruptions. When I got to my office, I was surprised to see Jill was already at her desk. She would sometimes come in early to get a jumpstart on the mounds of paperwork she had, but she would usually tell me beforehand so I was not caught off guard. This led me to wonder if she knew about Kelly as well. As soon as she saw me, Jill got up to greet me with a hug.

"I am so sorry, Sal," Jill said.

"Sorry about what?" I asked.

"Kelly. I can't imagine what that was like for you."

"How do you know about what happened?"

"It was sent out by email from an unknown source. There was a picture of you and her before she…before she," Jill said, as she began to cry.

"This went out to everyone?" I asked, bending down to look into her eyes.

"Yes," Jill answered. "Sal, is there anything I can do?"

"Yes. You can tell me if Alan is here. I saw his car in the parking garage."

"Yes, he is in his office."

"Thank you, Jill. I will be back down here as soon as I can and we can discuss this but right now, I need to see Alan."

I didn't wait for a response from Jill and bolted toward the stairs to climb the two flights up to Alan's office. I had so many wild thoughts running through my head of what to expect when I saw him. I was going to have to try and control my emotions because I was sure he was a mess. I also thought about the small chance that he did not know and him being here this early was a coincidence. Either way, I was preparing for what was sure to be a tough morning.

When I reached Alan's office, I paused for a moment before knocking on the door. I wanted to gather myself and prepare for what was to come. The last time I was this nervous entering Alan's office was when I was going to discuss what David Flores did after he was acquitted. That time, I had overreacted and had no reason to be so nervous. This time however, I knew things would be different. I knew that Alan was going to be an emotional wreck, if he was not one already. As soon as I was ready, I knocked on the door and waited for Alan to answer.

"You SON OF A BITCH!" Alan said, as he opened the door and pulled me inside by my tie. "How could you let this happen? I trusted you. I trusted you with her. How could you do this to me?"

"Alan, what are you talking about? You think I did that to Kelly?" I asked, shocked at the way Alan exploded on me.

"What am I talking about? Really? That is your question?" Alan yelled.

"Alan, I had no idea she was even there. And when they showed her to me, I didn't have any time to react. It just…happened."

"I got a message saying that she was shot because you couldn't follow directions. What the hell does that mean?"

"I was warned that if I asked questions about what was going on, I would pay a penalty. My job, my *career* is asking questions. It was an instinct. I had no idea that was the penalty they were talking about."

"That is bullshit, Sal. You can't come up with something better than that? My granddaughter is dead because you couldn't follow one fucking direction. And to top it all off, these bastards sent me pictures of my Kelly with her brains blown out. How am I supposed to deal with that image for the rest of my life?" Alan said, as he slumped in his chair.

I was expecting Alan to be an emotional wreck, but I certainly did not expect this kind of outburst. I knew that Alan did not mean to blame me for Kelly's death, but he needed to vent and I was not going to stop him. I also knew he was in a vulnerable state and I did not want to say the wrong thing that would make him feel worse. But I also knew that I had to comfort him and remind him that he was not the only one grieving over Kelly. No matter what decision I made, I felt it was going to be the wrong one.

"I am so sorry, Alan. I really am. I wish there was something I could do," I said, staying where I was.

"Resign," Alan said, softly.

"Excuse me?" I asked.

"Resign, so I never have to see your mug again. The worst mistake I ever made was making you partner. I didn't want to do it but you had that prick Thomas wrapped around your finger so tight that I had no say in the matter. Then when he died, I really had no choice but to honor his wishes. You put me in an impossible situation and now I have the opportunity to rectify that mistake. Resign to save your dignity. If you do not, I will take you to civil court and have you removed."

To say that I was shocked would be the understatement of the year. I knew Alan was upset but this was taking it way too far. He had said these things to me with such conviction that I wasn't sure if he was serious or just reacting to the situation. Either way, we were at a crossroads and about to enter territory that neither one of us could turn back from.

"You know Alan, you have some nerve," I said, with anger. "You think you are better than everyone else. You always have. I have had to put up with your shit for years and I have had about enough of it. I am terribly sorry for Kelly, I am. But for you to sit there in your executive leather fucking chair and blame me for what happened to her, aggravates the shit out of me. I did nothing but care for her and guide her the entire time she was here. I let her take the lead on the Millstone case, a case we lost by the way, and coached her every step of the way. I comforted her when she was scared to continue and wanted to quit. Where were you? Huh? Where were you when she was melting down after being threatened by Joseph in court after we lost? You never once were there for her. *NEVER!* And now you want to blame me for her death. Well fuck you Alan. You want to take me to court, go ahead. There are no grounds for you to get rid of me and you know it, you piece of shit."

After a few seconds of reflective thought, Alan responded to my tirade.

"You are right, Sal. I have been a prick to you and everyone else. It is just that Kelly was my baby and now she is gone and I don't know what to do. I know you did everything you could to help her and that is not your fault that she was killed. I just can't get to the point of acceptance."

"Alan, I know this is tough. I know what you are going through. Even though we were divorced, I still cared for Danielle and now, I have to bury her. I have to comfort my kids when they attend her funeral in two days. I want you to know that I will help you in any way I can. I will help plan the funeral, make any arrangements you need. Whatever you need Alan. I am there for you and your family," I said, hoping to comfort Alan.

"I know you will, Sal. I have no doubt about that. I am also sorry for what I said earlier. Please forgive me."

I do not know what I heard first. I do not know what I saw first. All I knew was that I had just witnessed one of the most horrific things I had ever seen in my life. I am not sure if it was the blood all over the desk or the ringing in my ears, but I was completely disoriented and in a state of shock. I was waiting for someone to come and bring me out of my funk but nobody came. There wouldn't be anyone to come to my rescue because there was only Jill in the office and she was two floors beneath me. I was on my own from this point on.

I looked at Alan's lifeless body on the floor and wondered why he had done what he did. I knew that he was distraught over Kelly, but that could not be the reason he put a bullet into his mouth. There had to be something else that was bothering him. Was he in trouble? Was he involved in something that nobody knew about? I needed the answers to these questions, but first I would have to call the police to report what I had just seen.

When the police arrived, they took my statement and closed off Alan's office as a crime scene. It was still early so not too many people were in the office building, but as people began to trickle in, word spread quickly and suddenly, there was a large congregation outside of Alan's office. There were rumblings amongst the crowd of what happened but nobody knew for sure what had taken place, which led to the uneasiness of the situation. After five or ten minutes, the lead detective told everyone to vacate the area and go back to their offices. Everyone was in compliance, leaving me once again, by myself. I finally called Jill and told her to come up to Alan's office but did not tell her why. When she arrived, she seemed a bit off.

"Jill, are you ok? You seem distracted," I said.

"Well...ugh, I really should not tell you this, but I have to."

"Tell me what?" I asked.

"About a week ago, Alan came to me with two documents. One was a signed affidavit stating gross misconduct. The other was a signed confession," Jill said.

"Signed confession by who and for what?" I asked.

"Alan. It was his confession of what he has been up to."

"Jill, stop playing games with me. What did Alan confess to?" I asked, growing inpatient.

"Conspiracy to commit murder."

Chapter 63

"Are you sure you read that right?" I asked Jill.

"Yes, I read it three times. He states that he was involved in a conspiracy to commit murder clear as day," Jill answered.

"Do you still have the document?"

"Yes. but not here. I put it in a safe deposit box at the bank," Jill said.

"Well, when the bank opens, I need you to go and get it. I want to read it for myself," I told Jill.

"Sal, please. Don't make me do this," Jill pleaded.

"What are you so afraid of Jill? What has you so spooked.?"

"It is what was in the letter. I will let you read it for yourself."

"Jill, you can't do this to me. What was in the letter? Who was he plotting to murder?"

"You, alright. It was you," Jill said, after hesitating for a few seconds.

Once again, I had to hold on to something in order to not to fall down. It seems all I have been doing the past few weeks is getting shocking news that rocks my world. Was my life completely different than what I thought it was? Why would Alan want me dead? What possible motive could he have? I did not want to believe what Jill was telling me, but I also knew that she had no reason to lie to me. All of the horror and guilt I felt watching Alan kill himself suddenly evaporated. I was now beginning to feel paranoia and fear. Who was Alan plotting with and when was this supposed to happen? I would need Jill's help to find the answers.

"Ok. Ok. Ok," I said, trying to regain my composure. "Jill, can you please help me get to the bottom of this? I need to go through Alan's personal files to see if I can find something. I just don't know how to do it."

"Of course I will help you, Sal. What do you need me to do?" Jill responded.

"First of all, I need Alan's password to his computer. Can you see if Gladys will give it to you?"

"Gladys just went out on maternity leave. Alan asked me if I knew anyone who could fill in as a temporary secretary for him while she was out but I did not know anyone. He was in the process of trying to get one from a temp agency."

"Do you have her number?"

"Yes. Let me call her now. What should I tell her?"

"Tell her exactly what happened and that as a partner, I need access to his files to keep the firm going," I instructed Jill.

"Ok. I will let you know what happens."

Jill went off to call Gladys, while I called Steven. When he picked up, I struggled to get the words out but was eventually able to tell him what happened. He had to pull over to the side of the road in order to avoid getting into an accident. He immediately began to ask questions that I could not answer, which enraged him further. He told me to stay in the office until he got there and together we would figure out what the next steps would be.

While I waited for Steven, I continued to think of why Alan would want me dead. The more I thought about it, the more I came up with nothing. We had a great relationship that went back years. Sure he was no Thomas to me, but he was still an integral part of my life and career. He was the one who was always so calm and seemed to have the right answer. How could things have gone so wrong for him? I became convinced that this was a mistake and set out to prove it once I had access to his records.

It took Steven another hour to finally make it to the office and get through the police barricade. During that time, Jill was able to get potential passwords from Gladys and I was looking through all of my communications with Alan. I was not able to find anything that would lead me to believe that I was in any type of danger. In fact, the last communication we had was centered around a gathering at Alan's house to watch a few movies. It still did not make sense to me what Alan had confessed to. Once I finished going through my records, Steven came into my office to get more details on what happened.

"Sal, what in the hell happened?" Steven asked me.

"I don't know Steven. We got into an argument about what happened to Kelly and we both said some things we probably should not have said, but there was nothing violent or troubling. He began to apologize, asked me to forgive him, then pulled out a pistol and put a bullet in his mouth. No warning, no nothing. That is it."

"He didn't say anything else? Didn't mention anything else?" Steven asked.

"No. I am telling you. He didn't say anything. Why?"

"I don't know. He seemed a little distracted the past few days."

"Steven, if you know something, you need to tell me," I demanded.

"How much did Alan fill you in on his and the firm's finances?"

"Not much. We never really talked about it. Why? What is going on?" I asked.

"Sal, what I am about to tell you has to, I mean *has to* stay between us. Ok?"

"Sure, yeah. What is it?" I asked, eager to know the truth.

"Alan was in deep financial trouble. He lost a lot of money on a few risky investments that went completely south. He invested in several hedge funds that did not produce the kinds of gains he was told they would. In fact, they all lost money. Everything he worked for was basically gone," Steven informed me.

"Go on. I know there is more."

"Now I did not know about this until it was brought to my attention that the firm was losing money about a year ago, right around the time you became partner. When I asked to see the books, I kept getting the runaround and never saw them. That was until Alan and I had a massive blow out and I threatened to expose his financial status to his family. He finally turned everything over to me and told me what was going on. Sal, he was embezzling money from the firm to make up for his losses."

I sat in my chair fuming at what Steven was telling me. I could not believe that this could have been going on without me knowing about it. How much more was there that I did not know? I was growing tired of all these questions popping in my head and not getting any answers. Even though Steven was telling me what seemed like the truth, I could tell he was leaving something out.

"You mean to tell me this has been going on for a year and nobody told me? Why?"

"Quite frankly Sal, I don't know. We should have and for that I apologize. You are right."

"Ok. Let's forget about that for now. How about you prove to me that you truly are sorry and tell me the rest," I said, giving Steven a death stare.

"What do you mean, the rest? I have told you everything."

"So you don't know about the confession letter Alan wrote and the affidavit he signed just yesterday?"

"Sal, I have no idea what you are talking about," Steven insisted.

"Steven. Alan wrote a confession letter stating he was part of a conspiracy to have me murdered. You seriously do not know anything about that?" I said, getting angrier by the second.

After pausing and looking down at the floor for a few seconds, Steven finally told me what possible motive Alan could have had to have me killed.

"I swear I did not know about that. I swear, Sal. But I may know why," Steven began. "When someone becomes partner in a law firm, it is standard practice to take out additional life insurance on that person, in the event that person should pass away. It is called a key employee life insurance policy and the beneficiary is the law firm. If something were to happen to that key employee, the firm would collect the death benefit."

"And how much is this policy worth?" I asked.

"Five million dollars," Steven answered.

"Again, how did I not know about this? Who pays the premiums?"

"The firm pays the premiums. A policy that size usually requires a complete physical but since you say you didn't know about it, Alan must have found a way to work around it."

"I did take a physical when I was promoted, but Alan said it was part of the process in promoting someone to an executive position. I guess that was a lie."

"I don't know what to say, Sal. I really do not. Is there anything I can do?"

"Steven, please do not take this the wrong way, but right now, I do not want anything from anyone at this firm. My former partner, my *friend*, wanted to have me murdered to collect on the insurance money so he can recoup losses he suffered making bad investments. Think about that for a minute. How wild and crazy does that sound?

And to make matters worse, you claim you didn't know about it. I am inclined to believe you but at this point, I am not sure who to believe. I need to process all of this. So, in light of all that has happened and what I need to do for myself, I am requesting an indefinite leave of absence. I am sorry Steven, but I need this."

"I understand, Sal. We will work out the logistics with human resources, don't worry about it. I know you may have a hard time believing me but trust me when I say I had no idea any of this was going on."

There was something about the way Steven was talking to me that made me want to trust him. He sounded very sincere and genuine, something he normally did not do. Part of me thought he was like this because now it would be just him at the firm but part of me also thought that he truly had no idea what Alan had going on and was just as shocked by all of this as I was.

I thanked Steven for understanding and told him I was going to pack some items up and speak with Jill. She would also be affected by this because she would now have to either take a leave with me or be assigned to someone else. I knew it was going to be tough for her because we had been together for so long, but in the end, I felt she would understand my position and why I did what I had to do.

When I returned to my office, I told Jill that I was taking a leave of absence and laid out her options. She was stunned by my decision, but also understood it, just as I thought she would. She asked me if I was going to do any consulting or legal work on the side and if I was, would she be able to help me with it. I told her I was not planning on it but would keep it in mind if I needed her. She then informed me she would rather resign then go work for another lawyer at Lowery, Hill, and Greenwood. I explained that it was not that easy, given that she is Steven's niece, but she promised me she would have a discussion with him. When the time came, we said our goodbyes and wished each other luck. It was tough to say goodbye to someone that has always been there for me and has put up with my shit over the years, but it was something I had to do in order to be there for the ones who needed me most, my children. Danielle's funeral would be the next day and despite the front they may have been putting on, I knew that this was going to be extremely difficult for them.

Chapter 64

There is no manual for preparing your children for their mother's funeral. It is something that has to be done in the moment and cannot be fully prepared for. Sure, I was going to be there to comfort Gio and Angela if they needed it, but to what extent do I take it? Do I tell them everything will be ok and that their mother loved them? Or do I tell them we are better off without her because she was an evil, manipulating person who conned her way into our lives? The first option seems to be the better and smarter choice, but the second option is what I really wanted to say. Thankfully, I had Nicole to guide me on how to handle this situation.

We had spent the previous night talking about the emotions the kids will probably go through and how I should react to each one. She also warned me that letting my emotions get out of control will have an adverse effect on the kids, so I need to stay calm for them. I chose not to tell her about the confession letter from Alan until after the funeral. Nicole had enough to deal with and she did not need another thing to worry about.

As I put my tie on, I began to reflect on my life with Danielle. We had been the perfect couple by everyone else's standards. We had the perfect home, great kids, and loved each other very much. I kept thinking if there were signs I had missed that would have led me to be suspicious of anything. It was frustrating because I could not think of one thing Danielle had done or said that would have raised a red flag. She was the perfect con artist and it angered me that I didn't see it. Today was going to be a challenge for me to not let my kids see my true feelings for Danielle.

I went into Gio's room to see if he was getting ready because I had not heard anything coming from his room. I was shocked when I saw he was still playing video games and was still in his pajamas. He has had a tough time dealing with Danielle's death because he doesn't quite know how to process it all. On one hand, he is upset that she died because she was his mother, regardless of what she had done. On the other hand, he was old enough to know what she had done and was angry with her for lying to him. Recently, I have tried to be more careful with him because of how vulnerable he is, but no matter what I do, he always seems to have an attitude with me.

"Gio, I know you don't want to, but you need to get ready. We have to leave soon," I said.

"I am not going," Gio said, not looking at me.

"Yes, you are. Look, everyone is going through the same thing ok? We are all dealing with a whirlwind of emotions, but you need to go to your mother's funeral. Period," I said sternly.

"Why? She doesn't deserve to have a funeral. Why can't we just cremate her and forget her? It is not fair," Gio said, getting angry.

"I know, son. I know this sucks, but we have to do it. Think of Angela. Do it for her."

"Fine. I will go, but I don't want to."

"I understand. Thank you. Be downstairs in five minutes."

After I left Gio's room, I went to see how it was going with Nicole and Angela. With Nicole around all the time and taking an interest in what Angela likes, the two of them had gotten really close over the past few weeks. It was certainly a major help to me, given all that I was dealing with, that Nicole has been able to take some of the burden off of me. She has been able to use her knowledge of child psychology to help Angela deal with Danielle's death as best she can. When I peeked in the room. Nicole was putting on Angela's shoes and telling her how pretty she looked. I didn't want to ruin that moment, so I walked away and headed downstairs.

When the limousine arrived, we all gathered our things and headed out. Gio and Angela were excited to ride in a limo for the first time, which was a nice distraction for them. They both ran to the limo and jumped in the back seat as if they did not have a care in the world. Nicole and I were a bit less enthusiastic, but still excited to ride in such luxury. When we were all in the limo, I turned on the neon lights to surprise Gio and Angela. They both had smiles from ear to ear on their faces and were making ooh and aah sounds in amazement. It was nice to see that they could so easily be distracted and not constantly be thinking about where we were going.

After an enjoyable ride, we finally arrived at the church. The driver came around the backside of the limo and opened the door to let us out. As soon as he did, I began to hear heckling from the few people that were gathered outside the church. They were yelling at me for what Danielle did, even though they were not affected at all by her actions. I was not prepared for this type of reaction and when I saw the scared look on Angela's face, it enraged me that she had to listen to this nonsense.

"Daddy, why are they saying those things to you? Do they not like mommy?" Angela asked.

"Don't worry about them, angel, they are just miserable people," I said, as I put my arm around my family to usher them into the church.

As we walked into the church, I could hear the organs playing Ave Maria, which for some reason got me emotional. I was not expecting to be emotional at all because of how much I hated her, but I couldn't help it. She was, after all, my wife for thirteen years. We had made a lot of memories together and shared priceless moments as well. We had two terrific children and even though she was an evil person, she was a terrific mother. I knew that Gio and Angela would miss her and it was mainly because of that, that I felt these emotions.

We took our seats in the front row, waiting for the service to begin. I was not expecting a large crowd; however, the first six rows were filled with people who came to pay their respects to Danielle. I knew most of the people in attendance because they were family mainly from Danielle's father's side. I didn't want to engage in a conversation with any of them, so I just waved and gave a polite smile whenever I made eye contact with them. I am sure some of them could tell how fake I was but I really did not care. My main concern was to make sure that Gio and Angela were able to get through this and finally be able to move on with their lives.

Once everyone was seated, the service began with a prayer from the priest. I am not much of a religious person, neither was Danielle; however, we both agreed that we would have a proper religious service should one of us die before the other. It was the only request of Danielle's that I was willing to honor because I knew it would bring closure to this whole situation and allow everyone to move on. Once the priest finished the opening prayer, he moved on to making the service about Danielle, which was difficult to listen to.

"We meet here today to honor the life of Danielle Amici," the priest began. "For Danielle, the journey is just beginning, but for us, there is grief and pain."

I heard a few sniffles coming from a few rows back and figured it was from one of Danielle's relatives. As the priest went on, the sniffling became louder and more constant. I turned around to see who it was, not so much as to tell them to calm down, but to see who was still being duped by this evil bitch. Sure enough, if it was Danielle's Aunt Brianna. She had been the one person who refused to believe Danielle was capable of what she was accused of. All through her trial, Brianna kept claiming her innocence and begging for retrial. She even at one point blamed me for setting the whole thing up and that I should be on trial instead of her. When I made eye contact with Brianna, I rolled my eyes and made a gesture for her to be quiet. Nicole pinched my leg and told me to stop it and not cause a scene. I complied with her request and turned around to devote my attention to the priest who was trying his best to make Danielle sound like a good person. As I was turning around, I saw something out of the corner of my eye that grabbed my attention. When I looked back, I could see someone in the far back corner with their head bowed in prayer. Although it is not uncommon for strangers to attend a funeral and offer their condolences and prayers, it has never happened at any funeral I have attended.

As the service went on, I kept glancing back at the person in the back of the room to see if I could get a better look and see who it was, but the person kept their head down most of the time. I nudged Nicole and told her to look as well, but she also could not see much either. I am not sure why, but it was really beginning to bother me that this person was at Danielle's funeral and was sitting all the way in the back. It was almost as if they didn't want to be seen. Against my better judgment, I turned around again and the person was getting up to leave. I stared as intently as I could without bringing attention to myself to see if I could get a good look. The person had glasses, a black winter hat, a peacoat, and walked with a distinct limp. The more I looked the more the person looked familiar to me. Nicole once again nudged me but this time, I didn't pay attention. I kept staring trying to figure out where I knew this person from. Then it hit me.

"Sean," I whispered. "Nicole, that is Sean Lancaster."

"*What?* Are you sure?

"I am absolutely sure," I said, grinding my teeth. "I can't let him get away this time. I just can't. This has to end now."

Despite Nicole's desperate pleas to let it go, I awkwardly got up during the service and calmly made my way toward the back of the church via the side aisle. I tried not to make it obvious, so I took out my phone and pretended to text someone. While looking at my phone, I used my peripheral vision to keep an eye on who I thought was Sean and kept moving forward. The closer I came to this person, the more nervous I got. I did not want my kids to see what was going or what might happen, nor did I want to disrupt the service. When I reached the back of the church, the person who I had been keeping an eye on had vanished. How could this have happened? I knew that this person could not have gone far, so I picked up my pace as I made my way toward the exit.

Once I was out on the street, I looked to my left and to my right, but did not see the person I was hunting. I was beginning to feel anger creep up inside me when I looked straight ahead and saw someone with a limp cross the street. This was my chance to make up ground and confront this person, who I was sure was Sean. I did not care about stealth anymore, all I wanted to do was catch up to this person and ask what they were doing at Danielle's funeral. I weaved my way in and out of traffic, making up solid ground along the way. When I was within ten feet of the person, they took off running.

I was convinced now that this person was Sean and he was leading me on another chase through the streets of New York City, just like he had before; however, this time, I was not going to lose him. Adrenaline kicked in to give me the burst of energy I needed and I began to close the gap between me and Sean. He was hobbled a bit by the injury he sustained during our last chase but that didn't stop him from making his way through traffic and alleyways. I kept pursuing Sean, despite feeling my shins burning and not being able to breath well. At this point, I was fueled not only by adrenaline, but also by pure hate.

After two or three minutes of chasing Sean, I had narrowed the gap to half a block. It was only a matter of time before I would catch up with him and get my answers. There were not a lot of people on the sidewalk, which helped me keep a close eye on Sean as he tried to evade me. While I was running on the sidewalk trying to make up more ground, I kept looking for something I might be able to throw at Sean to knock him down. I had no idea what I was looking for, but I was confident that if I found something, I would know it. Eventually Sean turned down an alley that was a dead end. This was my chance.

I rounded the corner leading to the alley and saw Sean slumped over in the back corner. He had no place to go because the walls were too high to reach and I was blocking his way out of the alley. I stopped running and slowed my pace enough that I was able to catch my breath and alleviate some of the burning in my shins. I was concerned he might have a gun on him so I made sure to look at my surroundings and identify where I could go if that was the case. As I carefully approached Sean, I looked down to my left and saw a rusted tire iron. Without hesitation, I picked it up and began to slam it against the palm in my right hand, indicating to Sean I intended to use it. When I got to within five feet of Sean, I could tell he knew he was beaten. I did not care. I was not going to take mercy on him. This was the moment I had been waiting for.

"You miserable fuck. I got you now Sean. Nowhere to hide," I said, teasing him.

"You don't have it in you Sally baby," Sean said between deep, heavy breaths. "You have had so many chances and you have bitched out on all of them. You are weak, Sal."

"Oh, I may have been before but see, I have changed. The whole Joseph Millstone experience has changed me. It opened my eyes to what the world is really like. What evil is like. What people like you are like. It also made me realize that the world is a much better place when assholes like you aren't in it."

"Sally. Baby. You have grown a pair! I am proud of you. What's next? You going to run for governor? Try to change the world?" Sean asked.

"Nah, I could never run for governor after doing this," I said, as I swung the tire iron and hit Sean in the left knee, sending him crumbling to the ground. "Or this." hitting Sean in the back with the tire iron.

It is hard to describe the feeling I had knowing that I finally had the upper hand on Sean and that there was nothing he could do about it. I stared down at Sean and revelled in the fact that he was writhing in pain. He had caused so much damage and pain to me and my family that it felt like justice was finally being served, although not in the manner in which I was used to. As Sean continued to lay on the ground trying to get up, I kicked him in the stomach two times and then once in the groin.

"Got anything to say now tough guy?" I said.

"You think this is bothering me? I took worse beatings in prison," Sean said, laughing.

"You think I am done with you? Not even close, you prick," I said, kicking him again in the stomach.

I knew Sean was tough but I did not know he was this tough. Anyone else that took the beating I was giving them would have either begged for mercy or passed out. I did not want to hurt Sean anymore than I already had, but the more he tried to goad me, the angrier I got. He always knew how to get under my skin, especially when I least expected it. I needed to find a way to not let him get to me and end this so I can get back to my family.

"You ruined my life. I know you don't care, but you need to hear it. You and Danielle both can go to hell," I said.

"See, that is what I am talking about Sal. You can't finish anything. What do you think is going to happen when I get away? You assaulted me, but I can't exactly tell the cops, now can I? There are other ways to get payback Sally baby. You know how resourceful I am. You will never know when or where it will happen, but one day you will be eating dinner with that gorgeous piece of ass you live with now and your kids, and that will be the last meal you will ever have."

I didn't even think about hitting Sean at that point, it was instinct. I hit him in the back two more times with the tire iron, then kicked him in the face. There was blood all over the place but I did not care. I was sick of Sean and all his wise ass remarks. I wanted to teach him a lesson he would never forget. If I did permanent damage to him in the process, so be it. I also began to think of what he said, when he asked what would happen next. He was right that he could not go to the cops but in a way, not being able to go to the police was actually worse.

"I am done with you Sean. I don't ever want to see you again. Go ruin someone else's life," I said and began to walk away.

It was then that I heard one of the most evil laughs I have ever heard. I knew I should not have stopped to turn around but I wanted to know what Sean could possibly be laughing about after getting such a bad beating.

"What's so funny?" I asked.

"You think you have it all figured out huh? You think that by beating me here you are in control? Think again pal. I finish things, unlike you. In fact, you should appreciate me for helping you out."

"What are you talking about you psycho?"

Once again, Sean began to laugh. "Danielle never stood a chance."

"*What did you say?*" I asked, walking slowly back toward Sean.

"She never stood a chance. I paralyzed her then choked the life out of her. I really didn't want to, but I have to admit, that bitch needed to go," Sean said with an evil smirk.

There are certain times in life when instinct and emotion take over. Sometimes a person can control these actions and other times there is no chance. This instance was the latter for me. Something inside me snapped. I went to a place I had never been before, which gave me no hope to control anything. I grabbed the tire iron from the ground where I dropped it and began smashing Sean over the head again and again. I was filled with such anger and rage I did not know what was going on. Blood was splattering all over my face and clothes but I didn't care.

"You fuck. You evil twisted fuck. Die you son of a bitch. *DIE*," I said, continuing to smash in Sean's head.

When I finally ran out of energy, I fell to the ground from exhaustion. My back was turned to Sean and when I turned around, I saw what I had done. His face was swollen so bad, I could not tell it was him. His skull had been cracked open and blood was pouring out onto the pavement. I knew he was dead and I had killed him but it didn't faze me. I was still in a state of rage and anger that I took the tire iron and started smashing his head again. After five to ten minutes, I was able to finally calm down and assess what to do next. I knew I couldn't go back to the church, and I knew I couldn't call the cops, so I did the only thing I could think of. I ran.

When I exited the alleyway, I looked both ways to make sure I would be able to escape. I made a quick left and then a quick right. I saw a clear path in front of me that was as inviting as a hot cup of coffee on a cold winter day. In that moment, I kept thinking to myself that things are oftentimes not what they seem. I was also nervous someone heard the beating I gave Sean and would call the police, so I continued to make my back toward the church. After I went two blocks undetected, I suddenly realized that I could not go back to the church wearing the clothes I had on. Sean's blood was all over my shirt and pants and my shoes were scuffed up. My house was nowhere near where I was, and I could not exactly walk into a store and buy new clothes. I decided to text Nicole to let her know that Sean had gotten away, and I was going to go home to change my clothes because they were soaked with sweat.

Having bought myself some time, I made my way back to my car by the church and drove home. I had managed to avoid detection on the streets, which was a miracle. On the drive home, I was sure to not violate any traffic laws and I kept both hands on the steering wheel. As I pulled into my driveway, I found myself unable to get out and go into the house. I felt a tsunami of emotion come over me; something I had never experienced before. Suddenly, I began to pound the steering wheel in frustration and rage. After two to three minutes of taking my anger out on the innocent car, I finally managed to calm down and get out the car.

Once I was in my house, I immediately took my clothes off, put them into a garbage bag, and put the bag in my trunk to dispose of. I text Nicole that I was home and that I was going to take s shower. She responded to meet everyone at the grave site and to hurry up. While I was in the shower, I kept trying to reflect on what had just happened, but for some odd reason, my brain would not allow myself to replay my beating of Sean in my head. All I was able to think of was what I needed to do to get away with it. How would I hide this from my family, the police, and Steven? I knew I had bought myself time to figure it out, but I was also concerned that once Sean's body was discovered, I would not be able to sustain my calmness.

After my shower, I got dressed and tried to prepare myself to be around my family. I had been through so much over the last few days and began to wonder when I would get a break. I do not like to feel sorry for myself, but I had dealt with more than anyone should have to in an entire lifetime over the last few days. The emotions of having to bury the mother of my children was going to take precedent within the next thirty minutes and I had to make sure that was where my focus was. It was going to be challenging to put what I did to Sean behind me, but I also knew that my family would help me through, whether they knew it or not. The road ahead was sure to be bumpy and unpredictable; however, I was confident that I would meet the challenge with the same tenacity and determination as I do everything else. Bring it on!

Epilogue

"**S**al, come on. We have six o'clock reservations and I don't want to me late." Nicole yelled at me.

For the past three months, she had been as supportive and caring as a girlfriend can be. No matter what I was feeling or going through, Nicole was there for me. She had the uncanny ability to make me forget all the problems I had and everything I had been through with just a few words and strokes of my hair. I never thought I would be able to love someone after Danielle, but Nicole has enabled me to do just that.

We had not had a chance to go out by ourselves in what seemed like an eternity, which is what made this night so special. I had arranged for my mother to watch the kids and made a reservation at Ai Fiori on Fifth Avenue, one of the most elegant restaurants in New York City. People have been known to drop between three and five hundred dollars for dinner and wine, but I wanted this evening to be not only memorable and as perfect as it could be.

We arrived by limousine at the restaurant five minutes early and decided to wait until it was exactly six o'clock to make our way into the restaurant. We finished our champagne and caviar, then gave each other one of the most passionate kisses ever. The evening was already shaping up better than I had imagined, and I was hoping it would get even better.

As soon as we entered the restaurant, the maître d' greeted us with a smile and grand welcome. He showed us to our table in the corner, like I requested, and pulled out the chair for Nicole. Once we were both seated, he handed me the wine menu and made a few suggestions. I already knew I wanted to order the 1928 Madeira Sercial, D'Oliveiras for both of us, which ran two-hundred thirty dollars a glass. After looking over the menu for a good ten minutes, we made our selections and relayed them to the waiter. Nicole went with the ravioli, while I chose the risotto.

While waiting for our appetizers to arrive, I began to feel a lump in my throat, as well as an increase in heart rate. The moment was perfect, and I felt there was no better time to begin my speech. I lifted my glass of wine and motioned for Nicole to lift hers as well. When both of our glasses were raised and next to each other, I began.

"Nicole, I wanted this evening to be perfect. I wanted you to have the evening you deserve for everything you have done for me and my kids. I hope to this point, I have succeeded," I began nervously. "The last few months have been absolutely incredible, and I have you to thank for that. Sure, there have been bumps in the road and unexpected people showing up at funerals, but for the most part, I have been blown away at how you have shown me that it is possible to love again. What I am trying to say is, you have made me so happy over the past few months and if you let me, I would love to spend the rest of my life returning the favor. Nicole, will you do me the honor of being my wife?"

The look on Nicole's face was something out of a Thomas Kinkade painting. The pure joy and excitement she exuded was exactly what I was wishing for, but also was fearful I would not get. She was so surprised, that she almost dropped her glass of wine. As I continued to look deep into her eyes, my cell phone begam to buzz in my pocket. This was not the time to check my phone, but it kept going on and on.

"Well, what do you say?" I asked Nicole, as my phone continued to buzz.

"Sal, why don't you answer your phone. It sounds like it is important." Nicole said to me.

"I will, but I have to tell you, I am a little concerned over here because you haven't answered me yet."

"I will, I promise, but first get rid of that damn phone call."

"Ok," I said. "Hello, this is Sal."

On the other end was a voice that was spoken through a voice scrambler. Immediately, all the excitement and romance I had when I asked Nicole to marry me was gone. The first thought that came to my mind was what now? Sean was dead so there was no way that this could be him.

"Sal Amici. Oh, Sal Amici. You think you are home free don't you. You think your troubles are over now that Sean Lancaster is dead, don't you? Well, I have news for you. It isn't."

"Who is this? What do you want?" I said, as I got up from the table.

"You know I won't tell you that. However, what I will tell you is that I bet right about now you should be wishing that the police had covered the front door of the King's home. Why you ask? Well, because Joseph Millstone wasn't acting alone. I want to thank you for allowing the opportunity to continue my hobby. You have no idea what that means to me."

"What are you talking about? Joseph worked alone. He admitted to it. You are just trying to get me riled up." I said, clearly not believing what I was saying.

"If that is what you think, then you need to hire better investigators. I will be back. I will terrorize New York City again. Oh, it will be worse than before. Just one more thing Sal."

"What is that psycho?"

"Catch me if you can."

www.ingramcontent.com/pod-product-compliance
Lightning Source LLC
Chambersburg PA
CBHW060529160726
47991CB00001B/249